REVEREND ON THE RUN

It was then that he noticed the figure behind him.

Why the hell hadn't he seen him before? Although the man was keeping distance and stopping into doorways so as not to be obvious, Lucas Holt knew he himself was the object of the man's surveillance. But who was it?

It could be one of Susan's officers, but she still thought he was back on South Congress. Or was this Nikky's idea of keeping tabs on him? The man did not look like anyone he knew from the God Squad and in fact seemed too old to be doing this kind of thing.

Holt's heart suddenly got a shot of adrenaline. He walked faster as the man started to catch up with him. As they moved quickly up to Seventh Street, the crowd thinned to only one or two other persons. Lucas Holt readied his master key for the plunge into the safe darkness of the church.

Just before entering, Holt glanced behind at his pursuer. The man was clearly winded but was also closing the distance between them . . .

MORE MYSTERIES FROM THE BERKLEY PUBLISHING GROUP . . .

THE SAINTS OF GOD MURDERS

CHARLES MEYER

BERKLEY PRIME CRIME, NEW YORK

THE SAINTS OF GOD MURDERS

A Berkley Prime Crime Book / published by arrangement with the author

PRINTING HISTORY
Berkley Prime Crime edition / July 1995

ISBN: 0-425-14869-6

Berkley Prime Crime Books are published
by The Berkley Publishing Group,
200 Madison Avenue, New York, NY 10016.
The name BERKLEY PRIME CRIME and the BERKLEY PRIME CRIME
design are trademarks belonging to Berkley Publishing Corporation.

PRINTED IN THE UNITED STATES OF AMERICA

10 9 8 7 6 5 4 3 2 1

For the saints of God in my life,
1982–87

HYMNS FOR CHILDREN
#243

I sing a song of the saints of God
Patient and brave and true.
Who toiled and fought and lived and died
For the Lord they loved and knew.
And one was a doctor, and one was a queen,
And one was a shepherdess on the green:
They were all of them saints of God—and I mean,
God helping, to be one too.

They loved their Lord so dear, so dear,
And his love made them strong;
And they followed the right, for Jesus' sake,
The whole of their good lives long.
And one was a soldier and one was a priest,
And one was slain by a fierce wild beast:
And there's not any reason—no, not the least—
Why I shouldn't be one too.

They lived not only in ages past,
There are hundreds of thousands still,
The world is bright with the joyous saints
Who love to do Jesus' will.
You can meet them in school, or in lanes, or at sea.
In church, or in trains, or in shops, or at tea,
For the saints of God are just folk like me,
And I mean to be one too.

Lesbia Scott
1940 Episcopal Church Hymnal

• Prologue •

The old man stood at the sink and washed the rivulets of blood from his aching hands. Momentarily mesmerized by the swirling pattern against the stainless gray drain, he forced his eyes to widen as his huge foot squashed the plastic pedal on the floor. Antiseptic soap foamed like shaving cream from the small spigot above the sink, covered his hairy hands, and added white bubbles to the whirlpool of red.

Blood used to be a sign of life, he thought as he frowned and scrubbed more vigorously; a sign that the surgeon had done his best in the battle for the patient's existence, a badge of victory. Putting your hands into someone's chest cavity and massaging his heart, slashing out his diseased appendix or cancerous colon, these used to be heroic, life-saving gestures. Now, he shook his head ruefully, now blood was a hated substance, terrifying to touch, something to be shunned, a symbol not of life but of death itself.

Even though, in forty years of practice, he had never been infected, Dr. Walter Hargrive scrubbed as if each drop of the patient's blood could kill him—because it could. The scrub suits, caps, shoes, and latex surgeon's gloves usually protected him. But the occasional slip of the scalpel, the tear in the glove, the airborne germ, these were persistent enemies, and he bore constant vigilance against them. He was, of all his aging colleagues, the most meticulous in cleanliness. As he left the doctor's dressing room, he looked one last time in the mirror, combing the out-of-place white hair, positioning the limp cotton handkerchief correctly in his suit pocket, preparing for his histrionic exit.

Walter Hargrive walked stiffly down the surgery corridor, his back straight, his countenance somber. He nodded to the nurses and technicians awaiting his command. His speech was practiced. He had given it many times before. Too many times.

"There's nothing more to do. The man had no family left. I've doctored him for thirty years. I'll call the funeral home from the lounge. Thank you very much for your help. You all did your best. So did I." He started to walk away, then turned and flashed his winning FDR smile. "Good night."

A few muffled responses of "Good night, Doctor" followed him down the brightly lighted hall. He entered the muted calm of the physician's lounge and dropped the smile. A quick cup of coffee and he'd call it a night. Funny how caffeine had never kept him up, even at these late hours. Somehow it seemed to strengthen him, give him courage to drive the long distance to his lake home without thinking of the corpse he had left in the O.R.

He poured the coffee and was about to sit in the plush leather chair when he noticed the other figure in the room. The surgeon's hands fumbled the cup.

"God! Where did *you* come from?"

"Oh, I've been sitting here all the time," the person replied calmly. "Didn't you see me when you came in?"

"Of course not. My back was to you." The physician took a small sip of the hot coffee and grimaced. "This stuff is worse than usual tonight. Did you make it or did that stupid nur—"

"No. I made it. And I'm sorry if I startled you. Like you, I often make late-night rounds." Eyes stared deliberately at the doctor. "How did the surgery turn out?"

"Just like the joke." Walter Hargrive smiled nervously. "'The surgery was successful. The patient died.' I guess his eighty-nine-year-old organs just weren't meant to be cut."

He shrugged his shoulders. "Oh, well. It could have been worse. If he'd lived we'd have put him on a respirator and he would have died anyway. Maybe my decision to operate on the old man was a favor. Maybe it was the will of God."

The other person's voice developed an edge. "That's a strange phrase, isn't it, Walter—'The will of God'? If people live, it's God's will; and if they die, it's God's will. I guess you could cover almost anything with that, couldn't you?"

"What do you mean 'cover'? Are you accusing me of something?" The surgeon's face reddened in the lamplight as he sat forward on the chair. "You've got a lot of nerve to sit there and accuse *me*. You of *all* people. As a matter of fact, that reminds me." He looked at his watch. "What day is this? Isn't it about time for you to . . . ?"

The other sat calmly opposite him and replied flatly, "No, Walter. It isn't."

The surgeon's eyes narrowed. "What do you mean 'no'? You'd damn well better keep up those payments." The FDR grin was back. "On second thought, forget it. I've been looking for an excuse to—"

"Easy, Walter." The remark was quiet, monotoned. "Don't get too excited with your self-satisfaction. I think you'll soon find you need all the energy you can conserve."

Walter Hargrive slowly edged back in his chair. A cold sweat dampened his starched, white shirt. His physician's mind noted the dull pounding in his head. His heart began to race.

"What's going on here?" He looked down at the cup in his right hand. He was aware that it seemed to be getting very heavy. "What did you put in this coffee?" he said to the passive, shadowed figure in the other chair. "What are you doing here?"

The figure stood as the surgeon gazed up through a thickening, hazy fog.

"Too many questions, Walter. Far too many questions."

The tone was calm, like a parent comforting a frightened child.

The aged surgeon watched helplessly as the cup of coffee was removed from his shaking hand.

"Let me have that before you spill it on yourself. We wouldn't want you to be found all messy now, would we?" The voice was deadly kind.

"What . . . are . . . you talking about? You . . . you drugged the coffee." The surgeon tried desperately to lift his body from the chair. His bones felt like cement, and he could not move. He could barely shape the words in his tightening mouth. "Why . . . are . . . you putting on . . . those . . . those gloves?"

"Merely a precaution, Walter. Standard double-glove technique." Latex stretched over screeching latex. "A double prophylactic, if you will, so we don't swap body fluids. I wouldn't want your blood on me, and of course I wouldn't want to leave any souvenirs like fingerprints, would I?"

The hand grasped a thin metal object and stepped behind the immobile doctor's chair.

"No! . . . No!" Hargrive whispered hoarsely. "Why . . . are you . . . ? Listen . . . to me . . . we . . . can make . . ."

One hand yanked back the surgeon's forehead as the other swept across his neck. Blood trickled, then spewed down the doctor's sweat-soaked shirt and puddled in his lap on the leather seat. His suit pocket handkerchief became red and sodden.

Not waiting for the gasping to cease, the figure rinsed the scalpel and placed it beside the coffee cup, which was also wiped clean. The double gloves were rinsed, then reverse-removed to fold one set into the other, dry side out, before sticking them in a pocket for later burning.

The lamp by the lifeless body was switched off with the help of a small, cotton handkerchief.

About to leave the silent room, the killer stopped at the door and removed the cap from a black felt marker. The sweet ether smell mingled with the heavy scent of venous blood as three numerals were deliberately drawn on the wall above the switch plate.

A nurse down the hall heard the lounge door close. She turned to catch a glimpse of long coattails rounding the corridor corner, and she knew Dr. Walter Hargrive had had his ritual coffee and left for the night. In a few minutes she would go make sure he had turned off the warmer.

Outside the hospital, a solitary form strode quickly away into the darkness, replaying again and again the surgeon's words: "The will of God. Maybe it *was* the will of God."

• One •

The Reverend Lucas Holt sat slumped in his chair with his feet propped up on the office windowsill, his chin resting on interlaced fingers. He stared blindly over his gray Tony Lama bullhides at the figures moving on Austin's famous Sixth Street.

"Old Pecan Street," as it was known before the city council decided numbers were easier to remember than trees, had been just another area of decaying turn-of-the-century buildings until the historical society started resurrecting them. One by one refurbishing turned the stone and wood two-story structures into trendy restaurants and boutiques. They catered to the wide range of Austin tastes, from the redneck Longhorn Massage Parlour to the lesbian Juno-books and the yuppie University Pub.

It was appropriate, Holt thought, for St. Margaret's Episcopal Church to be located on the small hill overlooking this scene. The church and the street were identical.

Sixth Street welcomed patrons of various interests and persuasions. People with money to spend descended onto the Street on evenings and weekends from far wealthier areas of town, leaving the transient, homeless locals to sleep in doorways after club hours and during the day, except when they were scattered to make way for a business lunch.

St. Margaret's parishioners covered the psychological and theological spectrum from charismatic fundamentalists to social justice liberals and all the perversions in between. It was the church to belong to for business and social ties, so the powerful—and those who used them—journeyed downtown from The Hills at night and on weekends, as the locals slept in the stone safety of its Gothic vaulted doorways.

The din of street construction fell on Holt's deaf ears. He observed but did not see the late morning crowd; old alkies, slowly waking, squinted at the pain of the sunlight, salivated at the thought of that first drink and cigarette; hookers primping near the Langhorn readied themselves for the afternoon trade; tourists waiting to pay too much in the tiny shops looked in windows and nudged each other; businesspeople hurried to the next vapid appointment.

The Street was a silent film that flickered before him. But the new, modern movie with high-decibel THX sound was playing in his head, though instead of words, numbers screeched out at him. The numbers—all in parentheses—were from a neatly bound audit that lay open on the desk behind him.

The Rev. Lucas Holt had just found out his church was bankrupt.

He wondered why he had left the penitentiary. Twenty years he had been chaplain to the male and female inmates there. Pimps, hit men, drug dealers, the kid who killed twenty-four people in a fire, the guy with hair implants who raped children, the prostitute who tried to seduce the Rev and nearly succeeded—he had left all that behind for a parish, something he said he had never wanted, wasn't cut out for, would fail miserably in if he took one. Why the hell had he done it? He was two months into St. Margaret's and ready to go back behind the high walls where he felt safe and the few dangers were known and familiar.

He missed the realness of the people there, the incredible stories of their lives, their childhoods, the families they came out of—and survived—and the families they created, or, more often, re-created. He missed the lies they swapped and the stories they told, their playfulness and their candor.

Most of all, and Lucas Holt could admit this to no one but
himself and God, he missed what he called the Dark Edge.

The Dark Edge was that part of human beings that was
kept most under wraps. At St. Margaret's it was hidden
deep under the furs and starched shirts and the best psychological insulation money could buy. At the penitentiary it
was raw, always near the surface, ready to erupt at any time
over some minuscule thing like cutting in line or glancing
the wrong way at someone. It was the part that was capable
of murder, arson, and theft; the part that was capable of
doing bodily harm, of lying, cheating, and taking whatever
one wanted, whenever one wanted it.

Holt enjoyed being around the Dark Edge in his prison
"parishioners." He liked the danger of imminent explo-
sions, the challenge of walking into high-tension cellblocks
armed with nothing more than his wits, like walking into a
minefield with only your instincts.

He liked it because he knew the Dark Edge within himself. He identified with the rule breakers, the sociopaths,
the outcasts of an affluent society, and he knew but for his
commitment to God he could have been in the next cell.
Sometimes that commitment barely constrained him, sometimes it gave him license to loose his Dark Edge in righteous indignation against greed, injustice, or prejudice. He
was, admittedly, a child of the sixties, reared on heroes and
superheroes, ready to break rules in defense of the power-
less. He had done his own small amounts of time from
protests and demonstrations, enough to know the depth of
his feeling must be confined within the black robes of the
church, enough to hope that his own darkness might be able
to defuse it in others, to bend his and theirs to a different
end.

He sighed and pursed his lips. It was not like leaving
there was much of a choice. The bishop—ah, the dear
bishop—told him he was needed elsewhere. It was more
than a polite invitation. It was a way of saying Lucas Holt
was crossing the line too often in the Diocese, becoming

too independent, too radical, too outspoken, too sympathetic with the criminals he was supposed to be rehabilitating.

Holt had argued vehemently with Bishop Casas to reconsider. There had even been a hint of a threat from disgruntled inmates who, sooner or later, would be back on the streets. His streets. The streets in front of the Bishop's office, and the Bishop's house.

But Holt knew it was futile. If he didn't take the offer of the parish, the Church hierarchy would begin its monolithic grind to put him out of a job, out of a career, and out of a life. It was St. Margaret's or nothing.

So here he sat, staring at Sixth Street and wondering what to do with the news he'd just received from the auditors. A grin slowly took shape on his face as the irony dawned on him. Maybe this parish was, after all, just a small version of the pen. Maybe the audit was something he could turn and use.

Still gazing out the window, he absently reached for the intercom button, punched it, and spoke slowly:

"Max?"

"Whatcha need, Rev?" came the raspy reply from the outer office.

"Get me 'Boom Boom' down at the God Box."

"Rev, you're not supposed to talk about the Bishop that way. Even *I* know that. Now, whatever it is you want I'll bet I can sweet-talk him out of—"

"Max, you could sweet-talk the man out of his boxer shorts, and I may need you to do that. But for now would you just get him on the phone for me?"

"You got it, Rev. But give me a few minutes. You know how difficult it is to get through to the man."

"Take your time," Holt replied, punching the button off.

Lucas Holt smiled at the thought of a scantily clad Maxine Blackwell welcoming Bishop Emilio Casas to her small room in the massage parlor. The bishop had not wanted the former prostitute to work at the church in the first place, but

Lucas had arranged the job as a part of her parole and insisted she come as part of the package. Maxine was getting older, disease had changed the business, and the "house" was being lost to urban renewal. She needed the job to get out. Even Emilio Casas had to admit it was a smart move, one which he could hardly reject without criticism.

Maxine was like a mother to Lucas Holt, and he enjoyed the attention. He had met her years ago in the Women's Unit of the prison. He had been young, attractive, and brand-new to the world of prison cons; she was twenty years his senior, stunningly attractive even in shapeless prison blues, and read him like a book. He saw her almost daily, tentatively fascinated as much by her lifestyle as her looks. Her initial flirtations with him turned to deeper interest as he politely kept his emotional distance, or thought he did.

He never saw her outside the pen, but, as she continued to get busted for prostitution over the years, he saw her through each lengthening sentence. They watched each other's careers advance. Lucas Holt became a powerful fixture at the prison; Maxine Blackwell worked a famous house in South Austin where she became the favorite of state legislators, college students, and cowboys.

She became his inmate secretary in the chaplain's office where they spent increasing time together. Early one morning, making sure the door was closed and no guards were near, Maxine brought him his Earl Grey tea and set it on the desk in front of him. Her faded, blue smock hung limply over her bosomy frame, unbuttoned enough to assure his attention. Her shoulder-length red hair framed her perfectly made-up face. Her underwear was in her cell.

She walked behind the desk and took his hands in hers. He pulled her into his arms and they kissed deeply, passionately, and then, eyes wide open, they both pushed away—and began to laugh.

When she could speak, Maxine said: "I been waitin' fifteen years to do that with you, Rev. . . ."

"So have I, Max," Holt replied, recovering his breath. "And you know what?"

"Hell, yes, I know what!" She laughed. "I feel like I just kissed my kid!"

"Well . . . it wasn't *quite* that way for me," he said. "But there was something too familiar about it for comfort."

"Shit, Rev, what a disappointment." Maxine sat on the desk and propped her feet on an open drawer. "I'm sorry," she said, reaching into her dress pocket, "but I gotta have a cigarette."

"Do it outside, Max," he said, reaching for his cup.

"Okay," Maxine replied, taking his hand and putting it on her bare knee. "But if we ever get over this, the offer's still open."

He took her hand and kissed it. "Go type some letters or something, will you?"

"Sure thing, Rev," she said, opening the office door. "Oh, and before you make your rounds this morning, you might want to get that red stuff off your lips. Though it would be a lot more interesting around here if you didn't."

They never had another encounter, though their attraction was obvious, and everyone assumed their relationship was sexual. So it was no wonder that the Diocesan grapevine had told Bishop Casas to oppose Max's employment at St. Margaret's. He secretly hoped she would bust her parole and make both Holt and herself look bad.

The Rev smiled as he remembered the Vestry's initial opposition to her. As the governing board of the parish, they expressed disbelief that a woman "with her credentials" would be considered for such a delicate and confidential position. It turned out to be politically fortunate that eight of the ten Vestry members were men, most of whom Maxine or her friends had "known" in the Biblical sense. They voted to affirm her hiring at the next meeting.

Holt's smile vanished at the serious sound of her voice:

"Bishop Casas on line three, Father Holt."

Maxine could be very convincing, he thought as he picked up the cordless phone.

"Hello, Bishop. How are things at the God Box?"

"Hello, Lucas. Things here at Diocesan House are just fine," the irritated voice replied. "But I'm sure you did not call to check on the well-being of the Diocese. I'm a busy man. What's on your mind?"

"Glad to see you and I are still on the same footing, Emil. I didn't relish placing this call any more than you did accepting it. I called to tell you what you can do with this broken down museum you locked me into."

"Now, Lucas," the bishop said in the patronizing tone he knew Holt hated. "You haven't even given it a fair try. It's only been two months and you're just getting ready for Christmas services. Of course things are going to seem hectic, but it's better than that stink-hole I got you out of, isn't it?"

"No, it's not. And furthermore—"

"Don't 'furthermore' me, Lucas," came the angry reply. "It was St. Margaret's or the street. And if I'd had my way it would have been—"

"Well, it may still be, Bishop," Lucas Holt interrupted. "That's why I called."

"What are you talking about? Come to the point. I have a finance meeting to get to in ten minutes."

"Okay, Emil. Here's the point. And you can take it to your fancy finance meeting. This morning I was paid a visit by the new auditors I asked to review the finances of this place when I came on board. They came by personally and announced to me that St. Margaret's is flat busted. *Bankrupt.* It seems the assets we thought we had—or at least *I* was told by *you* we had—were mere figments of the former rector's vivid imagination. It looks like the old boy had his hand in the till for quite some time. No wonder he vacationed so well and so often. Too bad he died last year with that heart attack; I'd like to give him one now."

There was an audible silence on the other end of the line.

"So . . . what do you intend to do about it, Lucas?" The unconcerned tone registered in Holt's mind. He could almost *hear* the smile.

"What do *I* intend to do about it?" He stood and paced around his chair. "*You're* the bishop of the Diocese of Austin. *You* tell *me*!"

"I don't know what to tell you, Lucas. I'm sure you'll come up with something." There was a slight pause. "You always *do*, don't you?" Emilio Casas was enjoying this.

Lucas Holt stopped pacing.

"Wait a minute," he said, sitting down and looking into the plastic blankness of the phone. "You knew about this all the time, didn't you?"

The pause on the other end extended into silence.

"This whole parish deal was a setup to get me out all along, wasn't it?" He raised his voice to the silence. "Wasn't it?!"

"Well, let's just say, Lucas, that I knew it would either make you or break you. Of course I prefer the latter." The bishop sighed deeply. "You are an embarrassment to me, Father Holt. Simply put, you and your liberal ideas are an embarrassment to the entire Church. There really is no room for a person with your background and your politics in this Diocese. On the other hand, if you do manage to salvage St. Margaret's, it would make a lot of people happy. Either way I win."

Lucas Holt gripped the receiver in a tight fist and spoke slowly.

"Listen to me, Emil. I don't like being set up. I don't like your right-wing, nationalistic, mealy-mouthed, pietistic religion. But most of all I don't like *you*. I only hope that I find out your hand was in the cookie jar, too. But I doubt it. You're not that smart."

"Are you finished?"

"Not quite. I *am* going to find a way to keep this place open and then I'm going to run it *my* way, Emil. We'll have soup kitchens, demonstrations, AIDS groups, homeless people sleeping in the pews and classrooms at night. All the things that get your hands and your name dirty. This church will be a constant embarrassment to you from here on out, Emil. Count on it."

"You are a big talker, Father Holt. And you are in no financial position to do any of that. I can assure you, much to your dismay, that you will not find me involved in the embezzlement of any church funds. We knew at Diocesan House that there were strange goings-on up at St. Margaret's. Your predecessor was good at choosing his own auditors—and paying them off—so that we could never catch him. And as for your plans, well, all that remains to be seen. My guess is that you will fail. But if you *do* succeed, you will have helped my career advance immensely. It would be a big boost toward my becoming Presiding Bishop of the entire Church. So whether you win or lose, I win. But all that is useless speculation, Lucas, because you will undoubtedly fail. People like you always do."

The bishop paused for a rebuttal. Getting none, he continued. "I really must go now."

"Just one more thing, Bishop."

"What's that, Lucas?"

"A bit of penitentiary wisdom."

"Spare me."

"'What goes around comes around.' And I intend to be there when it does."

"Your heretical theology is entertaining, I must admit, but I believe there was something else you told me you learned at your beloved prison, Father Holt."

"What was that?"

"'Money talks, and bullshit walks.'" The stern voice paused. "Don't call me until you have results."

The monotone buzzed in Lucas Holt's ear. He lowered the receiver close to the phone and slammed it down on the set. His office door opened, and Maxine entered with a steaming mug in her hand.

"Thought you might want some Earl Grey to calm you

down, Rev," she said, setting it in front of him. "I know how those little chats with the bishop can excite you."

Lucas Holt fell back into his chair.

"Damn," he said, looking up at Maxine, who had a worried look on her face. "Thanks, Max. I guess you heard all that?"

"Most of it. I got in on the part where you were getting dumped. Can he really do that?"

"If we don't find a way to get the church on a financial footing again, Bishop Casas can circulate rumors that I failed here—with the implication that I can fail anywhere. He'd love it, too."

Maxine sat on the desk and pulled her skirt up over her thigh. "Maybe we should open up a little, uh, *business* to supplement our Sunday donations?"

Holt laughed. "With the legislature in session we'd make enough to build a parking garage here." He pulled her skirt over her leg and brushed her off the desk. "We'll have to think of something else."

"What about all that 'Treasury' stuff in the glass cases downstairs? It's supposed to be worth a lot."

"I thought about that as soon as I found out about the bankruptcy. But those pieces have been collected for 150 years, Max. Some of them date back to Cortez's time. People donated them to the church not only for use as memorial pieces, but also for viewing. It's one of the most priceless collections in the West."

He sipped his tea.

"The University of Texas would love to get their little archival hands on it," he said. "But there's a lot of emotional attachment to those things, especially the old gold and silver items. Some people would rather see the church go down the tubes than sell the Treasury.

"I don't know. I'll have to ask the Vestry about it. They run the church and it has to be their decision. We'll think of something."

"Let me know if I can help." She winked.

Lucas Holt propped his boots back up in the windowsill and put the steaming cup to his lips. He was about to say something to Maxine when the phone rang.

"Would you get that, Max? I'm not here."

"Sure, Rev." She picked up the phone. "St. Margaret's Episcopal Church. May I help you? No, he's not . . . What? Oh! Well, uh, just a minute—he just walked in the door."

Holt wheeled around in his chair. "I thought I said—"

"I think you'd better take this one, Rev. It's Lieutenant Granger from APD." Maxine handed him the phone. "One of your parishioners is dead."

• TWO •

Lucas Holt walked into the brown brick, fortress-like Austin Police Department headquarters shaking his head. He still could not get the conversation with Casas out of his mind. He kept replaying it on his way down the street to APD, thinking of all the clever cutting things he wished he had said, reliving the anger at being set up, mixing the anger with the shock and confusion about the murder of his parishioner, Dr. Walter Hargrive. Preoccupied, he did not hear the first time the man called to him from the jail bull pen.

"*Yo! Rev!* It's *me*, man!"

Lucas Holt continued up the steps toward his destination.

"*Yo! Hey, Rev!* It's *Joey*, man; from the *joint*! From *The Squad*, man!"

The Rev stopped. A part of his memory was suddenly jarred. A familiar tone reached deep into his consciousness and began to attach the voice to a name from years past. He turned to see a small scruffy white man with jailhouse tattoos on his forearms reaching out from behind the bars and smiling. Holt observed the jagged lines proclaiming never-ending love for several different women and recognized Joey Brison, his inmate clerk from the state prison at Huntsville. He also saw the discolored marks in the tattoos and knew what Joey wanted.

"Hey, Joey," he said, grabbing the small man's hands and holding them for a moment. Joey was cold already. He would need to make bail soon before the sickness started. "How you doing?"

"Not so good, Rev, not so good. But now that I seen you I'm doin' better."

"What are you doing in Austin? I thought your turf was Dallas?"

"Dallas is bust, man. Winters are too cold, anyway. Besides that, The Squad heard you were in Austin, so we thought . . ."

Holt didn't know whether to laugh or cry. The group of inmates, mostly long-timers, who had attached themselves to him at the pen were derisively known as "the God Squad." Their antics were legend by now in the Texas prison system. They could be prankishly funny when there was little else to do, or they could be lethally serious if any of their members, especially Lucas Holt, was threatened. That they were in town was both the good news and the bad news.

"Who else is here?"

"Well, I been here a few months, just before you started up the street at Maggie Mae's." Lucas Holt smiled. Despite himself, he was beginning to like a church with a nickname. "Eddie Shelton hit town last week, and Dorati—"

"*Nikky*? Nikky Dorati's here?"

"Shit, yes, Rev." Brison caught himself. "Oh, sorry. Anyway, sure he is. We couldn't get along without our Fearless Leader, could we?"

Oh, God, what are you doing to me? Holt prayed.

The police guard walked over to the bull pen. His burr haircut made his hammy face look even larger, and his dark blue APD shirt bulged over the huge silver rodeo buckle precariously holding in his belly, like a dam about to burst. Many former prison guards took less strenuous jail jobs when they retired. Holt vaguely recognized him from Huntsville, though the recognition apparently was not returned.

"Listen, Father . . ."

A good sign, Holt thought. The collar carried more weight with Catholics.

"I really have to keep visitors away from this holding tank. So if you don't mind?"

"Yes, sir," Holt replied. "I just want a minute with my parishioner for a word of prayer, if that's okay?"

"Yeah, sure, Father. Little Joey's blown his parole with this drug charge. So where he's going he'll need all the prayers he can get." He glanced around for his superiors. "But make it short." He walked away, nervously fingering his nightstick.

Lucas Holt bowed his head and moved closer to Joey Brison.

"Yo, Rev! My man!" Brison lowered his voice. "You don't think you could lend me a little chump change to get me outta here for a while, do ya? I can make it worth your while with some, some info you might could use."

"Listen, Joey, you know I don't put up bail for anybody. You got yourself into this mess and you're going to have to get yourself out. I will put some coins in your commissary, though. How's that?"

Joey Brison said, too loudly, "*Yes*, Lord. *Thank* ya, Jesus."

The Rev whispered, "Easy, Joey, easy. You're going to call that guy back here."

"Sorry, Rev. And I apologize for hittin' on ya for the bail. I know you can't do that. I'm not feelin' too well and I just panicked when I saw a friendly face. Hell, the info's free to you anyway."

"What info? Make it quick."

"That dude that got snuffed this morning, Rev, the one from Maggie Mae's?" Joey's voice lowered.

"Walter Hargrive? What about him? How do *you* know about that?"

"It's all over the street, man. Crap like that brings down the heat on all of us. So lots of dudes are splittin' before they get dragged in on meatball charges like they got me on."

The guard walked near the two men who had their heads bowed and eyes closed.

"I'm sorry, Father Holt, but I must insist—"

"Of course, Officer. We were just finishing."

Joey Brison said loudly, "*A-man!* Yes, Lord! Thank ya, Father Holt. Could I just give you a short hug before ya go, Rev?"

"Sure, Joey." He reached his arms between the bars and embraced the gate and the man.

"Here's the poop, Rev," Joey whispered. "That doc was dealin'. I know because I bought from him a time or two."

"Okay, okay, that's enough," the guard said.

"Thanks, Joey. I'll be sure and remember you on my way out."

"Oh, you don't need to do that," he said, tossing Lucas Holt a black leather object. "I took a ten spot outta your wallet. You really oughta be more careful, Rev. There's some sneaky dudes out there on the street." Joey Brison smirked.

The guard grabbed the ten-dollar bill out of his hand and crashed the nightstick against the bars. "That's another charge on you, Joey."

"No, it's not," Holt replied.

The guard shook his head. "But, Father . . ."

"I want that money put in his commissary." He looked at Joey and walked away. "He earned it."

Lucas Holt already knew what he would find as he opened the door. Susan Granger's office reflected her lifestyle. It was meticulously messy. There on her desk was the long-neglected flower he had sent her, hanging its brown brittle head on the lip of the vase. A cup of cold coffee with circles of colors shimmering on the scum seemed anchored to the top of the file cabinet. Months of magazine articles lay piled on the floor beneath the window overlooking the alley. On the bulletin board were the usual cop cartoons from the usual cop magazines. Tacked loosely to the wooden frame at the top was the bumper sticker announcing "Hate cops? Next time you need help—call a Hippie."

The lieutenant was on the phone and motioned him into a wooden chair in front of her large desk. As she argued with what must have been her superior officer, he watched her and remembered their first meeting. It had been at a secluded section of Lake Travis known for its attraction to nude bathers. Ironically, it was called Hippie Hollow. She had come there on a dare.

They both had been students at the University of Texas back in the turbulent sixties. Even then they stood toe to toe on opposite sides of the issues; he was SDS, she a Goldwater Republican; he burned his draft card and she wanted him arrested for it; he took her to hear Hoffman and Dylan, she retaliated by dragging him to hear Nixon and Up With People. The latter he still recalled with nausea.

As opposites attract, so theirs had been a passionate and stormy encounter. He hesitated to call it a "relationship." They were incessantly in and out of "like" with each other. Words like *relationship* and *love* were too permanent, too committed, too middle class for both of them. And of course they could not let feelings get in the way of careers. They drifted, then split and lost contact as they pursued different vocations.

It was years later when he was called at the prison to do the invocation for an Austin police cadet graduation ceremony that he learned she was now "Lieutenant" Susan Granger. He remembered her surprise at seeing him approach her with his clerical collar. He wondered, looking closely at her soft brown hair sternly pulled back to expose her striking features, if either one of them had really changed since then.

Susan Granger hung up the phone.

"What are you staring at? What's the matter with you?" She swung around in her chair to glance at the small round mirror taped on the wall.

"Oh, sorry." Lucas Holt snapped out of his time lapse. "I was just thinking of Hippie Hollow."

Granger's face reddened in the mirror. "Well, don't." She pretended to put a hair back in place. "That was a long time ago, Lucas." She swiveled back around to him. "So what are you doing here, bailing all your hoodlum friends out of my jail?"

Nice try, he thought. He had seen her blush. "Actually, since you were so nice to call and notify me, I thought I'd ride over to the murder scene with you, if you don't mind, Lieutenant."

"Actually, *Father* Holt, I *do* mind. That was a courtesy call." She shook her head and suppressed a smile. "Though I must grudgingly admit that it is sort of good to see you again."

"A major concession on your part."

"And the only one you'll get from me today. Look, Lucas, I realize that Dr. Hargrive was a parishioner of yours, but I'd prefer you keep your clerical hands out of this mess."

"But, Susan—"

"Listen, Lucas." The hint of a smile vanished. "If you want to involve yourself with known criminals in your spare time, that's your business. *My* business is to put them behind bars and keep them there. But you'd better realize that this isn't the pen anymore. You don't have the clout that you had in the joint, and you don't have that gaggle of cons around to protect your every move. So you're vulnerable on both counts: You mess with criminals on the street and you're liable to get hurt; you mess with the legal system on the street and you're liable to get in *my* way. And I won't protect you, either, because after the reaming I just got from the captain about this prominent physician's untimely demise, I sure as hell won't put up with trouble from *you* now."

"But, Susan—"

"I *knew* you'd be down here as soon as I called the

church. That's why I almost didn't do it." She paced behind the desk and reached for the mug of hot coffee. "I *know* you, Lucas. You can't leave well enough alone. You never could."

"Susan, I'm the rector at St. Margaret's Episcopal Church now. Walter Hargrive was my parishioner. I have a duty to be involved."

"You have a duty to do the man's funeral and leave the investigation to APD—meaning *me*."

"So what makes you think—?"

"What makes me think you'll be in this thing up to your clerical collar?"

"Yes."

"I had a little chat with the warden at Huntsville this morning."

Holt grimaced. "Uh-oh."

"And he told me about the plans of a certain group of inmates that had been recently released from his fine establishment."

"So?" The priest stared blankly at her.

"Forget it, Lucas. Every time you look like you *don't* know something, I know you *do know* something." She shook her head. "That face has never worked with me."

Holt grinned. She was the only woman who knew him well enough to see behind the collar.

"'T'ain't funny, McGee.' He told me that three or four of them . . . what did they call themselves . . . ?"

"The . . . uh . . . God Squad."

"How quaint." She frowned. "A living oxymoron."

"Now, Susan—"

"Listen, Lucas, I don't need more ex-cons to contend with while I'm in the middle of a murder investigation."

"But how do you know?"

"I know they're on their way here because the warden told me they all requested—and got—assignments to parole officers in Austin. And I know they did that to stay in contact with you—"

"So what's wrong with that? They have a right to go anywhere they want to. And, assuming they *do* contact me, why wouldn't that be a *positive* influence on them?"

Susan Granger crossed her arms and leaned over her desk. "Because you know as well as I do that they're going to want to *help* their favorite priest, and the next thing I know I'll be tripping over them in the middle of this damned investigation."

Holt sighed. "Susan, all I want to do is to go to the murder scene with you to see what happened to my parishioner."

"Then promise you'll keep those cons out from under foot."

"Come on, Susan, you're being unreasonable. I haven't even been contacted by them. I just happened to see Joey Brison in your holding tank out front. And anyway, those guys will be harmless. They've done their time. That's all they'll do here—a little more time."

"Oh, that's not *all* they'll do here, Lucas."

"Of course they'll do some odd jobs around town."

"Yeah, like breaking and entering, auto theft, public intox, and the occasional assault and battery, not to mention trying to assist *you*—in ways that I don't even want to imagine."

"Come on, Susan. The worst thing that could happen is that—assuming I even run into them—they maybe can provide information that you'd never get in a million years."

Susan Granger smiled at the Rev and said, "Sure thing, Lucas. Like *what*?"

Lucas Holt leaned forward in his chair and whispered across the desk.

"Like the reason our eminent Dr. Hargrive was so well to do is that he dealt a little drugs on the side."

Susan Granger's smile tightened into a thin line. She sat down at the desk, opened a drawer, and retrieved her purse. "Let's go." She stood, slung the purse over her shoulder, and walked toward the door. "I know I'll regret this, but with any luck you will, too."

Holt stood to follow her. "No, you won't, Susan."

"Uh-huh. Meet me in the car out front in five minutes. But before you go . . ."

"Yes?"

"Get that damned dead flower off my desk."

"I sent that to you two months ago when I got to Austin." Holt smiled and reached for the dried, crumbling rose. "I thought you were keeping it for sentimental reasons."

Granger stopped at the door. "On second thought," she ordered, "leave it there. It will remind me of what happens when I'm around you too long."

An uncomfortable silence accompanied them to the hospital. Attempts at idle chatter were answered in grunts as feelings were left unarticulated. It was not until they got into the hospital elevator that their business took precedence over their dissatisfaction with each other's presence.

"Fourth floor, I think," Lucas Holt offered, staring at the elevator doors. He punched the button.

"Second, actually," Susan Granger replied, also staring straight ahead. She punched two. "Listen, Lucas . . . I—"

"Forget it. We'll talk about it later." The doors opened. "Looks like this is the place. I don't think all that blood is from surgery."

"Not *official* surgery anyway."

The area was busy with the day shift of Homicide searching for clues, dusting small parts of the room for prints, taking close-up photographs of bloodstains and other macabre reminders of the murder. Their cohorts had been there all night, since Hargrive's body was first found by the horrified surgery nurse. Though the evening team's findings were packed and ready for the lab, the day crew hoped to find things that were missed in the sleepless dark of night.

"That's the murder weapon," Granger said, pointing to the scalpel in the plastic bag. "We think it will have minute particles of skin on it from the victim's neck."

"Charming. I saw a murder like this in a cell block once, but it wasn't done with a clean-cutting surgical instrument." Holt glanced around the room. "What do you think happened?"

"We're not sure. It looks like Hargrive sat here drinking coffee after surgery. The murderer snuck up on him, pulled his head back, and slit his throat."

"I can see how you'd think that." Holt stood in one spot and turned behind the dead man's chair. "But you're wrong about the 'sneaking up' business."

Several cops looked up from their gruesome tasks. Instinctively they did not like this outsider priest invading their private inner sanctum any more than he would like them invading his. But they did enjoy seeing their boss put on the defensive. Noticing Granger's indignant expression, they returned to their work.

"Okay, Sherlock, clue in all of us poor, dimwitted Watsons."

"Listen, Lieutenant," Holt explained. "I don't know squat about crime from the cop's point of view. But I do know a lot about it from the criminal's point of view—and from the victim's."

"I'm listening." She looked around the room. "We're *all* listening, even though we're pretending not to be."

"Well . . ." Holt imagined holding a cup in his hand. "It just seems that if the late Dr. Hargrive had been drinking his coffee—of which I assume you've taken a sample?"

Susan Granger nodded to one of her men. He shook his head. She frowned and squinted her eyes at him.

"He would have obviously dropped it when that scalpel was so expertly applied to his neck."

"Brilliant deduction, Lucas. But what about the possibility that he was finished drinking his coffee and just sitting there when—"

"Sitting there doing what? There are no magazines around. The television is located behind the chair, so he wasn't watching that."

"Why couldn't he have been just *sitting* there, Lucas?

People *do* that, you know. Present company excepted, of course."

"Because he wasn't." The Rev led her around the side of the chair. "He was sitting there talking to someone he knew."

"What?"

The other detectives again looked up.

"I got to know a guy on Death Row at the pen who was a major drug broker. Not a dealer, a broker. This guy was Mr. Paranoid when it came to making deals. Obviously not paranoid enough because he got caught and took out three undercover cops when the trap sprung. Anyway, I learned a couple of things from him." Holt pointed to the chair opposite the one soaked with blood. "The indentation in the soft leather cushion indicates someone was sitting there. My drug broker con could have told you the exact weight of the person if the indent was fresh. And if your surefooted sleuths hadn't ruffled the carpet there in front of the chair, we might have had an indication of shoe size."

"So you're saying?"

"That Walter Hargrive was murdered by someone he *knew*."

Susan Granger knew he was right. She knew also that she and her staff eventually would have come to the same conclusion. It annoyed her that Lucas Holt had done it so quickly and in front of her subordinates, and that he obviously enjoyed it. She did not know whether to thank him or apply the murder weapon to *his* throat. She thought of doing both.

"Good job, Lucas," she said reluctantly. "Now for the hard stuff."

Lieutenant Granger led him over to the light switch on the wall. She pointed to the carefully drawn numerals.

"What would your druggie pal say about that?"

Lucas Holt stared at the three numbers.

"'Two . . . four . . . three' . . . Hmmmmmm. Could be a lot of things."

"We've already thought of most of them. Presumably, it looks like the number two forty-three. But it could also be a date."

"'February, nineteen forty-three?'"

"Right."

"Unless the killer was European, Susan, in which case it would be March twenty-fourth."

The lieutenant frowned. The Rev grinned. She had not considered that and he knew it.

"Regardless, Lucas, this is November, so neither date makes sense."

"How about taking it literally?"

"What do you mean?"

"Maybe the murderer is saying 'two for three'?"

"'Two for three' what? He . . ."

"Or 'she.'"

". . . or *she* . . . is going two for three rounds with us?"

"Could it be that whoever it is is killing two people for three?"

"Don't do that to me."

"Do what?"

"Don't even imply we haven't heard the last of this kind of thing."

Lucas Holt looked intently at her. He spoke softly but clearly. The officers in the room strained to hear.

"You know as well as I do there's more of this to come."

"I was trying to unconvince myself."

"Won't work, Susan." Lucas Holt motioned to the numbers. "We had serial killers at Huntsville. The only time they leave calling cards is when they want to be stopped."

"Or when it's a game."

Lucas Holt looked at the drying pool of blood on the floor.

"Hell of a game, Lieutenant," he said, writing down the number. "Unless you hurry up and win, somebody else is going to lose."

• Three •

The man walked down the busy sidewalk of Austin's famous Sixth Street. It was only eight P.M. and the real
crowds had not yet started to gather for the music, food,
and other sensual delights "Old Pecan Street" had to offer.
An unusual combination of excitement and nervousness
swept over him as he hurriedly approached a side street that
would take him to his destination. Though he kept his head
down, there were surprised looks on the one or two people
who recognized him, nodded, and whispered to their com-
panions when he had passed by.

He breathed a deep sigh when he turned the corner onto
Neches Street and saw the sign of the club. Why had he
ever agreed to meet down here? Why couldn't he have been
more persuasive and arranged a less public arena? Did Ashton Willis suspect? No. That was impossible. In fact, Willis
would feel more secure here, in his own element, with his
own friends around. That security would be used to advantage. That was always the game, wasn't it? Use people's
strengths to play on their weakness? This man had done it
before; he merely needed to convince himself he could do it
here, in a place so foreign to his own senses and inclina-
tions.

Taking a deep breath and glancing once around the
street, the man opened the door and casually advanced to
the only empty seat at the bar. To the right was a thin, older
man; to his left a young woman.

"Good evening." The bartender smiled and cleared the
place in front of his customer. "What'll it be tonight?"

"Bourbon and branch. Light on the branch."

"Coming right up, sir."

The bartender walked away, and the man carefully surveyed the room behind him by looking indirectly into the mirror behind the bar. So far he was safe. No one he knew, even vaguely, was in the club.

He sipped at his drink. It would be his only one, as he would have to maintain a clear head for the task of the night. He listened to the conversation of the young woman with her friend. It was a heated discussion of the latest City Council fiasco with the land developers and environmentalists.

The man smiled to himself. The same scenarios. Austin, for all its growth, remained a small town at heart. But the power brokers were beginning to expand their base to include new high-tech money in their decisions for the city's future. The base of community groups was putting pressure on the old line to change and open itself to zoning and tighter regulation. It would be a battle for years to come. As with other battles, the crafty would win again. Just as he would tonight.

The man glanced at his watch and knew his chances of recognition increased with each passing minute. He cleared his throat twice as a signal and started to get out his wallet when the man on the next stool turned around and touched his arm.

"Have you a cold, or is it that nasty cedar fever that's beginning to start again?"

"Must be the cedar. Just started tonight. I think I'll go home and take care of it."

"Good idea. Please, put your wallet away. You were nice enough to come down here and meet me. I wasn't sure you'd come, actually. But I thought we might begin our talk here among my . . . kind." Ashton Willis crushed his cigarette in the metal ashtray and exhaled with obvious enjoyment. "It has been a long time since we've done business. I was, quite frankly, surprised at your call."

"Well, I've been meaning to talk with you, Ashton. There may be some more business for us to do, assuming you haven't lost your touch."

"My friend, just because I haven't seen *you* doesn't mean I haven't been—*busy*—shall we say? There are many people in this town who require the same service as you. And there are so few real . . . artists left." He lit another cigarette and gestured into the mirror. "Except—perhaps here." He cleared his throat. "No, I haven't lost my touch. What did you have in mind?"

"The first thing I had in mind was moving out of here." The man nervously lowered his voice. "You never know who else is listening, or what they will do with the information."

"Of course that's wise. But seldom does conversation carry over the noise of the crowd in here."

The man looked in the mirror at a table behind them. "Then how is it that I can tell you which side your friend over there was on in the last city council campaign?"

"I see. Then let me pay for your drink and we shall go."

Still not looking at him, the man finished his drink. "No, thanks, Ashton. Bartenders have long memories." He put money on the bar and turned to go. Almost absently he said, "Wait ten minutes, then leave. I'll meet you at your house in half an hour."

The street that led to the exclusive Cat Mountain section of Austin was winding and hilly. The man easily negotiated the curves in his BMW and felt right at home here. He noticed his head was a bit stuffy, and he opened the sunroof to let the cool November air circulate and clear his thoughts.

He had successfully maneuvered himself out of Sixth Street and back to his own familiar ground. He would have to be careful, though, even here. Ashton Willis was not as old or as vain as Walter Hargrive. Still, the plan would work. The act of surprise was on his side.

The mailbox read "Ashton C. Willis." The house,

perched atop Cat Mountain, overlooked the Colorado River on one side and the Austin skyline on the other. Willis had invested wisely in real estate in the days before Austin became a boomtown. Simply by owning land he had made fortunes. He was one of the few who had maintained those fortunes when everybody else in town went bankrupt. Now his money was financing new business growth as well as continuing to allow him to indulge his own private interests, and there were many of those.

The man parked in front of the house and waited. He had stopped at his own house to pick up a small cardboard box and to be certain Willis would arrive first. He picked up the box from the trunk of the car, walked to the front door, and rang the bell.

Ashton Willis, dressed in a smoking jacket and holding a drink, welcomed him into the house.

"Come in, my friend. The small box you have there has already excited my interest. Sit down and I'll fix you a drink."

"No, thanks, Ashton," the man said. "This is business." He looked around the familiar living room. It was richly furnished with custom-made furniture. Original paintings hung on every wall. Priceless objects of porcelain, gold, crystal, and silver adorned tables and display stands. "I'm in a bit of a hurry tonight. I just want you to take a look at this and tell me what you think."

The man opened a small cardboard box and carefully lifted out a compact gold case. Biblical scenes were delicately hand-engraved on all sides. Ashton Willis gently took the case from the man and sat down to examine it further. He removed his spectacles from his smoking jacket pocket and put them on, then opened the case and found its interior equally beautiful.

"This is superb, my friend. Exquisite. It may be the best one yet."

The man walked around in front of the fireplace and talked absently to Ashton Willis. "So what do you think?"

"I think it's probably worth about twenty thousand."

"But can you *do* it?" The voice came from behind Willis as the man inched closer to the brass fireplace set. The poker was silently removed from its stand.

Willis remained entranced by the beauty of the case. He wanted it and knew he would have to bargain skillfully to get it.

"Of course. Of course I can do it. Just look around you. But this . . . this will take some time. Not like the others. This will surely take . . ."

It was only a glint in the rim of his glasses, but it was enough to cause Ashton Willis to turn around just as the man behind him raised the poker. Confusion, then terror overcame him in an instant as he knew he could not escape. Raising his arms in a reflex action deflected the first blow and allowed him time to lunge at his attacker. But surprise was on the attacker's side, and as Willis lunged, the poker found its target again and again. His glasses shattered as he fell onto the splattered blue carpet.

The man, breathing heavily, donned gloves and wiped clean everything he had touched. He repositioned the poker and retrieved the gold case and cardboard box. He started to move toward the door when he stopped, set the box down, and walked back to pick up the fireplace poker. Thrice dipping it in the pool of blood on the rug, he smeared three large numbers on the painting above the fireplace.

He pulled the door shut behind him and wondered if they knew yet what it meant.

• Four •

At six o'clock in the morning the black Mazda 626 pulled into the open parking lot behind St. Margaret's Episcopal Church. Lucas Holt emerged, bleary eyed, and fumbled in his jacket for the separate set of keys for the building. Though the Eucharist wasn't until seven A.M., he liked to arrive early, down a small pot of tea to get his eyes open and voice intact, and be sure everything was set for the service.

Sometimes, as he approached the back door of the church at this hour, someone would be asleep in the shelter of the porch that overhung that entrance. Usually the sexton had taken care of them when he came in at five. Ricardo Valdez, known to everyone as R.V., was supposed to get there early enough to make coffee, direct the homeless to morning food, and set up the altar for the early service.

In the dark of this morning, however, Lucas Holt wondered if R.V. had done his job. Someone seemed to be waiting—*lurking* would be too strong a word, Holt thought—in the shadow of the porch. The Rev resolved to have R.V. replace the burned-out bulb above the door with an even brighter one today.

About halfway across the lot Holt caught the unmistakable aroma of a cigar and saw the distinctive red glow in the darkness. Judging the height of the person from the site of the glow, Holt quickened his step.

As he approached the porch, the cigar moved toward him.

"Yo, Rev," the deep voice said.

"I *thought* that was you, Nikky," Holt replied with obvious relief.

"By the height of the cigar, right?"

"Right."

"I taught you good, didn't I?"

"You taught me *real* good, Nikky." Lucas Holt put his key in the lock and opened the back door. "You got time for coffee?"

"Always got time for coffee with you, Rev," Dorati said, crumbling the cigar ash with the bottom of his shoe. He put the remaining unsmoked piece in his coat pocket and followed Holt inside.

They took the elevator down two floors and sat in the back of the kitchen. R.V. had made a pot of coffee and a separate small pot of Earl Grey tea.

"Where's Ricardo?" Dorati asked.

"Upstairs getting coffee and breakfast ready for the morning crowd."

"He's all right, you know."

"I know. I hired him the first day I came here. The guy we had was a crook."

"So's Ricardo."

"I know. But his momma's a parishioner here, and he needed the job to get out of jail—and he was raised Catholic, so he won't steal from the church, anyway."

"Great logic, Rev." Dorati bumped his cup against Holt's. "Good to see ya."

"You, too, Nikky," the Rev replied as their first meeting flashed through his mind. It was at The Walls unit in Huntsville State Prison—the section reserved for hardened criminals doing big time—twenty-five to life. Dorati's five-foot-six frame was neatly dressed in a starched tan uniform with tight creases in the shirt and pants. His black hair and bushy mustache made his dark eyes and complexion blend into the khaki uniform, like an explorer needing a pith helmet.

"Dorati," the short man had said, extending his hand. "I'm the warden's trusty."

Holt learned that "trusties" were long termers who, by good behavior, earned the privilege of being assigned to a prison official. Trusties had free rein of the prison, ran errands, and tended the grounds of senior guards' houses. Nikky Dorati, by his behavior and his rep, had been assigned directly to the warden.

They were both younger then. Nikky Dorati was doing thirty years for a hit that was reduced to manslaughter. Lucas Holt was two years into what would turn out to be twenty as chaplain. Both recognized in the other an unswerving sense of purpose and loyalty—and both determined to convince the other of the superiority of their ways.

Dorati came to Holt's nightly Bible study, dragging others with him to liven up the discussion. As the months passed, Nikky heard a side of the Bible he had never heard before, much less believed—a realistic, down-to-earth side, presented by a man absolutely convinced of its meaning today, not millennia ago. Much to his surprise, the stories started making sense to him.

Likewise, Lucas Holt learned of a way of life foreign to his own beliefs and customs. He listened to a side of crime and poverty and abuse that he had only read about in school. And he came to appreciate the coping, survival skills that these men and women had used to stay alive in a society where most of the chips were against them.

As they shared their stories from their own backgrounds, they came to respect and like each other over the years. Eventually Holt and Dorati crossed the boundary line into territory they both knew was extremely dangerous. They became friends.

And the risk paid off. Dorati, "The Mafia Midget," became the leader of The God Squad. He remained the Warden's trusty but spent all his free time either with Holt or the selected inmates in that group. Lucas Holt became the leader of the informal prison network, a powerful role in the functioning of the institution that was usually reserved for a high-ranking or greatly feared guard.

Now that they were both "out of the joint," they would see whether their friendship could withstand the pressures of the alleged "real world," or rather "real worlds" to which they separately belonged.

"You got a job yet?"

"I just hit town a coupla days ago, Rev. Cut me some slack. I did have enough money to get a room down at the Alamo Hotel."

"Nice old hotel."

"It ain't the Four Seasons, but it'll do for starters."

"Let me know if I can help. We've got a lot of good folks in this parish who—"

"I ain't been on the streets in twenty-two years, Rev." Dorati poured himself another cup of coffee and refilled Holt's cup from the teapot. "And I'd still be rottin' away the last eight in there if it wasn't for you."

"Not so, Nikky. You bought the good behavior and commendations all by yourself."

"All the same, Rev, I owe ya a few." He handed Holt a piece of paper. "Here's my private line." Dorati laughed. "If a woman answers, hang up and call me back in a coupla days."

"I assume you've got my home number already?"

"Number, house, car—I got you scoped, Rev. And as soon as a few more of the boys get into town, we're gonna have a little reunion at your place." He pulled the cigar out of his pocket. "On us, of course."

Holt pictured the occasion and started worrying already.

"Don't worry, Rev, we'll be good."

"Right . . . but . . ."

The intercom barked from the wall.

"Father Holt?"

"Yes, R.V.?"

"We're ready up here. You comin' up?"

"In a second. Thanks."

"I know you gotta go, Rev. I just wanted to stop by and say hello. And let you know how to get me if you ever need my help."

Holt stood and walked to the elevator with the short, greasy-haired man. As the elevator doors closed, Dorati said, "Somethin' I need to tell you about a guy that got offed last night."

The doors opened on the second floor and the two men hugged as they parted.

"Thanks, Nikky."

"Ain't nothin' to it, Rev." Dorati headed out the back door past cologned and perfumed parishioners coming to Communion before work.

Lucas Holt watched him relight his cigar in the parking lot. If what Dorati had told him was true, their relationship was taking a different turn that would use both their skills, and connections, in a new way.

And Susan Granger would hate it.

The report of the new auditors lay like a thousand-pound weight on Lucas Holt's desk. He could hardly pick it up. Each page seemed thicker and heavier as he moved through it.

The figures were clear and clean, the report neatly printed and bound with a plastic spiral. How was it that something supposedly so benign, even attractive, could be so devastating?

Maybe that was the way of the world, he thought. We expect attractive things always to be pleasant and only ugly things to be bad. That was how seductiveness worked; that was how the flimflam artists scored; that was how the con men won their games. Present an attractive package, play on people's expectations that pleasantness means goodness, then when their eyes are focused only on their own assumptions, pull the switch and escape.

That was exactly what the previous rector had done.

Books were juggled, payoffs made, glowing reports of full coffers given to the Vestry and the annual parish meeting. Ostensibly the church was in the best shape ever. So the Vestry, on the alleged strength of those finances, had voted to renovate and rebuild the sanctuary—much to the surprised chagrin of the rector.

Of course he had fought them every step of the way, knowing what the ultimate outcome would be. It was perhaps the effort of this battle that, along with his diet and exercise habits—or lack thereof—led to his heart attack, hospitalization, and eventual death.

Lucas Holt looked again at the red numbers in parentheses at the end of the report. He hoped his predecessor was frying in Hell for the sins of greed and weakness. Unfortunately the man had made his last confession with his dying breath, so there would be no comfort in imagining coals and pitchforks. Often the Rev thought the mercy of God was entirely unfair. This was one more case in point.

Jotting notes on a pad by the report, Holt had begun to estimate the value of the Treasury. With the price of gold as high as it currently had been, the sale of the Treasury would easily cover the church's basic operating expenses for the year, including the start-up costs already incurred for the sanctuary renovation. During that time he and the Vestry would have to launch an aggressive fund-raising effort if they were to keep St. Margaret's afloat. The Treasury was clearly the key to salvaging the church and, literally, buying time for the future.

But even if they sold it to collectors, invested the money, and tried to live off the interest while they raised the next year's budget, many parishioners would leave the church in disgust. Those artifacts were sacred to some, emotionally tied to family members long deceased for others, and the source of church popularity and distinction for many. It would be difficult to wrench the pieces out of the hands of these stolid and often powerful people. But the choice was clear: sell the Treasury and maintain the church's presence and ministry in downtown Austin, or keep the Treasury and display it in a museum open nine to five and closed weekends.

Holt wondered how the Vestry would vote. He began writing down their names to devise a lobbying strategy for each member. He had gotten only to the third name on the list when his office door opened and a familiar presence burst through with his mug in her hand.

"Come right in, Susan, and have a cup of coffee, why don't you?"

"I *am* in, I'm drinking your insipid church-coffee, and I am about to take a seat. I would suggest you keep yours. You're going to need it."

"Don't be so reticent, Lieutenant Granger," Holt said with a straight face. "Tell me how you *really* feel."

Maxine stepped through the open door with a steaming cup of tea. "I was just bringing this in to you when your . . . uh . . . friend stormed in ahead of me. Sorry, Rev, I usually announce your visitors." She put the cup on his desk.

"That's okay, Maxine. The lieutenant here is just practicing her assertiveness training. When she finishes her coffee, she will eat the mug. I am privileged to be the one chosen to observe. Thanks for the tea."

"I'll close the door and try to keep other intruders out," she said, not looking at Susan Granger.

"Thanks, Max."

The door closed and Susan Granger sipped her coffee. "I don't know how you can trust that woman to work for you, Lucas. I busted her once a month before she finally went down to prison. The money she had stashed around her room would have choked a horse."

"And did you ever find drugs there?"

"Well, no, but that doesn't mean—"

"And did you ever find her or any of the women she worked with diseased?"

"No, but—"

"Then blame the johns that patronized the place, not her

THE SAINTS OF GOD MURDERS 41

for providing a much-demanded community service. I never understood why you busted the women but not the patrons, anyway."

"Because most of the patrons had diplomatic immunity and you know it. They were either legislators or rich kids from U.T. whose parents could raise plenty of political hell for my department."

"Best justice money can buy. That's the American way."

Susan Granger eyed him suspiciously. "Is that why you opted out of the system?"

"I didn't opt out, Susan. We just have different approaches to it. You think you can work from within it by following all the rules, and I know I can't, at least not the way you do." They had had this discussion before, and he knew where it would end if they let it. "I worked within the system at the prison."

"Not the way *I* heard it. The way I heard it you *worked the system* at the prison."

"Nasty rumors, Susan." Holt grinned. "But I doubt that you came down here to argue with me about the American justice system. What's going on?"

Susan Granger crossed her legs and lounged back in her chair. "Did you know an Ashton Willis?"

"Ashton Willis . . . Ashton Willis . . . sure, he was an art buff around town. Supported all the galleries and even adopted some starving artists." Lucas Holt put the hot cup to his lips. "I take it from your question that Mr. Willis is now somewhere in the past tense."

"Excellent deduction. He is, in fact, in the past-perfect-very-dead-murdered tense. And do you know who killed him?"

"No. Do you?" He hated it when she was smug like this. "Who *was* it, for crying out loud?"

"The same one that killed Walter Hargrive."

Lucas Holt put the cup back down on his desk. He asked her to explain what had occurred, then proceeded to listen with only one ear. His triggered mind raced back through prison memories of mass murderers. They were always smarter than the usual criminal, more calculating, more precise and logical. They liked to play cat-and-mouse games with police, leave clues, sometimes even send letters or call radio shows. They took more risks than ordinary thieves or drug dealers. They would come out in the light of day, strike at unorthodox times or places, and then repeat the pattern to embarrass their pursuers. They were nearly always loners. And, he remembered with some fright, they were frequently well known and liked by their neighbors and friends.

"Lucas, are you listening to me?"

"Huh? Oh, yeah, sure, Susan."

"What did I just say then?"

"Something about a painting?"

"Yes, the painting. It was defaced with the same three numbers we found in the room where Hargrive was killed."

"Has any of this leaked to the press yet?"

"Nothing about the numbers. We made sure of that. The only people who know are in the department. If we let that one out, there'd be a dozen cover-ups using that insignia, just like they did with Son of Sam in New York. No, Lucas, we've been very careful about . . ."

From the intercom Maxine's voice interrupted: "Father Holt, I hate to bother you, but I have Burt Lister out here saying he just *has* to see you about the children's service for Sunday."

"Excuse me a minute while I run my church, Susan. It's these important matters like arguing over which hymns to choose that I love most about parish work."

Holt walked to the door and opened it to find his temperamental choirmaster leaning over the desk pointing to a service schedule.

"See, Maxine, if you just change this hymn here at the end, it will all work out the way I want it." He noticed the door open and stood to face Lucas Holt. "Oh, hello, Father. Thank you for clearing this little matter up for me."

"What 'little matter' is that, Burt?"

"Well, you see, this Sunday is the special children's service. The adult choir has the day off and all the services are being sung by the children. Won't that be wonderful?"

"*Wonderful* is certainly one word for it." Lucas Holt tried to restrain his excitement. He dreaded the day. Kids drove him crazy. He disliked intensely their screechy little voices ruining the hymns of the church. It was difficult to ruin the songs in the Episcopal Church Hymnal, but they managed. And they were always squirming and picking their noses and giggling and distracting people—usually their parents—who for some unknown reason thought they were cute. "What seems to be the problem?"

"Well . . ."

Holt noted to himself that Burt Lister always seemed to begin his sentences with the word *well*, just like Ronald Reagan, except Burt's voice was high and nasal.

"Well . . . it seems there is some disagreement about the closing hymn. Some of the parents want us to sing one of the new hymns, and I want to use one of the traditional 'Hymns for Children.' "

For this I left the prison, he thought. "Which 'new' hymn do they want, Burt?"

"Well, I don't know. It doesn't matter to them. But you *know* that the new songs don't rhyme or make any musical sense at all. So you can imagine what those kids will do to the recessional hymn, can't you?"

Lucas Holt had visions of midgets in red and white robes carrying him out of the service like Munchkins in *The Wizard of Oz*. They sang, or rather yelled, unintelligible words in inexplicable rhythms.

"I think you're being perfectly sensible about this, Burt. Which hymn did *you* want to use? Some of those about sheep and birdies are pretty sickening."

"Well, nothing like that, Father. I wanted to use 'The Saints of God,' if that's okay with you?"

"Fine, Burt—on one condition."

"Well, what's that?"

"That they only sing one or two verses of any hymn during the service."

"Well, Father Holt, you *can't* do that. This is their *big* day. Their parents will be out there watching their little darlings perform. What will I tell them?"

"Tell them two verses of screaming dwarfs is all I can take on a Sunday morning. It's either that or the new hymnal, Burt."

"Well . . . okay, Father. We'll do 'Saints of God.' And I'll give it my *best* to keep them on key."

"Anything else?"

"Well . . . no, Father. Thanks for your help."

Burt Lister turned to the secretary. "Verses one and two, Maxine," he said quietly.

The Rev rolled his eyes and pretended not to hear. Just as he was about to close the door, he heard the choirmaster give final instructions to the secretary.

"Well, you'll need to retype the hymn number in the bulletin, Maxine. It needs to be changed to two forty-three."

Lucas Holt yanked the door open and stared at Burt Lister. "What was that hymn number?" His eyes were open wide and he was beginning to breathe quickly.

"Well . . . uh . . . it was . . . two forty-three, Father Holt. Is anything wrong?"

"No. Nothing. Thank you very much." He slowly turned around, slammed the door shut and yelled at his visitor.

"SUSAN!"

Nearly spilling her coffee, Susan Granger responded, "My God, Lucas! Don't do that to me! What is it, for God's sake?"

"That's it!" he said, rushing across the office and picking up a book from his desk. It was labeled "Hymnal 1940."

"*What's* it? What the hell are you doing? Have you lost your—?"

"Look here! Read these lines!"

Susan Granger stood and took the book from him. She started reading the verses when he stopped her.

"No! Do it out loud!" He waved at her. "Out *loud*!"

"Okay, okay. Calm down," she said as she focused on the page in front of her. "'I sing a song of the saints of God, Patient and brave and true. Who toiled and fought and lived and died, For the Lord they loved and knew.' So what's the big deal, Lucas? It's not quite like you to get excited about this theology stuff."

"Keep reading! Keep reading!"

Susan Granger shook her head and continued. "'And one was a doctor, and one was a queen, And one was a shepherdess on the green: They were all of them saints of God—and I mean, God helping, to be one, too.'"

"Now look at the number."

"It's number two forty . . . Oh my God, Lucas." Susan Granger sat down and studied the hymn in detail.

"What's the matter?"

"Do you remember verse two?"

"It's been a long time. What is it?" He looked over her shoulder as she read it to him.

"I'll skip the first part. Here's the section we worry about."

"What do you mean?"

"Listen: 'And one was a soldier and one was a priest, And one was slain by a fierce wild beast: And there's not any reason—no, not the least—Why I shouldn't be one, too.'"

A minute of silence passed between them as they considered the implications of their find. Susan Granger was the first to speak.

"I count six." She looked up at him. "Right?"

"Right. Two down and four to go. Unless we catch the killer or he makes some unusual mistake."

"Which he probably won't, Lucas. You know that as well as I do."

"We also know we're dealing with a seriously ill person

here. And one who is desperate to be included as a Christian, if the hymn is any indication."

"But one thing so far doesn't fit."

"What's that, Susan?"

"These types usually don't act out of sequence. And he did."

"I don't understand."

"The first one was Walter Hargrive—the 'doctor.' But now he's jumped to the second verse and killed the 'soldier.' Ashton Willis had a distinguished military record. He was decorated by Eisenhower for his bravery in World War II. So unless the murderer owns a Chinese restaurant . . ."

Lucas Holt gave her an incredulous look.

"Chinese? Susan, have you lost your—?"

Lieutenant Granger smiled at him. "You know: 'One from column A and one from column B.'"

The Rev frowned, thought a second, then said, "No, Susan. The killer is taking them directly in order."

Susan Granger stared at him. "In which case . . ."

"That's right. Ashton Willis was gay."

• Five •

Granger stared at Holt in disbelief. "That's hard for me to buy, Lucas. He was a prominent man about town. And I've lived here long enough to know almost everything about almost every prominent body. There would have been lots of rumors about him if he were gay."

"Not necessarily, Susan. He was from that generation where it was still socially incorrect to be homosexual. So he had the perfect cover. He was forever taking in artists to live in that studio in back of his house. He lived on Cat Mountain and hobnobbed with all the people who consider themselves the movers and shakers of Austin society. Being a bachelor seemed appropriate for him; he was constantly joking about his previous marriages. But nobody ever asked 'to whom?' He always had a beautiful woman on his arm at the parties and bars. He made Lee Kelly's society column and made sure his name was always paired with a woman's. He was very discreet about his sexual preference, unlike many of his contemporaries who paid the price for it. If you didn't know better you'd swear he was straight."

"So that's my next question, Lucas. How is it that *you* 'know better'?"

"I'll tell you on one condition."

"No conditions, Lucas. Just shoot."

"Nope. You'd probably find out anyway, but I'll save you a lot of time if you promise one thing."

"What's that?"

"You promise you won't yell."

"Well, at least I know who it involves. It's that damned 'God Squad' of yours, isn't it? Okay, which one was it?"

"You promise?"

"Yes, I promise."

"Nikky Dorati."

Susan Granger stood from her chair and walked around the room with her hands on her hips. Finally she stopped in front of the Rev's desk.

"NIKKY DORATI?"

"You promised."

"Nikky Dorati is back in Austin again? That three-time loser is running loose on *my* streets? And *you* have the audacity to imply you've actually been *hanging out* with him?"

"Susan, you promised not to—"

"I *lied*!" she said, pacing in front of him. "Sometimes I can't believe you, Lucas Holt. Don't you give a damn about your reputation? Don't you think you're supposed to be setting an example in this community? And who do you associate your name with? Nikky Dorati, for God's sake."

"I think he's changed his act some, Susan."

"Damned right he has, Lucas! He graduated from Mafia hit man to chief enforcer and coke salesman for the Austin organized crime scene."

"The only organized crime in Austin is the bus system."

"The *subject* here is Nikky Dorati!"

"Okay! I'll grant you he was all of those things and more. But that was a *long* time ago, Susan. I'm telling you he's made some changes since that last time in prison."

Susan Granger calmed down and sat in a chair by the desk.

"Look, Lucas, I know Dorati and some of the other hoods in this town are here because of you. I know you are loyal to them and they to you. But that doesn't stop what they do from being illegal, immoral, and sometimes deadly. I just think you ought to be more careful of your reputation, that's all."

"Shucks, Susan. And here I thought you were worried about my body."

"All right, smart ass. Get yourself canned out of this church. Get yourself messed up in drugs and thefts and muggings. Just remember who warned you from the beginning."

"Lieutenant Granger, your concern and interest warm the very cockles of my heart. I will surely watch my back and not 'hang out,' as you put it, with the likes of hardened criminals."

"So when did you meet with Dorati?"

"It wasn't exactly a planned meeting," the Rev said between sips of tea. "He stopped by this morning to let me know he was here."

"And to tell you he murdered Ashton Willis?"

"And to tell me he *heard* that Willis was dead, but word on the street was nothing."

"What about the 'MOM' rule?"

"We already know two out of three—'Method' was the poker and 'Opportunity' must have knocked once real hard and Willis let it in. It's the third one—'Motive'—that even the street can't figure."

"Sure thing. And I think the street's got it figured out just fine. I think they'll use you as a patsy any way they can and then toss you out the way somebody tossed out Ashton Willis and Walter Hargrive." Her voice was rising again. "Dammit, Lucas, you know druggies never change."

"Of course I know that, Susan. What you fail to understand is that the guys we're talking about are entirely out of the drug scene. They *have* to be. They have an agreement with me that we associate as long as they're clean. If they're into any gaming at all—drugs especially—they don't come around."

"And you believe them?"

"Professional hazard."

"What about Joey Brison?"

"Until I saw him at your place today, I hadn't laid eyes on Joey since he was my clerk at the prison."

"And you think Dorati is clean?"

"As clean as he's going to get, and that's good enough for me. Besides, what makes you think half of the prominent business people in this town are 'clean'? They just dress better, deal in bigger dollar amounts, and can buy their way out of trouble. If we're going to talk 'criminal' here, Susan, let's make sure we define our terms."

Susan Granger smiled.

"You know we're at it again, Lucas. You want me to be a Socialist and I want you to be a Republican." She reached over and touched his hand. "I am worried about your bod, but I also give a damn about your reputation. I have to keep you around to fight with, don't I?"

He squeezed her hand. "Okay. Check and checkmate—at least for now." He rose and came around the desk. "I need to send you on your way in a few minutes. I have an emergency Vestry meeting this afternoon to talk about salvaging this whole outfit."

"The bankruptcy you told me about?"

"Yes. We're trying to come up with some ways to prevent going under."

"Okay." She stood to leave, then turned around. "Just one more thing, Lucas."

"What's that?"

"When you mentioned the word *prevent* just now, I wondered if we could figure out how to stop this killer before he strikes again."

"What did you have in mind?"

"Well, assuming we're right about this 'two forty-three' thing, and assuming we've got the sequence correct, then the next victim on the list has to be—"

"A 'shepherdess'? Who in the world could *that* be?"

"Maybe it's a gay rancher."

"Very funny, Susan." Lucas Holt opened a drawer and pulled out the listing of Austin clergy.

"What are you doing, reviewing your list of shep-herdesses?"

"Sort of." He put the list on his desk. "I was wondering if that could mean any of the women ministers in town."

"Very good, Father Holt." She walked behind him to re-view the list. "But that would mean skipping categories and doing the priest *and* the shepherdess at the same time. Somehow I think this guy's not into economy murder."

"Probably not, but it wouldn't hurt to have your people keep an extra eye on these people's houses over the next few days."

Susan Granger took the list. "I'll do that. Any other ideas?"

"Well, yes, as a matter of fact. I have a family in the parish that seems uniquely qualified for the category."

"Who's that?"

"Do you know the Hampton sisters? They inherited the Deep River Ranch out by Liberty Hill."

"Yeah, but they don't still run it, do they?"

"One of them does. One sister, Meredith, lives here in a condo down on First Street. You could put an undercover guard on her without much problem. But let me talk with her first. I understand she's pretty good with the gun she carries."

"Done. What about the other sister?"

"Stirling still works the ranch."

"By herself?"

"No. She's got some hands, but they don't live there, so she's pretty much alone. But, again, let me call her first. Their daddy taught them to be self-sufficient—and more than a little skittish."

"We'll put a couple of our officers on the ranch. Liberty Hill only has one cop, and he's still driving the town's seventy-six Ford pickup. Not a lot happens crime-wise in Liberty Hill."

"Let's hope it stays that way."

"Father Holt?" Maxine's voice rasped through the intercom.

"Yes, Max?"

"Mr. Travis Layton, Esquire, is out here to see you." Her smiling tone of voice indicated her like for the person at her desk. "Says he's early for the Vestry meeting and needs to talk with you beforehand."

"I'll be right out, Max. See if he'd like some coffee or something."

"I'd like the 'or something,'" Layton barked. "But you don't carry my brand at this waterin' hole."

The intercom clicked off.

"I'll be going, Lucas. If you think of anything else, remember you promised to let me know *first*."

"Right, Susan." He winked at her.

As Susan Granger closed the door behind her, Lucas Holt picked up his private line and dialed an unlisted number.

"Hello, Nikky?" He spoke softly into the phone. "I need some help. Here's what I want you to do. . . ."

• Six •

"I just don't know, Lucas." Travis Layton sat across the small table from the Rev. "You're going to have to do some damned hard convincin' to get me to let loose of that Treasury."

Lucas Holt knew it was hard for Travis Layton to "let loose" of anything once he got hold of it. The sixty-two-year-old attorney was known for his tenacity when he took a case. Part of a vanishing breed, a native Austinite, Layton built a career taking the cases nobody wanted. He'd fought with almost everyone in town and had enemies and friends in powerful places. Often they were the same people. The only battle he hadn't won was with the bottle.

"I mean, some of that stuff is from my family from generations back. We were here when this chunk of real estate you're sittin' on was still Mexico and settlers were invited by the government to farm the land. One of those jeweled crosses downstairs is from a mission my great-granddaddy salvaged when that band of Texan upstarts started talkin' rebellion. He moved the church to his ranch where it'd be safe. Matter of fact, a lot of that Treasury is from that old mission of his."

"I know that, Travis, but—"

"No *buts* about it, boy. If my great-granddaddy ever thought you-all would be sellin' his stuff, he'd a hid it out instead of donatin' it to this collection."

"I suppose a lot of the others on the Vestry feel the same way?"

"Damned right they do, son. And you can start right at the top with your senior warden."

"Harris Lambert?" Holt looked puzzled. "He's not from anywhere *around* here. I thought he migrated from Georgia or Tennessee and started a second career in insurance here. I know he's committed to the church, but what's his investment in the Treasury?"

"Well, first off he's senior warden and likes the position. He ain't likely to do much to damage his chances of gettin' reelected to it for another three-year term."

"He does do a good job of running church business."

"Don't hurt his insurance trade any, either." Travis Layton grinned. "The more people he comes into contact with, the more business he seems to do."

"How much more *can* he do? He seems to have built up an empire in his thirty-some years here."

"You don't know Harris, son. There's *always* another client to get into the coffers. He's been ambitious as long as I've known him. I've worked both for and against him over the years in insurance suits, and there's no finer ally and no worse opponent than Harris Lambert."

"And you think he won't want to see us lose the Treasury?"

"Ninety-nine percent sure. In the first place he's got the whole damned thing insured to the teeth. And he has it appraised every year to update its worth."

"Not by the same firm that brought us Bankruptcy, Inc., I hope."

"Not hardly. In fact, I think he hires out a different firm every year, just to be safe. Plus he sees that Treasury as a way to get people into the church. They come out of curiosity and stay 'cause of our programs. Nope. No way in hell you're goin' to convince Harris Lambert to let loose of that gold mine we got on display in the basement."

Lucas Holt put a check mark next to Lambert's name on his list. The next Vestry member brought a smile to his face.

"Now, Cora Mae Hartwig will certainly vote in favor."

"Boy, if it meant sellin' her eighty-nine-year-old body on Sixth Street to keep this place open, she'd do it. And she'd sell yours, too, if she thought it would help."

"Is *that* how old she is? Nobody I ask around here seems to be sure."

"That's my best guess. The only thing I know for certain that's older than her is a live oak tree over on Salado Street."

Lucas Holt laughed and refilled Layton's coffee mug from the pitcher Max had left with them.

"Thank ya, son. No, Cora Mae is so devoted to St. Margaret's Episcopal Church she'd rob, kill, and maim to keep it here. I think that's why that old lady never married. She was too much in love with this church to give her time to anyone else."

"So that's one yes vote." Holt put a plus by the name of Cora Mae Hartwig. "Who else is a yes?"

"Well . . . let me see."

"How about Toni Lord? She's fairly new to Austin and can't have many ties to the Treasury."

"That's true, Lucas. But she does have ties in the African-American community. She's made a lot of her real-estate fortune over there developin' those neighborhoods and makin' lots of money for some powerful people besides herself."

"I don't get the connection."

"Bein' from Smithville, you wouldn't. I don't think they tell you all the juicy stuff in Smithville High."

"So educate me."

"Quiet as it's kept, boy, there were a lot of blacks found their way to the Underground Railroad through this church. And some of them came back to Austin feelin' mighty grateful. Their families today still go to church here, and I think you'll find some interestin' names on the donor list for a lot of the things in that Treasury if you go to lookin' it up."

"You're right. That never did come up in my Texas History class. But Toni's a tough businesswoman. I still think she'd be in favor of selling it if she could be convinced it was the only way to survive." Lucas Holt picked up his pen. "I'm going to mark her down as a yes."

"Then I can tell you another definite no for your list."

"Who's that? Besides *you,* I mean."

"I ain't made up my mind yet, boy. Don't go gettin' so sure of yourself. I was talkin' about the other minority we got on the Vestry."

"Luis Arredondo? I suppose you're going to tell me his granddaddy ran the mission on your granddaddy's ranch. Or maybe he's Castilian instead of Mexican and donated some Communion cups from Spain?"

"Wrong on both counts, Lucas. Luis's family is from the Valley. He's built that family grocery where he started working as a kid into the biggest produce distributor between San Antone and Dallas. He grew up Catholic but went to St. Stephen's Episcopal Boarding School on a scholarship. When he graduated from there, he came to St. Margaret's because we're downtown and close to his business."

"I think you're building your case wrong, Counselor. You've just about got me convinced he's in favor of selling the Treasury."

"He probably would be."

"Except for what?"

"Except for his buyers are all Catholic, and most of his family's friends are all Catholic, and half the people who do business with him are Catholic."

"So . . . ?"

"So when word hits the front page of *The American-Statesman* that Luis Arredondo was in favor of selling religious relics to the highest bidder, thus breaking up the oldest and most complete collection of Spanish and early Texan mission objects west of the Mississippi, nearly all of which are from Catholic churches and are viewed by hundreds of Catholic schoolchildren on field trips from around the state every year—"

"Okay, okay. I get the picture." Lucas Holt frowned and marked on his list. "So I'll assume for the time being Luis is a tentative no."

"That's what I like about you, boy. You're such an optimist."

"I'm a far cry from an optimist, Travis. I just think I may be able to convince Luis it's the right thing to do."

"Sure thing, son. And if a frog had wings, he wouldn't bump his ass so much."

The Rev smiled. "It's worth a shot, anyway." Lucas Holt took the final swallow of his now cold tea. "So who does that leave me?"

"The only one you do have a chance with, Lucas. Case Atkinson has only lived here a few years. He's got no family ties here—"

"Or on your granddaddy's ranch."

"There, either, son. And he's trying to build up—no pun intended, of course—his architectural practice."

Lucas Holt groaned under his breath, much to Layton's delight.

"To look like the swing vote that kept St. Margaret's Church alive and well in downtown Austin would win over a lot of potential customers. You know how powerful the Austin Heritage Society is around town. There are a lot of people in sympathy with them, and they'd love to keep this place as a historical building."

Travis Layton stroked his growing five o'clock shadow.

"Yep, I'd say Case Atkinson is a definite maybe."

"I'll put him down as a yes."

"Like I said, son—"

"I just think there's a higher probability of his voting in favor of the liquidation than you do." Lucas Holt reviewed his list a final time. "That tallies up to two in favor, two against, I'll give you Atkinson as a maybe, and then there's you."

"Looks like I might be the decidin' vote, boy. Wouldn't that be a hoot?"

Lucas Holt looked at the old attorney. The black pointy-toed boots were scuffed and faded, his gray Western suit was worn shiny in spots, his shirt torn at the pocket. Holt wondered what Layton had been like in his heyday, before he smelled of Bugler tobacco and Jack Daniel's whiskey. Probably a lot like his own dad as he remembered him from childhood, before he began to look and smell like Travis Layton.

Lucas knew it was part of his affection for this old man. It was, indeed, like seeing his father sitting there, full of bullshit and bravado, talking like Texas—cactus, horseflies, and gun smoke. A small-town lawyer with Austin aspirations, Ben James Holt made repeated tries for a seat in the Capitol, but was never quite willing to make the deals that would win it for him. Lucas remembered the late-night talks after political meetings, when his dad would come home exhausted, confused about his friends and their ability to compromise their lives for a taste of power.

And he remembered the final race, when it looked as if his dad would win decisively. Going into the last week of the campaign, a rumor emerged in the press that his dad had committed some personal indiscretion that, if known, would cause him to pull out of the election. There were hints at bribes, an affair, jury tampering in a murder trial from years before, but his dad took them all on with the righteous indignation he had passed along to his son.

Until two days before the vote.

It was well past midnight. Lucas had been up reading when he heard the phone ring. His mother answered and called for his father, not an unusual occurrence for the best attorney in town. He remembered hearing his father hang up, return to the bedroom and close the door. He thought he remembered hearing his mother cry. The next day at break-fast his dad announced to Lucas, and later to the press, that he was withdrawing his name from the ballot for "personal, family obligations." He swore to tell Lucas when the boy was older and would understand, but he never did.

His campaign leaked the story that Mrs. Holt was quite ill and would require her husband's full attention. It seemed to be confirmed when his mother died the following year. Only he and his father knew it was by her own hand. Even before that, after quitting the campaign, Ben James Holt was a different man. He had turned into the prototype of Travis Layton, whose tattered image sat before Lucas Holt now.

"Peso for your thoughts, boy! Where'd you go?" Layton asked.

"Huh? Oh, I was just thinking that your deciding vote could be the crowning point of your career, Travis."

"Shoot, boy, you know my career's been a roller-coaster ride ever since my daughter died twenty-five years ago. 'Life seen through the bottom of a whiskey glass'—that's been my story for a long time."

"You could beat it, you know."

"Hell, *I* know I could beat it, Lucas." The man's voice rose in anger. "Why the hell should I *want* to? Ruin a great reputation, you know. I been thrown out of more court-rooms than a dog has fleas. And I went right back and won all them cases just to show 'em I could." Travis Layton sat forward in his chair. "*Beat it*? What the hell do you think's kept me *goin'* all these years?"

"Sorry, Travis." Lucas Holt retreated. "I didn't mean—"

"I know it, son. And I'm sorry for losin' my temper." The attorney stood up. "Isn't it about time for that meetin' to start?"

Lucas Holt looked at his watch.

"Matter of fact, it is." He stood and walked to the door. "Come on, I'll walk up to the room with you."

"I'll be up in a minute, son. I left my briefcase in the car. I want to fetch it so I can take notes on what I'm sure will be your excellent presentation. Who knows, Lucas? Maybe you'll change my mind. I doubt it, but you're the optimist around here." He patted the Rev on the back. "Go on ahead. I'll meet you up there."

Lucas Holt walked up the stairs to the classroom where the Vestry would begin deliberations about the future of the church. Just as he had known with his father, Holt knew exactly what it was Travis Layton had gone back to his car to "fetch." From the second-story window, he saw the old lawyer reach for the brown bag in the backseat.

He only wished Layton would have invited him along.

The meetings were okay, it was the table he disliked. The long, dark mahogany board room table formalized the relationships, kept Vestry members at a distance from each other, and hid their nervous mannerisms that often gave away true feelings.

This was Lucas Holt's third Vestry meeting, and he was still ambivalent. On the one hand, it was good to have a group of concerned and seasoned parishioners helping guide St. Margaret's through the straits of this difficult decade. On the other, Holt was very used to running his own ship all alone, without the interference and advice of anyone else.

At least the number was small. Though there had been ten members when he started two months ago, they were now down to six. Austin's rapid population turnover accounted for three corporate managers leaving; the fourth had suffered a heart attack and resigned.

Holt looked around the table and found himself liking each person there for a different reason, beginning to trust them, though still chafing at the constraints of group decision making that were necessary here—especially now.

For the last hour he had made his plea about selling the Treasury. He had reviewed the audit line by line and had watched their reactions both as individuals and as a group. If Holt had learned anything at the prison, he had learned to read people the way cons did, looking for the fatal flaw, the not-so-obvious comment that revealed the protruding bit of ego on which to hang them up.

"So, that's about it. I think I've told you the whole story as I know it." As he finished his closing argument, feeling much like Travis Layton must have felt in his heyday, the Rev sized up his jury.

Layton, always the lawyer, shuffled through the papers, overdoing his attentiveness to cover the buzzing in his brain. At bottom he would see the reasoning behind selling and agree, unless his cantankerous side got control. Apparently Layton could be a mean drunk, at times dangerous with the gun he was known to carry in his briefcase.

"I'd entertain any questions or comments now," Holt said.

Next to Layton, the petite Toni Lord looked earnestly concerned. Her puffy round circle of a face with her shiny black hair pulled taut usually expressed willingness and openness to ideas—or so the strong-minded woman would have you believe. But tonight her brown satin skin crinkled in doubt, as though she had been hit in the face or had been forced to take unpleasant medicine.

"So you're sure the mortgage company will work with us?" Lord asked. "We would have to know that before we commit to selling the Treasury."

"They'll work with us," Harris Lambert spoke for the priest. "Because they don't want the publicity we can raise if they refuse us." Holt regarded the man as he talked. Now in his early sixties, Harris Lambert must have cut a dashing figure in his younger years, before his broad shoulders and thin waistline reversed positions. The thinning gray hair still had in it the dark black streaks that once had framed the rough Mount Rushmore face. "Besides, I've known that company for decades." Lambert smiled the ingratiating smile for which he was known. "We've done business on a handshake—and I think they still value my opinion somewhat."

"Even if we do have the mortgage payments worked

out"—Luis Arredondo leaned forward with coffee cup in
hand—"it doesn't mean we can pay our debts *and* keep the
doors open with our current expenses." For someone in the
produce business, Holt thought as he looked at the man,
Arredondo dressed like a riverboat gambler—three-piece
suit, his deceased Castilian father's gold watch in the vest
pocket, complete with chain and dangling PBK key. Luis
was a man on the way up in Austin politics, a Hispanic
popular with the masses who had been known to be "practi-
cal" with Anglo power brokers when necessary to advance
his business or political cause. And for all his sleek good
looks—the dark hair, eyes, and skin that so many women
seemed to find attractive—he was known to be a vicious
street fighter when forced into a corner. Holt hoped never
to push him there.

"We should do whatever we have to do," Cora Mae
Hartwig's scratchy voice spoke up. She cleared her throat
and took a drink of the coffee she had brought in her own
thermos. The Rev could not suppress a smile at the rife
speculation that she doctored her ubiquitous concoction
with a shot of schnapps. "The ministry of this parish means
a lot more than a bunch of dusty antiques. Once we're rid
of that stuff, we can get on with the business we're supposed to be *in* here."

Toni Lord started to reply, but was cut off.

"And don't think I have no investment in the Treasury."

"Just because you wrassled the original Mexicans for it . . ."
Travis Layton drawled.

The group laughed, and the old woman squinted her eyes
and pursed her lips toward him before she continued. "Stop
over to my house for some arsenic and old lace, Travis,"
she replied. "And the rest of you, listen to me. My ances-
tors are responsible for some of those beautiful old pieces,
too, but so what? All that is past history. When you get to
be my age, history looks a little less romantic than it does
to you young folks who seem to want to hold on to it. I just
want to get on with solving the present problems, and

we've got enough for Maggie Mae's to say grace over for years—but we need to get *to* them and we can't do that if we're not *here*."

"Case," the Rev said, "you've been awfully quiet tonight."

Toni Lord could no longer contain herself. "I've got to break in here," she said angrily. "I've been sitting and thinking and fuming inside for the whole meeting. I don't like selling that Treasury and I don't think we should do it." She leaned forward and tried not to appear the little girl that her petite frame portrayed. "Every church I've belonged to, the minorities get short shrift. I had hoped that wouldn't happen here at St. Margaret's—but it sure as hell looks like it is."

Her face was stern as she addressed the group. "That Treasury represents the handiwork of decades of native people, many of them Hispanic or Indian or African-American *slaves*. There's a story to be told there that hasn't even begun to be told. So I think it boils down to a choice between keeping open an institution that has helped suppress native peoples versus valuing and holding on to the very products that those peoples created."

"But, Toni—" Luis Arredondo started.

"Let me *finish*, Luis," she scolded. "To me, that's no contest. If this building is to stay here, then we'll have to find another way to keep it—but I for one will *not* vote to do it—once again—at the expense of destroying this incredible collection of minority artwork." She glanced at Arredondo. "Floor's yours."

"Thank you," he said coolly. "But don't think that you have a monopoly on harsh feelings about this situation." He sat back in the chair and shook his head. "I keep wondering who the hell was watching the store while our previous Rector embezzled us out of everything we had."

"Now, wait just a damned minute here," Harris Lambert said. Holt noticed that he kept his hands out of sight, so no one would see his clenched fists. "If you're implying that I was somehow remiss in my duties, Luis, I'll have you know that I scrutinized everything that old fool did, and I had it double-checked by the junior warden at the time—who was an accountant with Anderson. But the damned auditors he paid off made the books look absolutely sound."

Luis himself was now red-faced. It seemed to Holt that the display of anger was disproportionate to the size of the problem. At the pen that always meant some hole cards weren't showing.

"I am just saying," Arredondo continued vehemently, "that since most of us are businesspeople here, it makes me furious that we are now put in the position of destroying that collection. I have different reasons than Toni for not selling it. But, like her, I will *not* agree to consider breaking it up just to save this building and to clean up after the irresponsibility of a priest *and* his Vestry."

"Damn it, Luis." Lambert's fists were now on the table. "*You* were on the Vestry then."

"I *know* I was, Harris! And I feel like we just *sat* there and *let* him to it to us! We are *all* to blame! And I *will* not sacrifice that Treasury to our own stupidity! I will *not*!"

"We have been over this before, gentlemen," Cora Mae Hartwig pronounced quietly. "We were too trusting, Luis. Just too trusting. I was on the Vestry, too, Harris. And you'd think someone *my* age would have known better. But he was so convincing and smooth, and who would have thought that the *Rector* would have done such a thing?"

"Water over the dam, Cora," Travis Layton replied, pulling the meeting back to order. "Got to be water over the dam. What we have to do now is decide how we're going to get out of this damned situation that he put us into."

Lucas Holt noticed Case Atkinson fidget.

"Case? Did you have a comment on this?"

"Yeah, I guess I do. I mean, I know I'm the new kid on the block around here, so I don't feel like I have that much of a say." The tall, thin man with the runner's body leaned back in his chair and folded his hands on the table. His sandy-brown hair was always perfectly in place, his small mustache neatly trimmed. His crisp starched shirt was always open at the top button, revealing that the severe acne marks on his face extended downward.

"I'm newer than *you* are and I have a say in it," Holt replied. "It's a tough decision, any way you cut it."

"I guess I can see both sides of the issue."

"That may be a plus," Toni Lord remarked. "Most of the rest of us can only see our side."

"Or it just may be indecision," Atkinson answered. "Right this second I don't know what to do. But I have to tell you I'm leaning in the direction of selling." He unfolded his hands and picked up his cup. "I guess I need more time and information. But one thing's for sure. I don't feel good about making a decision under the pressure of a storm. I'd be a lot more comfortable with more time and more data." He glanced around the table. "And more peace."

"Good," the Rev said. "I hope all of you need that. I only wanted to raise the issue with you tonight and plead my argument for selling. I appreciate the deep feelings on all sides of this. We need to talk about those to come to the right strategy. Call me in the next two weeks as questions come up. Poll people at church when you see them. Pull together as much information as you can and I'll do the same. Then let's see if we can come to a final decision next month."

"Thank you, Father Holt," Harris Lambert spoke as senior warden. "By the way, I apologize for the expressive language of myself and my cohorts here, but we *are* Episcopalians with strong views on all sides."

"No apology necessary. The prophets did it all the time."

"Then I hope we meet with their success in leading people to the right decision," Toni Lord said.

"If there is no further business?" Lambert looked around inquiringly. "Then this Vestry meeting is adjourned."

Twenty minutes later the last car pulled out of the lot as

Lucas Holt locked the back door for the night. He noticed a
Sunday leaflet that Burt Lister must have dropped on the
way in from the printer's. In the glare of the outside light
he skimmed the Order of Service, stopping at the Recessional Hymn.

As he stuffed the leaflet into his coat pocket, he wondered how many of the Vestry knew the words to Hymn
243.

• Seven •

The North San Gabriel River meandered lazily through the piece of land on which the Deep River Ranch was situated. In its calmer, gentler moments the San Gabriel provided water for the stock and both beauty and entertainment for the Hampton sisters who swam and fished its muddy whirlpools. Occasionally it exceeded its banks, and once, in the Memorial Day Floods back in 1981, had nearly consumed the ranch house, which sat in a high bend thought to be safe from its fury. On this November night its rocky waters provided noisy cover for unsure footsteps slowly approaching that same house.

Stirling Hampton sat in plain sight of the kitchen window. Listening to the radio, she poured a second glass of Fall Creek wine from her neighbor's vineyard. Her natural blond hair shone brightly in the lamplight, and her fair, white skin rendered her nearly angelic, soft and feminine in her loose flannel shirt and Levi's.

Her gentle appearance, however, concealed her considerable physical strength and ability to run the ranch and the hands that kept it working. She had grown up on this land and was determined to keep it from the designs of local developers who desperately wanted to market the river and its seasonal fascinations. As she struggled with weather, disease, and governmental confusion, her sister remained the ever-silent partner. But the lonely struggle felt good to her, and the long days ended with a spent feeling of accomplishment. This day had begun at four A.M. and was only now winding down with a late supper, which she would be too tired to finish. Tomorrow would be the same—assuming there was one.

Stirling Hampton turned in her chair without getting up and reached for the volume knob of the radio. Flicking it off, she returned to eating her solitary dinner, preferring to hear the rush of the San Gabriel in the background. For others the flow of the river muted subtle sounds and rendered them inaudible. For her, the river's motion was a constant given. She knew its sound, could gauge the approach of coming storms by it, heard the change of seasons in its varying current, prepared for battle when its torrents raged. Its ever-present background was the baseline over which all other sounds were noticed by her, like the snap of the twig about twenty paces from the kitchen door.

Through the window, she appeared as nonchalant as she had been since entering the house. She had disregarded the call from that Lieutenant Granger as alarmist nonsense and had not really understood the reason for concern. It was not until later, after sundown, when the usual nocturnal creatures were unusually silent, that she began to listen more carefully and to take the necessary precautions.

Thanks to her daddy, not much frightened Stirling Hampton. With her older brother's childhood death she became the "son" of the family, accompanying her father on hunting and fishing trips, learning the land and the stock and the river from him. Their relationship was the source of envy from her sister, who competed in a losing battle for his closeness. Now her sister had left Stirling in charge of her share of the estate, hoping the latter would fail or die under the burden. With her daddy in mind, Stirling planned to do neither.

She lifted the crystal goblet up to the light, swirling the ruby liquid around slowly. While appearing to observe its color she glanced out the window, noting the shard of light reflecting from some small object in the stand of cedars nearby. Whoever it was had not moved, with the exception of shifting feet, for over thirty minutes.

She had waited for prey with her daddy before, and she knew she could outwait this one. The person out there was obviously unfamiliar with the land, nervous about the task, and probably in a hurry to bring it to conclusion. If she dallied long enough, the nervousness would be her ally and a mistake would be made.

With another noise, the movement of a branch on a window, she reached down to her lap and felt the cold steel object resting there. The long tablecloth hung close to the floor and neatly hid the double barrels from view. Still looking at the wineglass, she absently cocked the shotgun and rested it on the other chair under the table. She aimed directly at the door.

Even if the person did see the bulge, they would not suspect that such a delicate-looking woman as herself could heft such a weapon. The last intruder to make that mistake was walking the cement floors of Huntsville Prison with a permanent limp. There was another sound, and she cocked the second trigger.

From the corner of her eye she caught the glimpse of the man's face in the other window. She turned in time to see the pane explode inward with the force of the bullet. More out of instinct than sense she dropped from the chair to the floor and fired one barrel in his direction. The light above the sink shattered and electrical sparks glowed long enough to see the entire window disintegrate as the house went dark.

Stirling Hampton rolled to the wall for protection as more shots sounded from outside the house. The darkness was broken by shouts from the riverbank. There were several people out there, none of whose voices she recognized as safe. She quickly cracked and reloaded the empty chamber, cocked the shotgun, and aimed both barrels at the door.

Suddenly the doorknob turned and Stirling Hampton, her eye on the target, began to squeeze the double trigger. Just before she made her final pull, a voice shouted from the other side of the door.

"Miss Hampton, are you all right? It's Lieutenant Granger, APD."

"I'm terribly sorry about the mess, Miss Hampton."

"Call me Stirling. You ought to be able to call your almost-executioner by her first name."

"Yes . . . well . . . anyway, Stirling, when we saw this guy looking in your window and raising something metallic up to the glass, we couldn't hold our fire any longer."

Lieutenant Granger stood in the now-lighted kitchen with Stirling Hampton. The man they had captured was held by two officers, who were putting on handcuffs and reading his Miranda rights.

"Jeez, you all. I know them rights better than you do. I was just lookin' in the window and checkin' to see if she was *in* here. I couldn't see too good from out there, and she was takin' an awful long time with that dinner. It still smells pretty good, ma'am."

"How long were you out there, Eddie?" Susan Granger asked.

"Damned—I mean darned if I know. S'cuse me, ma'am," he said to Stirling Hampton. Her blond hair and blue eyes had entranced him. "I know better than to cuss in front of a lady."

"Never stopped you down at headquarters, Eddie."

"Like I said, Lieutenant." Eddie Shelton glanced at Susan Granger, then smiled at the other woman. He was in love.

"Lieutenant?" Stirling Hampton began. "Do you think this man could have something to eat? I mean, he wasn't armed or anything, except for that flashlight."

"So he says, anyway. I'll bet my officers find a little something in the bend of that river tonight. Either that or you've got some salmon jumping down there that nobody knows about."

"Well, what *were* you doing out there?" Stirling Hampton asked.

"I was just keepin' an eye on ya like they were. Makin' sure nothin', uh, happened to ya."

"But why? You don't know me."

Eddie Shelton blushed. "No, ma'am, I surely don't."

"Go ahead, Eddie," Lieutenant Granger said. "Tell her who put you up to this."

The slight man suddenly got quiet.

"Okay, Eddie. *I'll* tell her. It was Lucas Holt, wasn't it?"

Stirling Hampton looked at the lieutenant. "What's Father Holt got to do with this man? Why would he send him out here?"

"The Rev *didn't* send me," Eddie argued.

"No. Then who *did*, Eddie?" Susan Granger was getting progressively angry. She did not appreciate having her duties interrupted by the meddling of someone she knew very well. "Just who exactly *is* responsible for our shooting up this lady's property, nearly getting you killed, nearly getting *me* killed, and for preventing us from capturing the maniac who's already killed two people and may come back for Stirling after we're gone?" Her face was blotched with red. "Come on, Eddie," she said, pushing him into the two officers holding him. "Tell us who it was."

Eddie Shelton knew he was in trouble. If they made this bust stick, he could be doing a lot of time back in Huntsville, especially if they found his piece in the river. With his record, a gun charge, an attempted burglary charge or both would blow his parole and require that he finish out his ten-year felony term. Surely the Rev would understand that. But it wasn't the Rev he was worried about. It was the one who sent him here that he really hoped would understand. Maybe the Rev could fix that, too.

"What's it worth to ya?"

"No deals, Eddie," Lieutenant Granger snapped. "We got a good clean bust, and you're going back to the Walls to finish out that dime you got in the first place."

"What's a 'dime'?" Hampton asked.

"Sorry, Stirling. It's a ten-year sentence a sheriff friend

of mine sent him down for three years ago." The lieutenant frowned in the man's direction. "Eddie here has a little problem of sticky fingers that needs correcting. Right, Eddie?"

Eddie Shelton remained silent, his head down, staring at the floor.

"So this bust will make certain he finishes it."

"What if I don't press charges?"

Eddie Shelton raised his head. One look at Stirling Hampton proved to him that he had actually been killed a while ago and was now in heaven with a real angel.

Susan Granger tightened her grip on the flashlight they had taken from the intruder. "That certainly is your prerogative, Miss Hampton. Of course, it is difficult to keep filth like this off the streets when we don't get citizen cooperation."

"Well, he was out there checking on me just like you were. And you do seem to know who sent him, so it's not like he's the killer you say you want to catch."

"Fine, Miss Hampton. We'll take him back to Austin on a parole violation that probably won't stick. He'll be back on the streets in twenty-four hours looking for someone else's house to break into. I'm sure that doesn't bother you, but it bothers the hell out of me. I'm the one who has to catch him again and press charges again."

"I understand your concern, Lieutenant," Stirling Hampton said, "but in this particular case the man has done nothing wrong, I *would* like him to come back and replace that window, though."

"I'd be glad to, ma'am. Just as soon as I get out of their fine jail."

"Shut up, Shelton," Susan Granger said. "You can make whatever arrangements you like, Miss Hampton. We're going now. I am sorry for the inconvenience." She looked at the two officers holding Eddie Shelton. "Take him to the car."

The two hurried the man out the door and out of sight. Susan Granger also turned to leave.

"I hope you don't regret this, Miss Hampton."

"I won't."

"I'm not so sure. I will continue to keep a plainclothes officer posted down the road a piece. If he hears anything, he will come to check with you."

"Thanks, Lieutenant. I can take care of myself."

That's what they all say, she thought. "Good night."

Susan Granger took her time returning down the gravel road to the car. Too much was happening too fast, and she had the feeling it was all slipping through her fingers, just like Eddie Shelton had, just like most of the criminals seemed to do lately.

She took a deep breath of the crisp night air and stopped to look up at the stars. Once you got out of the city, out here where there were no lights of any kind, you could even see the massive Milky Way. She remembered the first time she saw it, on a camping trip with her family to the Davis Mountains in west Texas. She must have been five or six, and it was one of the few times she had really been out of Dallas and the suburban sprawl around it that her father helped protect with DPD.

She had been surprised at the suddenness of the trip. Her mother had had to make arrangements for a substitute teacher to take classes at the high school and talk to Susan's principal about pulling her out of first grade for a week. As they drove the twelve hours through the flat barrenness of the west, Susan overheard the conversations, her father's anger, her mother's consolation, their anxiety at awaiting the outcome of the investigation of the shooting.

It would be years later before she would understand that her father's acquittal on all charges did not expunge the guilt from his soul. He would replay the scene in his mind, or have it replayed for him periodically by news media opening and reopening the documentary films of the event. And each time there was her father, smiling at some other cop's comment as Jack Ruby burst through the crowd to kill Lee Harvey Oswald.

Just as Ruby had slipped by her father, so many others had slipped through his daughter's tight grip, like grains of sand falling from a tightened fist. But for her it was not the result of negligence or lack of diligence on her part. She was a good cop, a play-by-the-book cop who was constantly frustrated by a system of alleged "justice" where the bad guys got better treatment and had more rights and protections than the good guys. She hated it when an ambivalent public demanded tougher action by police, then refused to cooperate by pressing charges. Just like tonight.

The constellations in her head spun wildly. Lucas Holt and ex-cons and a mass murderer orbited around her, held by her forceful gravity. She resented their questioning her integrity or her authority and the tight-fitting set of beliefs she relied upon to keep her world intact. But she had to admit it was that opposite side, the very threat to those rigid beliefs, the seemingly freer style of Lucas Holt that was attractive to her.

A familiar car door slammed and Susan Granger was back in the present. She sighed as if to take in the whole Milky Way, to remind her of another reality, another time when life was clearer, cleaner, more open to possibility, capable of being grasped and held by six-year-old hands.

Eddie Shelton was wedged uncomfortably between two officers in the back of the squad car. Lieutenant Granger sat in front with the driver and turned to face the man in handcuffs. She did a double take as the face in the darkness first looked like Jack Ruby.

"You're a lucky boy, aren't you, Mr. Ed?"

Eddie Shelton knew better than to say the response that went through his head. "Sure thing, Lieutenant."

"Yeah," she continued, only half addressing Eddie Shelton. "You might have slipped through the sieve tonight, but you'll be around again, and so will the guy who sent you.

It's your nature, you know, only next time maybe the sieve will be tighter, or maybe you'll miss the hole, or maybe you'll go through the hole again, but I'll get a piece of you—or maybe I'll *push* you straight through the hole into a box."

Shelton again restrained his tongue. The lieutenant's voice was too controlled and steady, as if she was using all her strength not to jump. "Sure thing, Lieutenant."

"And if anything happens to that lady out there, I'll nail you *and* Dorati for obstructing justice so fast you won't know what hit you."

"Uh-huh."

"That's right, Eddie," she said. "I'm in no mood to take any crap off of you or anyone else tonight." She turned around in her seat and reached for the radio. "Unit Twelve to headquarters. Over."

"HQ by. Over."

"Lieutenant Granger with a request for Communications. Over."

"Comm-Q by. Over."

"Patch me through to the officer tailing Lucas Holt."

• Eight •

The Bergstrom Air Force Base commissary was busier than usual for a rainy Friday night. Families with crying kids wanting to be home stood in line with baskets full of cereal, eggs, melting ice cream, and juices. Colonel Alvan Bradenberg watched them and was glad he could escape through the line labeled "10 Items or Less." He secretly cursed the soldier in front of him writing a check. Why the hell bother to call it "Express" if you allow idiots like that to hold us all up? he wondered. Then, of course, the soldier had picked the one bottle of laundry detergent that was not marked and the cashier had to call for a price check.

Alvan Bradenberg was not now, nor had he ever been, a patient man. His early career in World War II flying uncharted missions behind enemy lines had earned him quick promotions. His impatience had paid off in the early days of Vietnam as well, where he was one of the few pilots willing to fly the long hours of infiltration over areas not yet declared to be the enemy. The qualities of impatience and risk were highly valued by his superiors in those days. In more recent times, in the seventies and eighties, his superiors made good use of both the overt and covert contacts he had developed in wartime.

In the last twenty years his status had grown dramatically as the number of "missions" he carried out for them grew and became increasingly more dangerous. It was not a good thing to be caught dealing with what the general public still called "the enemy" in these post Cold War times. If he had ever been captured, especially in South America, the embarrassment would have been global, high-ranking officials publicly denounced (and privately compensated), military trust undermined.

The Pentagon knew it could count on the silence and the expertise of Bradenberg if they did not cramp his style, watch him too closely, demand a full accounting of his whereabouts. He was allowed to do some private business of his own on company time, deepen his contacts, make full use of the government's network of transport and communications to serve his own ends. And he did.

But that was all behind him now. As he pushed his way through the crowd to the parking lot, his impatience focused on getting through these next few days. His retirement date was fast approaching, and the "business" he had conducted over the years would now serve him well into his old age.

Driving past the gate guard he enjoyed the special salute due him. He turned right on Highway 71 and grimaced at the glare of the oncoming car lights on his rain-splotched windshield. He exceeded the speed limit by his normal ten miles per hour. A man of his importance had places to go, things to do. The excess was justified, as it always had been in every area of his life. Now he was one week away from that excess paying off indefinitely.

At first he was not sure about the car in the distance. It was hard to see the license or the make in this rain, but something about it looked familiar. There was someone waving him down, someone whose familiar outline he recognized even in the dark and rain, as he had recognized other outlines in other dark places and had maneuvered to save his own life and take theirs. This was not an enemy agent, though it was someone he had reckoned with from time to time, someone whose excesses he had shared and occasionally supported.

He wondered if he should stop. He did want to get home. It was late: he was in a hurry and impatient to get out of this weather. Stopping would probably mean helping with the damned car, maybe getting wet, certainly taking the man to a gas station and putting up with delay and inconvenience.

Before he knew what he was doing, he felt his foot press the brake pedal and slow down. What the hell, he thought, maybe it was time to temper the impatience, to slow his life down, to relax and help out an old business partner. After all, this stranded man had helped him with a percentage of the prices the colonel arranged. And those prices were always a bit below what he had actually negotiated. Maybe he did owe the man something.

The disabled car was pulled off the side of the road at the bottom of the hill just beyond a little-traveled Farm to Market Road. Alvan Bradenberg pulled up directly behind the car, whose flashing lights backlit the man's features like a neon advertisement.

The muddy London Fog raincoat was buttoned tight, and the man appeared to wear tight-fitting gloves. The colonel's mind flashed a discrepancy about those gloves, then ignored the instinctual but now unnecessary paranoia from his past. He flipped the switch that unlocked the doors and allowed the man to get in the front seat. He glimpsed and noted the unbending bulge in the man's pocket. But, with one week to go and his missions behind him, he ignored any internal warnings in his hurry to get home. Besides, the man had worn a gun before, just as the colonel had on their meetings.

"Alvan!" the man said loudly. "I thought maybe that was you when I started waving my arms to flag you down. God, I'm glad to see you."

"What the hell are you *doing* out here, anyway? And what seems to be the problem with your car?"

"Damned if I know. The thing just stopped. Maybe it's flooded. If I can wait here a minute I'll go and restart it in a little bit. I can't even get any heat going to sit in the damned thing. And this rain chills me to the bone."

Alvan Bradenberg knew he would be in for a longer

delay than he thought. The man wanted to shoot the shit and reminisce. He shouldn't have stopped. He could damned near be home by now in his nice warm house with his dinner and his dog. Instead here he sat, captured by an old "friend."

"How have you been, Alvan? It's been quite a while since we've gotten together."

"Fine. Just fine. Coming up to twenty for retirement next week." He hated this kind of idle chatter. "And you?"

"Fine, also. Business has never been better. Austin's become quite a boomtown, you know, and that always means more business for me."

There was an uncomfortable pause, broken by the man in the passenger's seat.

"Flown any . . . 'missions' lately, Alvan?"

"No. I've been entirely out of that for years now. Things aren't quite like they were in the old days. I don't think we could get away with half the deals we did in the past anymore." He hoped the man would leave soon and let him go home. He should have listened to his impatience one more time and avoided this ridiculous encounter that raised specters of the pleasantly dead past. He tried to push in that direction. "How about trying your car again. If it's flooded, the vapors ought to be worked out by now."

"In a minute, Alvan." The man pushed his hands deep into his coat pockets. "Damn, it's cold out here tonight. Reminds me of that time when you flew into, what country was it . . . ?"

"Which time?"

"The time you got the price on that jeweled Madonna for me."

"Czechoslovakia."

"Yes. I knew you cheated me then, Alvan, and I'm certain you'll be surprised to hear that I knew each time after that."

"What?" The colonel's eyes flashed in the darkness. "What the hell are you talking about? I took a hell of a lot of risk on those missions even taking your shit along with me. So what if I took a little extra to compensate for doing the dangerous part while you sat here in Austin safe and sound?" Alvan Bradenberg was beyond angry. "You've got a lot of balls sitting here in my car and accusing me."

It was then that the colonel's instincts forced his mind to put the previously ignored pieces together. But even as he did, he knew it was too late. He would either die sitting or fighting. He lunged at the man in a desperate attempt to deflect the gun. It was the last impatient move he would make.

Two silenced spits tore through the muddy pocket of the man's raincoat, jerking the colonel back against the door. His heavy numbing hand landed on the horn and was quickly removed by the passenger. The man removed the bulky gun from his pocket. One more spit to the chest and a trickle of blood spilled from Alvan Bradenberg's tightly clenched lips.

The man was about to grasp the colonel's right ring finger when the glare of headlights flashed in the outside mirror. He left the gun on the floor of the car, opened the passenger door and got out into the pouring rain.

The pickup truck stopped parallel to the two cars as the man made sure he was kept in the dark shadow with his own taillights behind him. The rancher in the truck rolled down the passenger window.

"Y'all okay here?"

"You bet! I was just getting back into my car to get it started. My friend and I were taking this car to trade in, and it stalled on me. It's fine now, partner."

"You want to make sure it starts for you? I got some cables in the back."

"I don't think we'll need 'em. Just let me get in here . . ."

The man easily turned over the engine and waved off the rancher. "Thanks a lot. We'll be fine now."

"Y'all take care now."

The man stayed in his car until the pickup disappeared

over the hill. He then walked quickly back to the steel tomb of Alvan Bradenberg, opened the passenger door, and got in. He reached again for the colonel's diamond ring when the hand grabbed his and pulled him toward the steering wheel.

Alvan Bradenberg's eyes opened in a wide death stare. His other hand produced the gun that the man had left on the floor. A quick spit sent the shocked intruder recoiling back in the seat. But the man knew he had the advantage. He used his living power against Bradenberg's ebbing strength to turn the gun back into the colonel's gut and force two final muffled shots into his now still body.

Breathing heavily, still overcoming his shakiness, the man pulled himself away from the slumping form that had tried to cheat him one last time. He felt his grazed shoulder and was relieved to find only a small flow of blood from the surface wound.

Being careful not to leave any more traces of his own blood, he rolled down all the windows and pulled the dead body down on the seat. The rain would take away some of the stains and mix the colonel's blood with his own.

With some strain he reached over for the dead man's right ring finger. He held the diamond inset up to the windshield and scratched three numbers faintly into the glass.

• Nine •

The two-story was one of the smaller luxury houses perched atop Las Ventanas. The exclusive, gated subdivision boasted views of Lake Austin to the east and of the hill country to the west. A cool fall breeze blew through the upper bedroom window, where a pale light shone.

The couple moved together on the soft Victorian bed, like a large patchwork caterpillar undulating beneath the quilt. The woman, on top, gently stroked the man's hair, kissed his cheek, and nuzzled his neck. She pulled the antique cover securely over them and felt his arms hold her tight, wanting her closer. She responded, pressing her body firmly against his, intertwining their legs more tightly. The man softly explored the back of her body with his searching hands.

"That's good," she said, snuggling down to his chest.

"Good," he murmured.

"Mmmmmmm. You've got great hands," she said as she began to slowly stroke her fingertips through the hair on his chest.

"Yours aren't bad, either. They go well with the rest of you. Nice match, actually."

She began moving on top of him. "Keep that up, right there."

"It already *is* up."

"I know."

Before she could finish her sentence, the phone on the reading table next to the bed rang.

"Damn," the man said. "Lousy timing."

"Forget it. It's probably my mother anyway. She always calls this late at night to see how I am."

The man smiled at her as the ringing continued insistently.

"Want me to answer and tell her you're coming?"

The woman ignored the phone and the comment. She concentrated on the feelings welling inside her. The man was also caught in the rising tide of the moment. He stopped talking and resumed his exploration and caressing of her body.

The phone continued with annoying persistence to intrude into their closeness. It was like a disinterested third party in the room, not participating, not even observing, just obnoxiously present and totally distracting. No matter how they tried, the couple could not seem to totally ignore the offensive sound from the table.

The woman spoke first. "I'm sorry . . . I've got to stop and answer."

"Now? You've *got* to be kidding."

"It must be important or they would have stopped."

"I don't believe this," the man said dejectedly.

"Maybe someone's in trouble." The woman looked at him wide-eyed.

"Only person in trouble around here is me," he moaned. "Here I am about to have cardiac arrest from your passion, and you stop so abruptly." He took a deep breath. "It's like they put heart paddles to my chest."

She pulled away from him just a little. "I'm sorry. I'm losing ground with that ringing. I *have* to answer it."

"Okay. Okay. I need a break anyway. Just don't go away."

She grinned and squeezed him with one arm while she reached over and fumbled the receiver to her ear.

"Hullo?" she said, trying to sound sleepy and not being good at it.

The voice from the other end was upset and demanding.

"Ms. Wade, would you please put the phone to Lucas Holt's ear?"

"What? Who *is* this?"

"This is Lieutenant Granger, APD."

"Jeez, Susan, I didn't recognize your voice. Did anybody ever tell you your timing was—"

"Just *do* it, Kristen," the lieutenant interrupted. "And do it *now*!"

Kristen Wade handed the receiver to the man lying next to her.

"It's for you, Lucas."

"You mean it's *not* your mother?" he said, putting the phone to his ear.

"No!" came the loud voice from the receiver. "And I'm not *your* mother, either, Lucas Holt."

"Well, you sure follow me around like her," he said. "What the hell do you *want*, Susan?"

"You're in no position—excuse the expression—to be the irate complainer, Lucas," the lieutenant explained. "Let me just say that we've got Eddie Shelton down here, and he's *real* scared about blowing his parole."

Lucas Holt sat up in the bed.

"What happened out there?"

"Not till you get down to APD, Lucas. Suffice it to say Eddie's not the only one who stepped in cow shit at the ranch tonight."

"What happened to 'the Shepherdess'?"

Kristen Wade frowned at him. He shook his head.

"*You* scared the killer away. So not only don't we know who he is, but he's probably out there right now looking for another one."

"Okay, Susan, that's enough."

"No, it's *not* enough, Lucas! I warned you about meddling in police business with these scumbags you call your friends. You haul ass down here right now, or I'll have you picked up so fast you won't know what hit you."

Lucas Holt restrained himself from retaliating. He knew she was angry. But he refused to feel bad for sending a member of the God Squad to guard Stirling Hampton. If

Eddie Shelton had screwed up, at least he had saved the woman's life.

He took a deep breath and, looking at Kristen, responded with a certain tiredness in his voice.

"Okay, Susan. I'll be down shortly."

"That does mean *tonight*?"

"Yes. Tonight," he said, rolling his eyes. "Promise."

Kristen Wade took the receiver from his hand.

"Good night, Lieutenant," she sang into the phone in her throatiest voice. "Pleasant dreams."

The only answer was a loud click.

Lucas Holt fell back onto the bed.

"I don't believe this," he said, staring at the ceiling. "I thought for sure I slipped that guy she had following me. . . ."

Kristen Wade rolled over and wrapped her body around him once again.

Holt felt her move and stopped staring at the ceiling. He reached down and pulled her close, kissing her neck and shoulders and moving his hands slowly over her flushing body.

"Know what?" he said softly.

"Hmmmm?"

"They're not going anywhere at that police station to-night. I'll bet they're all still around when I get there. You think?"

"Uh-huh," she whispered. "I'll bet they are."

He put his lips next to her ear and murmured: "Do you have a free hand, Kris? Mine both seem to be busy."

"Uh-huh." She moved her hand over his chest. "What would you like me to do with it?"

"Well, first of all . . ."

"Mmmm-hmmm?"

"Reach down there and . . ."

"Yes?"

"Unplug the phone."

• Ten •

"Where the hell have you been?" Susan Granger snapped as Lucas Holt walked into her office without knocking. "Don't answer that. I *know* where you've been."

"Does this mean I don't get a 'Hello and would you like something to drink?' "

"You're damned right it does, Lucas. Sit down. I need to ream—and you're the designated ream-ee."

Lucas Holt obediently sat in the wooden chair across from Granger's desk. He had been in this position many times before, with his parents, the school principal, dean of the seminary and lately his bishop. He knew what was coming and also knew she had two, make that three scores to settle with him. The first was to make sure her detectives outside heard the yelling. That would get him back for embarrassing her at the scene of the first murder. The second was to rail at him for what she called "interfering with police business" and using the God Squad to investigate a case. The third was a bit more complex. It involved Kristen Wade.

"It's hot in here," she said. "Or maybe it's just your overheated presence in this room that makes it that way," she continued, walking over to her office door. "I need this open a crack for air."

Holt checked the first goal off her list. As he suppressed a much-needed yawn, he wondered how long the harangue would take and hoped his mind would not wander too far. He had a sudden urge to prop up his feet on her desk. Fortunately, he resisted.

"Well, answer me!" the lieutenant said loud enough to be heard outside.

"I'm not sure what you meant," the Rev said, realizing he had already missed a couple of sentences of the speech. "Run that by me again, Susan?"

"I'll run it by you again, Lucas Holt. I'll run you by the county jail for a night if I catch you interfering with police business again."

Check two, he said to himself.

"I want a straight answer out of you now. Why did you send that half-baked burglar Eddie Shelton out to the Hampton ranch?"

Because nobody else was available? he thought. "I was just trying to be helpful, Susan."

"Helpful? You call shooting up that woman's house, nearly getting several people killed, and scaring off the murderer 'helpful'? No thanks, Lucas. Keep your help—and that misnamed 'God Squad'—out of my business. If you had any sense at all, you'd keep them out of *your* business, too."

"Are you about done so you can tell me what happened out there?" He started to get out of his chair.

"Not quite, Lucas. Sit down," she said, pushing him back into the chair. "I want you to know I've got the chief and the mayor breathing down my back about these two murders. I've got some irate neighborhood groups ready to picket out front here tomorrow morning, and I have six calls from six different reporters to return, including one from *Good Morning, Austin* where they want to put me on television for an hour to tell them what we're *doing*, for God's sake."

"I'll take the *Good Morning, Austin* spot for you. You see I need to raise some money for—"

"DAMMIT," she said out loud. She slammed her office door and stood over him. "You're not *listening* to me."

Well, he thought, she was right about that. And therein was the crux of the matter. As she continued to lecture, cast aspersions on his genetic heritage, and blow off steam from a lousy day, he did what he had always done in situations like this one. He looked intently with great interest at the speaker—and continued not to listen.

Instead he thought about Kristen Wade.

He had actually met her at the same cadet graduation where he had reconnected with Susan Granger. He had been about to leave the "reception" at a local watering hole when he turned and literally ran into the tall, auburn-haired woman in a white linen business suit, open at the neck. He had not found her particularly attractive the first time he saw her. It was difficult finding someone attractive who had just spilled Scotch down your chest.

Susan Granger had thought the incident quite humorous as she introduced them. He wished she would find some humor in the present situation. She looked as if her blood pressure was out of control.

Susan and Kristen had been friends from a local summer softball team. That was back when Kristen Wade worked for the attorney general. Now she was a successful candidate in the House representing the Austin district and was touted to run for the State Senate within the coming year. Her career seemed boundless.

Susan Granger intruded the present. "Dammit, Lucas, *listen* to me. . . ."

"I *am* listening. I just don't especially like what I'm hearing." Whatever it was.

Kristen Wade was everything Susan Granger was not. Progressive to liberal in her politics, she was sometimes too much even for Lucas. She was well tailored, in touch with major issues of her district, worked hard at her social graces, and had grown to be politically powerful in her own right. The oilman's daughter from Leander, Texas, had made it on her own, with a little start from Daddy's black gold.

The first few times they saw each other, they argued politics and people over long dinners at Jeffrey's Bistro. They drank margaritas at Casita Jorge's and ate health food at Mother's. Holt enjoyed her company, her independence, and her sense of adventure. He also knew, for all of their involvement together, sexual and otherwise, that the relationship would not "go anywhere." It was safe for them both; an exercise in staving off loneliness, passing time pleasantly playing and holding. Neither one would let it grow into love. Neither one could afford it.

As Susan wound down her lecture, Lucas saw the feeling in her eyes. She knew she could not compete with Kristen Wade, and she did not pretend to do so. Holt wondered if Susan knew how attracted he was to that feeling he saw, how worried he was that he might let himself move toward it to see if the relationship they once had could be rekindled in the present, given who they were now. Indeed, she *was* different from Kristen Wade, and the difference was that he might love her.

"So all I'm asking, Lucas, is that you stay the hell out of my way and let me do my job. Is that clear?"

"Clear as a church bell, Susan." He stood up from the chair. "Listen," he said, putting his arm around her, "I'm sorry if I caused you grief out there tonight. And I'm glad you didn't get hurt." He turned and faced her, his hands on her shoulders. "I know you've had a hard day and got lots of people on your back. And I know we've been down this road before."

"Yes, we have." She paused. "Among others."

"True. But I have to tell you that, in spite of your being upset, I'm not sorry about Eddie's being out at that ranch." Holt looked at her. "Though I do regret you had to call me at Kristen's."

Susan Granger pulled away from him.

"Lucas," she said, shaking her head. "I don't care who you see and when. I can't care. It's none of my business. Not anymore. It's just that it raises old ghosts that are too pleasant."

"The ghosts are pleasant for me, too." He reached for her

hand. "We seem to go in cycles, you and I." She took her hand away and planted it on her hip. "We see each other a while and then we don't. We've been that way since college. Given our histories, where we stand on things, we probably always will be that way." He stepped forward and took her hand off her hip. "Hell, I don't know. I just don't want to mess up a good friendship here."

"I presume you mean ours."

Holt smiled. "Of *course* I mean ours. You and I will be friends a long time. I think I want to leave it at that for now, but I'd be lying if I told you I was certain I wanted it to stay there."

"I don't know what I want, either, Lucas," she said, walking to the window and looking out at the alley. "It's tough having you here in Austin, seeing you, even having to stumble over you in this damned investigation. You're close but not close, present but not present." She turned to face him. "But right now I can't have it both ways. I guess I have to say either you're in my life or you're out of it—and I don't mean professionally."

Lucas Holt paused and went to her.

"Then include me 'in,' Susan. But for now it's got to be a limited partnership—for reasons we've talked about for years."

Susan Granger thought a moment, then turned to face him.

"Okay," she said blankly. "That will do until our next argument."

"Checkmate. And I promise I'll keep you informed," he said as he put his arms around her. "Had dinner yet?"

She breathed a relaxed sigh. "Yes."

Suddenly her office door opened and an embarrassed officer saw them.

"Don't you know how to knock, Mr. Blair?" Granger let go of Holt and crossed her arms at her chest.

The Rev tried not to smile. The lecture had just been canceled out.

"Sorry, Lieutenant."

"Well, now that you're in, what is it that's so damned important?"

Officer Blair handed her a piece of paper.

"This just came through, Lieutenant. I thought you'd want to see it right away." He turned to go.

"Wait a minute," Granger said, looking at the paper. "Go down and release Eddie Shapiro. Tell him not to leave town and to keep his nose clean or I'll find and bust his druggie ass and press charges later."

"Yes, sir, uh, Lieutenant, uh, ma'am."

"Do it now, Blair. And close the door behind you."

"Right, Lieutenant." The nervous officer gladly left the room.

Lucas Holt gave her a puzzled look as she handed him the paper and sat at her desk.

"What does *this* mean?" he said, staring at the unfamiliar name.

"It means he skipped around on us, Lucas."

"What?"

"Instead of the 'Shepherdess'—he killed the 'Soldier.'"

• Eleven •

Susan Granger drove the blue-and-white APD cruiser in the slow lane of Old Bastrop Highway. No lights. No sirens. Windshield wipers slapped the rain away. Wet caliche foamed white on the flat roadbed and momentarily recorded treadmarks of the heavy tires.

"Smells good," the Rev said, rolling the window down a crack. "Even out here in the traffic the rain smells good."

"Caliche dust and rainwater. West Texas cocktail."

The headlights bounced off the large green sign announcing the turn for Bergstrom Air Force Base.

"You going to stop at Bergstrom?"

"No. I've got officers there doing the routine checks. They won't find anything. I thought we'd go straight to Bradenberg's house."

"Where's he live?" the Rev said absently.

"Out by Garfield, down 973."

Lucas Holt gazed out the passenger window. "I've got a parishioner out there in Garfield. One of the Vestry, come to think of it. Case Atkinson. Architect. New to town."

"Have you given up complete sentences or did your drugs finally kick in?"

"Huh? Oh, no. I was just sort of mesmerized by the night." He continued to look out the window away from her. "And thinking. Atkinson is fairly new to town. Don't know much about him. Maybe from Houston . . . maybe from the West Coast. Can't remember right now. Something he said when I first got there. It was about the Treasury, some pejorative comment about how we needed to 'find a better home' for it."

"What *are* you mumbling about?"

"Oh, just thinking out loud. That little problem of no funds at the church."

"Are you sure Maggie Mae's is totally insolvent?" Granger laughed.

"'Insolvent' would be a step up. I had to present a plan to the Vestry a couple days ago. Only thing we can do is sell the Treasury. Only place we've got money." He opened his eyes wide and stretched in the seat. "Can you turn some heat on?"

Granger adjusted the controls. "Guess you've got to do what you've got to do—though it does seem a shame to end the tradition. Maybe you could sell it intact, instead of disbursing it to collectors or museums?"

"Yeah. I don't know. They're supposed to vote on it at next month's meeting."

"You'll think of something." She glanced over at him and smiled. "You always do." White tongues of light from oncoming cars licked her face as she spoke. "You remember the demonstration at the university over the Tet Offensive?"

"Unfortunately, I do."

"U.T. cops, APD, State Troopers."

"Don't forget the Rangers."

"Rang*er*, son," Susan said in her worst West Texas accent. "'One riot—one Ranger.'"

"We were really lucky, Susan."

"Yeah, we were. But you were good at negotiating, though I hate to admit it, even back then."

"The sudden thunderstorm didn't hurt any, either. It doused out the fire in everyone's eyes." Holt yawned. "I've always liked the rain for that reason. Seems to mellow people."

"Well, I can't afford to get mellow when it looks like our

murderer is getting a little careless." The sound of a landing F-16 drowned her voice and shook the car.

"What'd you say?" Holt pretended to shout. "The military industrial complex was being obstructionist."

Granger shook her head. "I said the murderer got careless."

"How so?"

"According to the officer at the scene, there was a bullet hole on the passenger's side of the car. The rain had washed all the blood off the bullet, but it was obviously meant for the killer. They did find a few cloth fragments and think they might have been from some kind of raincoat."

"I wonder if he was careless—or if Bradenberg was crafty enough to get a shot in? It would fit with the old man's rep."

"Either way, our man got wounded. And it does tarnish the image of perfection he's been trying to portray in leaving no clues."

"Same numbers present?"

"Same numbers. This time they were carved in the windshield with Bradenberg's diamond ring."

"Nice touch."

She slowed the car. "That's where it happened." She pointed to the shoulder of the road marked off with yellow and black crime-scene tape.

Lucas Holt looked intently at the bounded area. A man had taken another man's life here a short time ago. In one specious moment this small plot of ground was vacant, then filled with life, then death, now vacant again. It seemed to him a paradigm of Earth.

"Like a Psalm," he said pensively. "But it does make you wonder."

"What?" Susan Granger sped up the car and moved to the center lane. "Remind me never to go out in the rain with you, will you? What the hell are you talking about?"

"It makes you wonder what we're doing."

"Okay, Lucas," she said, flicking on her turn signal. "Fill me in on the last twenty sentences in your head. How did you get to that?"

He shifted in the seat to face her.

"I was just thinking we make a big deal out of individual murders."

"Why shouldn't we? And we're not just talking *individual* here, we're talking *multiple* murders now."

"Let me finish. And take a left at the next Farm to Market Road toward Garfield. It's easy to miss in the dark." He sat back in the seat. "So we make a big deal out of individual murders. There's panic and concern in the community—your chief and the mayor get morally outraged in front of TV cameras. We do our best to find the murderer and bring him or her to what we jokingly refer to as 'justice.'"

"Now, wait a minute, Lucas."

"No, come on, Susan. Hear me out before you start defending."

"Go on," she said reluctantly, thinking of her defense.

"We do all that for *one* individual—but we let massive numbers of people die all over the world from starvation, terrorism, imprisonment, famine, or a dozen other things like alcohol and abuse that we could prevent or change. We claim no moral resolve to do anything of the same intensity as what you and I are doing here tonight." He paused and looked out the front window at the opening blackness in front of them. "It's curious, that's all."

Susan Granger's defense had crumbled. Not only did she know he was right, she even agreed with him. She was quiet for a while so as not to interrupt either of their thoughts. The road narrowed from six to four lanes. The rain slowed to a fine mist.

"Maybe, Lucas . . ." she broke the silence. "Maybe what we do makes a small difference in all that."

"If we show it's important to catch this murderer, maybe

it will reinforce that it's really not okay for all those other deaths to happen, either."

"I don't know. I hope you're right."

Holt put his hand up on the seat behind Susan Granger's head and rubbed her neck.

"You can stop that next Thursday."

"Huh? Oh." He smiled. "Yeah."

"Damn!" she said as she braked abruptly. "You made me miss the turn."

"Sorry."

"Don't be." She backed up the car and turned down a southeast Travis County Farm to Market road. "Here's FM 973."

Two miles later she stopped at a gated cattle guard and ordered the officer standing watch to open the iron gate and let them through.

"Watch it, Lieutenant," the man warned. "The ruts are washing out with all the cars coming through here tonight."

"Got it. Thanks."

The bumpy, rock-rutted road led down through a swelling low water crossing.

"The one thing I hate about Texas ranches," Holt said, "is the low water crossings. Hope we can make it back out of here tonight."

"Rain's stopped," Granger replied, holding on to the steering wheel against the force of the water. "Should tone down before we leave. But they are unpredictable. Depends on how much water's coming from upstream."

The cruiser fishtailed coming out of the water and spun its tires on the rocks going back up the hill. Three tight turns later the mud-splattered vehicle arrived at the neatly paved driveway of Alvan Bradenberg's more than modest two-story hacienda.

Dark-colored military police vehicles parked next to Jeeps and civilian cars in the circular driveway. Two other APD blue-and-whites were conspicuously parked in the road.

"Let me guess who they think is in charge here," Lucas Holt said as he slammed the door shut. "And it's not you."

"That's only because they're scared we'll find out something they don't want us to know."

"What's to find out?" he asked as they proceeded to the front of the house.

"I don't want to get too dramatic, Lucas, but this guy was one hell of a spy. He did things nobody else wanted to do. He also did things nobody else *could* do. For those reasons they let him have his head and do things his own way."

"So the problem is that *they* don't even know some of the things he's done?"

"You got it. And if we find out before they do and it has something to do with the reason for his murder . . ."

Lucas Holt smiled. This could be fun, he thought.

"Don't smirk like that, Lucas Holt. You're here as my guest. Don't make an ass out of yourself with that military-industrial paranoia crap."

"Who's paranoid? They're out to get us all, Susan." He smiled in the dark.

"Don't start, Lucas."

"Okay. I'll be good," he promised. "Sort of."

The door opened before they could knock.

"Lieutenant Granger, I'm Colonel Royce."

First name "Rolls" from the size of that ring, the Rev thought. He endured the introductions and used the wasted time to scan the foyer and living room. It was the first thing the inmates had taught him to do. Never miss an opportunity to case a room.

Either the dead man made an inordinately large military salary, or he had a lucrative business in something or other on the side. Holt knew which one Nikky Dorati would choose to believe.

"Mind if I look around, Colonel?" Lucas Holt mumbled as he wandered up the thickly carpeted stairs to the second floor.

"Well, uh, if Lieutenant Granger—"

"Thanks, Colonel. I'll just be a minute." The Rev winked at Susan Granger and knew he had started her worrying. He was hoping she would have something to worry about.

It was always amazing to him how people automatically smiled at someone wearing a collar. The Boston Strangler could have invited people into his house and murdered them with smiling faces if he'd just had the foresight to wear a clerical collar. Even now the tough-looking military personnel guarding the rooms and searching through them took time to smile and speak to him. He spoke and smiled back as he absently glanced around each room.

"You his priest, Father?" one man asked.

"No, my son." Lucas Holt loved playing the "priest" role. Catholics always assumed he was one of them and so told him everything. This man was no exception.

"I didn't know him very well," the Rev continued. That was sort of true. He knew him better now than he had this morning, which was not at all. "Did you know the man?"

"Only by reputation, Father. He had a hell of a repu . . . I mean, excuse me, Father. I meant he had a really fantastic reputation as a . . ." The man lowered his voice and turned so he would not be seen talking to the Rev. "You know, Father. An undercover man."

"Really, my son?" The "my son" bit worked every time. "You mean he actually did dangerous work for our country?" This was getting difficult to say, even for him.

"Oh, yes, Father. He traveled in and out of more foreign countries than you could guess. Rumor has it that he smuggled people and, uh, things into and out of both Eastern and Western cities."

"Soldier!" A command came from farther down the hallway.

"Yes, sir," the man replied.

"This is not a social event! Stop talking to civilians and get back to your post!"

"Yes, sir!" The soldier looked apologetically at the Rev

and returned to the stiff guard position by the bedroom door.

Lucas Holt walked through the door and whispered out the side of his mouth: "That's okay, my son. I had a mother once, too. But you spell *his* with a *capital M*."

The soldier snickered as Holt shut the bedroom door and heard another bellow from the senior officer.

This room was different from the rest. It was a bedroom that had been converted into a kind of study. The soldiers in the room were oblivious to his looking around. They were more concerned about the APD officers and their incessant opening of drawers, leafing through magazines, feeling behind pictures. A priest was the least of their worries.

For an alleged super spy, Holt thought Alvan Bradenberg was pretty clumsy. The APD people were finding a wealth of papers hidden behind paintings or under books. As a matter of fact, he noted, they were finding *too* many things.

Huntsville Prison. Tuesday afternoon group. Jimmie (two-to-ten burglary) Brickhouse speaking: "Sometimes, Rev, before I exit a joint, I'll leave lots of things tossed around, like I took a bunch of different stuff, to cover up what I *did* take, so they'll never miss it."

Just like now. Bradenburg, the consummate spy, left lots of things to be found.

Holt ambled over to the rolltop desk with the wooden lamp casting shadows on the scattered papers. Ostensibly looking at the painting over the desk, he glanced down to see if the papers seemed of any importance. It was then that he saw what he wanted. Apparently, Bradenberg also knew if you really wanted to hide something where it would never be found in all these papers, all you had to do was put it out in the open where it would be seen and overlooked.

Lucas Holt backed away from the desk, casually took off his overcoat and slung it over his arm. He strolled to the other side of the room and nonchalantly looked at the paintings and certificates on the wall.

"This boy was more decorated than the White House

Christmas Tree," he said to no one and everyone. Call attention to yourself so they'll all be watching you. It works like Bradenberg's ploy.

One man responded. "Yes, Father, he was."

Good, he thought. I snagged one. "Must've been quite a guy, huh?" And then, without stopping, "Say, could you tell me what this painting is over here by the desk? I noticed it before, and I couldn't make out the place. It looks so familiar."

"Well, uh, I'll try, Father." The soldier nervously left his position.

"Thank you. Here it is, right here."

"Let's see, Father."

As they stood by the desk, Lucas Holt tossed his coat on top of the papers. The soldier was startled.

"Oh, I'm sorry, Father. You can't leave your coat there."

"No problem at all, my son." He very carefully grasped the coat, and hopefully the object underneath it, and slung it back over his arm. "Now, about this painting."

"I think it's the castle at Heidelberg, Father, but I'm not at all sure."

"Yes! That's it exactly! I was there once a long time ago. I guess Colonel Bradenberg must have been there at one time or another in his career. It's such a tourist attraction."

Lucas Holt continued the small talk as he casually made his way back to the door of the room. He smiled and once again silently mouthed the word "Mother" to the outside guard's delight. Soon he found himself back downstairs in the foyer.

Susan Granger, still accompanied by the protective eye of Colonel Royce, was just returning from her brief tour of the first floor.

"Well, Father Holt, did you have a good look at the upstairs rooms?" the colonel asked.

"Yes, I did. This is a wonderful house. There are some fine people up there doing a very thorough job. And the military guys aren't bad, either."

Susan Granger had to resist a smile. She knew she had better get him out of there.

"Thank you very much for the information, Colonel Royce," she said, extending her hand. "Father Holt and I are most grateful for all you've shown us. If we are able to piece anything together, we will call you, and of course we ask you to do the same."

Colonel Royce was still back on Holt's remark. "Oh, uh, you're welcome of course, Lieutenant. And we will certainly call you if we find anything." He was still looking at the Rev as he shook Susan Granger's hand.

"Pleasure meeting you, Colonel." Lucas Holt carefully rearranged the coat onto his left arm as he shook the man's hand. He was aware that the colonel had observed the shift of the coat, and he tried to change the subject. "Stop by St. Margaret's some time and see our Treasury collection of religious artifacts, Colonel. I think you'd enjoy it."

"Thank you, Father Holt. I just might do that." He was now looking directly at the raincoat on the Rev's arm.

Susan Granger started out the door.

"Don't you want to put your coat on, Lucas? It's pretty wet out here."

"No, thanks. I got kind of hot in there."

Colonel Royce stepped up behind him and reached for the coat.

"Oh, I insist, Father," he said, taking the coat from Lucas Holt and shaking it out firmly by the shoulders.

The Rev backed into the coat, held by the colonel, and smiled as he walked through the door into the rain.

"Thanks very much, Colonel," he said, looking directly at the military man's disappointed face. "Have a pleasant evening anyway."

Susan Granger started the cruiser and bounced through the muddy, flooding ruts. Lightning streaked in the distance, but the storm was now ahead and to the east of them.

"What the hell was that last bit about, Lucas?" she asked, squinting against the sudden flashes of bright light.

"I guess he thought I was hiding something under my raincoat."

"Good grief!" she said, steering carefully around some loose rocks. "Those guys are as paranoid about you as you are about them. What could you possibly hide under your raincoat?"

Lucas Holt reached back into his hip pocket and retrieved a small square object he had placed there when coming down the stairs. He had looked to all observers like he was merely checking his wallet.

"How 'bout this?" he said, holding it up in front of her.

"My God, Lucas!" she yelled at him. "You removed *evidence* without a warrant?"

"Removed? What if I just 'borrowed' it?"

"'*Borrowed*' it! You *stole* it, for God's sake!" She nearly hit a large boulder that had washed down the creek bed. "Dammit, Lucas, what *is* it, anyway?"

"Something I think may lead us to our killer."

"This better be good. Damned good."

"It is," he said, putting the object back in his pocket as they approached the guard at the gate. "We've got Alvan Bradenberg's little black book."

• Twelve •

"West Sixth" was the opposite end of Old Pecan Street in more than geography. Crossing the north-south dividing line of Congress Avenue, Sixth Street became lined with more sedate restaurants and gift stores and eventually, farther from downtown, with small, two-bedroom older homes, badly in need of repair and nurture. Fortunately for the local homeowners who were regularly set upon by eager developers, restoration was currently more prestigious than demolition; thus, many of the old homes that faced on West Sixth had been refurbished for businesses ranging from hair salons to law and architectural firms.

But the side streets off West Sixth were still graced with slightly larger houses erected in the 1920s when the area was a prestigious suburb. Wealthy business and professional families entertained each other and discussed politics and economics on their front porches with their University of Texas faculty neighbors. Much like West Sixth itself, these houses had been "gentrified" over the years, returned to their former quaintness by the same sorts of people who had first built them seventy years ago.

A mud-splattered blue-and-white vehicle sat in the driveway of one such house. Soft brown globs dripped from the car's underbelly onto the blacktop as light rain cleansed it from its night's work. Inside the neatly restored two-bedroom dwelling, the smell of newly refinished oak floors complemented the pungent cedar log burning in the small tiled fireplace. Lucas Holt and Susan Granger sat on the couch facing the fire but not each other. A small, black address book lay before them on the coffee table.

"Dammit, Lucas, I told you all the way over here I can't look at that book."

"What time is it?"

"I don't *care* what time it is. To look at the names in there with you is to become an accomplice to a felony. You stole the damned *evidence*, Lucas!"

"What time is it?"

"Even being in your *house* with you and that book makes me an accomplice."

"Susan, what time is it?"

She reluctantly looked at her watch.

"It's five past twelve. Time for me to get going."

"You got off work officially at seven. We went out to the Bradenberg house at ten. Anything that 'happened' did so while you were off duty, and it didn't happen to you anyway, it happened to me, and besides, it's merely information from a confidential source—not evidence for the court."

She glanced at him.

"And what exactly would you tell the district attorney if—no, make that *when*—she asks you what 'happened' out there?"

"I'd tell her the truth of course."

"Which 'truth' is that?"

"Look, can I help it if I tossed my coat on the desk, and when I went to take it off the desk, this book fell into the lining and I didn't notice it till I got home?"

"And I just *happened* to be here with you dropping you off at midnight when you found it?"

Lucas Holt smiled like a Cheshire cat.

"Exactly!"

"Your rationalizations sound more and more sociopathic, Lucas Holt. It's a good thing you got out of that prison when you did." She kicked off her shoes and pulled her legs up underneath her on the cushion. "Okay, bozo . . . I'm off duty and we'll pretend for the sake of argument that it's confidential information from an unknown source." She glanced at the book. "It really doesn't look like 'evidence' to me."

"Me, either."

"Just remember to come and visit me in Huntsville."

"Be honest, Susan, you know you're drooling to see what's in here as much as I am."

"Of course I do. It just worries me when I begin to use your logic." She waved him off the couch. "So go get some drinks and let's look at the damned thing."

"Wine okay?"

She nodded and the Rev uncorked a bottle of Fall Creek Cabernet. He filled their glasses and sat down next to her. The faint smell of her rain-damp hair mixed vaguely with the remains of her morning's cologne. He clicked his glass against hers.

"May we find the murderer of 'The Saints of God.' " He sat down next to her.

"I'll drink to that," she said. "God, I can't believe I'm sitting in this house with you again."

"It's a nice house."

"I didn't mean that. I meant the last time I was here . . ."

"My dad was in it."

"Right."

"I had just moved him here from Smithville so I could keep an eye on him while I went to U.T." Holt poured more wine. "He liked you."

"I liked him." She smiled at him. "He was softer than you. You kept the house after he died?"

"Yes. It was during my second year at Union Seminary."

"I think I remember seeing your dad's obit when I was in cadet school."

"He died six years after Mom did—almost exactly to the date."

"Sorry."

"It was a bad time for me, trying to take care of him long

distance from New York. But he wanted me to go there rather than closer to home. I came back to Austin for quick weekends and sort of watched him age and die."

"And the house?"

"I stored most of this furniture, hoping someday I might come back, and leased the house to students while I was at Huntsville."

"All those years."

"Yep." Lucas put another log on the fireplace and sat back down on the couch. "When I knew I was coming back here, I didn't renew the lease and had the whole place renovated before I arrived."

"It looks like you—and your dad."

"I'll take that as a compliment."

"Do." Granger put her glass on the wooden coffee table. "So can we get down to business now?"

"Go for it."

She eagerly reached for the small black book, hunched next to Holt, and opened the pages slowly. "Any of these names familiar to you?"

"Not so far," the Rev replied, though he was not sure he would tell her if they were.

They sifted through each page and went over each name. Many were foreign with addresses in Zurich, London, Vienna, Rio de Janeiro, San Salvador, Hong Kong. There were also more obscure places with small town names like Hinterzarten, Looe, Melk, and Costa. It was clear—and also quite logical that Bradonberg had connections all over the world. Most listings were innocuously straightforward, as they would be in any address book. But some were marked with asterisks, stars, or crosses that had meaning only to the owner.

An hour later Holt poured the last of the wine into their glasses. Susan Granger tossed the book back on the table and slumped back into the cushions.

"Another dead soldier," she pronounced over the bottle.

"Bad image."

"Oops." She smiled. "You're right."

"How about a dead address book?" Holt replied. "I guess it shouldn't surprise us that all our best friends weren't in there." He leaned back next to her and propped his feet on the table.

"All that for nothing," Susan Granger moaned. "I guess I could run these through the BCI computer and see what we get."

"You do and we'll both end up in Huntsville, Susan. Don't you know that those military people over at Bradenberg's house are looking like crazy for this little dandy?" He put his bare foot on top of the book. "Their computer is going to be monitoring the Bureau of Criminal Information computer—especially for searches done from Austin—to tell them where to find it." He took a swallow of the red wine. "And, of course, us."

"I get it." Granger smirked. "Have your computer call my computer and we'll do lunch."

"Yeah, except that *we're* lunch."

"Thank you, Lucas Holt, for absolutely confirming all of my internal gut instincts not to let you get involved with this case."

Holt sat up and picked up the book. "It's not over yet, Susan."

"Sure it is. Those military investigators are going to figure out where that book went . . ."

"No, they won't. Bradenberg could have destroyed it. As long as we don't surface any of the names in it—like through the computer—they can't track it. We're safe, so far."

"*You're* safe," she said, raising her tired body from the pillows. "*I'm* tired and going home."

Holt stared at the book, as if trying to communicate with it.

"Lucas, what are you doing?"

"I don't know. Something about this book bothers me."

"Like what?" she said sleepily. She pulled a pillow in front of her and hunched over it.

"Maybe we went through it too fast." He leaned forward next to her. "I keep thinking something in there looked familiar—like it hit a Gestalt image in my brain or something—but I know I missed it. Give me that thing again."

She handed him the book and slumped down more on the couch, warming her toes against the fire. Holt flipped through the pages again, letting his unconscious observe the names.

"I know it's in here somewhere. I'm sure I saw something that . . ." Suddenly he stopped and looked carefully at the page of names under the letter *H*. "Susan . . ."

"What?" The nearly comatose voice next to him had been warmed close to sleep by the wine and the fire.

"Susan, wake up. And hand me the phone."

"What?" she said, sitting up on the couch and shaking herself awake. "What did you find?" She looked over his shoulder at the small writing.

"Just hand me the phone. I need to make a call."

"At this hour of the night?" She reached over and put the set on his lap. "Whose name did you find?"

"I knew this was it." Lucas Holt tapped the seven numbers and listened for an answer. "Bradenberg listed some of the names in reverse order. But I guess I recognized the combination of the letters in the name along with the local phone exchange."

"But who?"

"Listen." He held the phone out from his ear so she could hear the conversation. "It's ringing a long time. I guess he's asleep."

"No shit, Sherlock. It's after one A.M."

The ringing stopped, and the Rev's heart pounded. A sleepy voice came through the line.

"Hello?"

"Hello. Is this Harris Lambert?"

Susan Granger grabbed the address book and reviewed

the name. It was written "L. Harris" with the phone number also scrambled, probably according to a coded sequence.

"Uh, yes. Who is this?"

"I'm sorry to wake you, Harris. This is Lucas Holt."

"Lucas? What's the matter? Are you all right?"

"Yes, I'm fine."

"Is the church okay? It's not burned down, is it?"

"No, Harris. I'm not calling you on Vestry business. The church is fine and you're still senior warden. I'm calling to check out a name with you."

"What do you mean?"

"I ran into my friend Lieutenant Granger tonight, and she said there had been a murder out by Bergstrom."

"My God! That's awful, Lucas. Was it someone we know from church?"

"That's what I'm calling to find out." He looked at Susan Granger. "You see, your number was found among his belongings."

"Really? Who was it?"

"The man's name was . . . Alvan Bradenberg."

There followed a long silence on the other end of the line. Holt and Granger waited for a response.

"Harris?"

"Yes . . . I'm thinking. I'm not quite awake yet . . . but I believe the name rings a bell somewhere. Can you wait just a minute?"

"Sure."

Lucas Holt whispered as he held his hand over the receiver.

"What do you think?"

Susan Granger whispered back. "Hard to tell. If he's lying he's damned convincing."

The tired voice sounded more intact now.

"I'm back, Lucas. I glanced through my file cards and found the name. I know I'm old-fashioned, I just haven't mastered that computer filing stuff yet. But I'm still pretty good at my clients' names. I was certain I remembered it. I hardly ever forget a client's name, you know. Not like these young fellas."

"Alvan Bradenberg was a client of yours?"

"Yes, he was. He had a rather large life insurance policy with my agency. He took it out a long time ago; it says here 1958. I guess the premiums have all been paid up because there's no notation to the contrary on my card. If you don't mind my asking, how was he killed?"

Holt looked at Granger, who stuck her ear up to the phone. "I believe the lieutenant said he was shot. Why?"

"Sorry to be so crass, Lucas, but I'm always checking for double indemnity. My agency couldn't take many losses like this one, especially at double the price."

"Well, I'm sorry to have disturbed you, Harris. Hope you can go back to sleep now."

"I'm sure I can, Lucas. Actually, I'm used to being awakened with calls like this. And now that I'm semi-awake I want to tell you something if you still have a minute?"

"I disturbed *you*, remember? Go ahead."

"I gave a lot of thought to what you said at the Vestry meeting today, and I want you to know I'm leaning in the direction of selling the Treasury."

Lucas Holt looked stunned.

"Oh . . . well, I'm glad you see it that way, Harris."

"I haven't made up my mind yet, Lucas, but I did want you to know I appreciate the dilemma we're in, and I am open to the liquidation of that entire collection."

"Okay, Harris. Thanks for the information. I'll be in touch as soon as the next meeting is set. Good night."

"Good night, Lucas."

Susan Granger put the phone back on the end table.

"I've got to be going, Lucas," she said. "I'm so tired I don't know what to think about that call. And besides that, your fire's going out and the wine's gone."

"I don't know what to think, either. It could be totally legit or it could be a damned good ploy."

Susan Granger pulled on her shoes and walked to the door. The Rev put his arm around her.

"Be careful going home." He kissed her on the forehead. "I hear there are a lot of criminals out there."

"Yeah," she replied. "And half of them are your friends."

"Good night, Lieutenant."

"Good night, Reverend Holt." As she walked down the front steps, she noticed that the rain had stopped and the night was colder. Remembering something important, she turned before getting into the car. "Before I forget, Lucas . . ."

"Yes?"

"I want you to know I'm keeping that tail on you."

"But why?"

"I reread that hymn this afternoon."

"And . . . ?"

"And, as you already know, we've got the 'shepherdess' covered. God only knows what the 'fierce wild beast' could mean. So there's only one category left."

"I already thought of that, Susan. But I'm afraid they'll have to get their 'priest' from another denomination. I don't fit onto anybody's hit list."

Susan Granger got into her car and was about to close the door. She looked back up at Lucas Holt standing on the porch.

"Neither did the other three."

Holt poked out the fire and closed the glass doors on the fireplace. Sitting on the couch, he drained his glass of red wine. He then picked up the telephone and dialed a number. He let it ring twice and hung up. Five minutes later his phone rang.

"Nikky?" he said.

"Evenin', Rev. You caught me in the middle of a hot card game."

"Sorry, Nikky. Did you find out anything?"

"Nothin' I can tell you right this second."

"I see. How about at Mother's in an hour?"

"I can make it there sooner than that, Rev."

"I can't."

"You got some company?"

"Yep." Lucas Holt looked out his front window. "In an unmarked car down the street from my house."

"The boys'll take care of that, Rev. See you there at two."

Holt hung up the phone and stared at the dying embers. Much to his chagrin, he had enjoyed Susan Granger's company tonight. He liked the smell of her hair, her sleepy softness against the glow of the fire.

Watch it, he told himself. Stay on task here.

He turned the lights off on the first floor, then went upstairs and turned his bedroom light on. Returning to the darkened kitchen, he put on his jacket and stepped outside the back door. He waited until he heard the shouting from the street.

Then he ran.

• Thirteen •

The first cabbie saw the man running and ignored the attempt to be flagged down. The second cruised down West Sixth as the man appeared to be walking normally and pulled over on request.

"Forty-third and Duval, please," Lucas Holt said as he closed the door.

"Sure thing, mister." The cabbie flipped the meter lever down and concentrated on turning the car around to head toward his destination.

Trying to keep a low profile, the Rev leaned back hard into the seat to obscure his head from other drivers. He knew the only other persons out at this hour were drunks and cops looking for each other. He was, therefore, not surprised when a patrol car slowly drifted up even on the right side of the cab at the stoplight.

The police officer glanced disinterestedly in the direction of the cab, then seemed to notice something. She rolled down her window and tapped on the front passenger's window with her stick. Lucas Holt felt the sweat running down his back as he pressed farther into the seat, trying to become invisible. The cabbie reached over and rolled down the window.

"Hey, Marty!" the officer yelled. "What're you doing downtown? I thought your run was the airport."

"Hiya, Runt! I might ask you the same thing. I'm just killin' time till the mornin' rush starts. The wife's out of town this week and I'm gettin' some extra fares by stayin' out longer. So what's *your* excuse? This ain't *your* beat, either."

Lucas Holt was certain the light had changed six times by now.

"Oh, we're supposed to be chasing down some idiot friend of the lieutenant's. She thinks he's going to get offed by that space cadet who's been killing people the last few days."

"No kiddin'? What's he look like? I'm always glad to help you guys out if I see anything."

The officer held up a 4x6 picture of Lucas Holt, and the cabbie studied it at a distance. The Rev hoped he was far-sighted with cataracts and needed corrective lenses, which he had left at home. Contemplating how quickly he could get out the other door and into the darkness, Lucas Holt held his breath and poised to escape. He was about to make the lunge when the cabbie spoke.

"No, Runt. I ain't seen nobody like this all night tonight. But if I do, you count on me callin' you on my radio."

"Thanks, Marty! You better get going or that fare back there's going to make me pay for his ride. Right, mister?"

Lucas Holt smiled in the darkness and waved his hand.

"Okay, Runt. You take care of yourself now, you hear? And tell your folks 'howdy' for me."

He rolled up the window, and the two cars turned in separate directions. Lucas Holt waited for his heart to stop pounding and his breathing to become regular again before he ventured to speak. The cabbie spoke first.

"Known that little kid since she was born. She was the youngest and the runt of the litter. Why, they didn't even expect her to live, she was so small. Spent the first month or two in an incubator."

He paused, and the Rev wondered if he should reply. Before he could decide, the cabbie continued.

"Yep, I been lookin' after her in one way or another all my life. She ain't nothin' like my kid. Nothin' but trouble he is. Been in and out of jail long as I can remember."

Lucas Holt glanced up at the picture and name of the cabbie.

"Since you just now read my name, you probably know why I told her I hadn't seen you, Father Holt. You did my kid a favor once in the joint. It wasn't no big thing to you, but he wrote and told me about how you got him out of the hole. I ain't never been able to do for him like that. Probably why I take care of the runt like I do. Anyway, I appreciated somebody takin' the time to be good to my kid."

Lucas Holt sighed deeply.

"Thank you. I can explain all of this."

"No need to, Rev. It don't make any difference to me what they think you done, or who they think's out to get you. All I know is what you did for my kid."

"I remember J.J. well. He was a bright kid. You would be surprised to hear how much he thought of you, and how often."

The cabbie's voice cracked.

"I wish his mother and I would have known that side of him. She was really broken up when he overdosed on that junk. He was all she ever had, you know. She worshiped the ground he walked on. He never did any wrong where she was concerned."

"I think you had a soft spot for him too."

"Yeah. Maybe . . . in a different way . . ." The cabbie's voice trailed off.

Lucas Holt let the silence carry the two of them through the empty streets.

"Well, thanks for the help, anyway. I just need some time away from the police, to get hold of some information."

"Like I said, Rev. I ain't heard nothin' and I ain't seen nothin'." The driver flipped the meter off and picked up his log book. "And I dropped this fare downtown—on my way to the airport."

The back door to Mother's Café and Garden was bolted shut. The pounding on the door brought a shout from a frightened employee.

"Who is it? What do you want?"

"It's Lucas Holt. Is Charles around?"

Another voice sounded muffled through the door. "I'll get it, Robert."

The heavy door opened and a smiling, bearded man welcomed Holt inside.

"Lucas! What in the world are you doing here at this hour? We're just cleaning things up."

"Must've had a busy night, Charles."

"Very busy. Plus this is our night for a major cleaning. But we're just about finished. And now you show up. Want to help?" He handed the Rev a wet towel.

"I'll pass this time. What I need is a table for two and some setups."

"Uh, Lucas, like I said, we're about to go home."

"Charles." The Rev put his arm around the man's shoulder and walked him into the darkened restaurant. "I need some time away from, uh, everybody."

"'Everybody' wouldn't mean 'the police,' would it?"

"Yes, them, too. And I've got another person meeting me here."

The two heard the knocking on the kitchen door and turned to see Nikky Dorati walking toward them.

"Charles, I'd like you to meet—"

"Nikky Dorati's the name. Glad to meet ya. Any friend of the Rev's is a friend of mine." The short man stuck out his hand.

"I'm Charles Hayes. Pleased to meet you, too." He turned to Lucas Holt. "I don't know what it is you two have to talk about, but I can guess it's not for anyone else to hear." He headed back toward the kitchen. "Go take a table in the back where the light won't show outside. I'll bring you some nachos and you can help yourself to the beer. There's plenty of Negra in there for you. I know it's your favorite."

Lucas Holt and Nikky Dorati moved to a corner table under a dim light. Each man looked tired in his own way and for his own reasons. For both it had been a long day and was getting to be an even longer night. They exchanged their stories and brought each other up to date with things they had found and not found.

"Sorry about Eddie, Rev. I didn't want to send him out to that ranch, but he was the only one of the boys who was available on such short notice."

"It worked out okay. He just damned near got himself taken off the count."

"Yeah, Eddie ain't known for his Boy Scout skills, Rev. He's a city boy, born and bred in downtown Houston. That 'scout in the forest' crap ain't his style."

The Rev took a sip of his Negra Modela.

"What did you do to my 'escort' down the street from the house?"

"Oh, the usual 'hit and run' number. They stuck a potato on the exhaust pipe, then pelted the car with eggs. Relatively harmless stuff, just like you'd want. But enough to distract them so you could slip out."

They helped themselves to the nachos and opened another bottle of Negra.

"Okay, Nikky, what have you managed to find out so far about the 'Saints of God'?"

Nikky Dorati smiled. He knew he had information that only he could find, and he hoped some of it would be shocking. Lucas Holt had gotten pretty inured to his sordid tales over the years, but he felt sure tonight's encounter would be different.

"Well, first of all I found out they weren't exactly 'saints.'"

"And who is?"

"Not me and you, Rev, that's for sure. But these boys were *big*-time sinners."

"How do you mean?"

"Take old Doc Hargrive for instance. He was writin' scrips for every dope fiend in town. He had 'em on uppers, downers and in-betweeners."

"But what would he get out of that? He was a wealthy man in his own right, wasn't he?"

"The important word there is *was* a wealthy man. Seems he had a little personal problem with dope that didn't help his already lousy surgery skills, Rev. He had more suits than Sears and Roebuck. And he'd already lost a couple of big ones. The scrip business was startin' to heat up with the Feds, so he was beginnin' to cool that one some. Street talk has it he was blackmailin' somebody to make up the extra bucks he'd lost on the dope fiend trade."

"I heard from another Vestry member that he never was the same after his kid was killed in Vietnam."

"Rev, I hate to tell you this, but he wasn't all that hot *before* that kid died. It was only the man's reputation and connections that kept him out of court before that. After his son's death he just got sloppier. The old man was probably even a failure at blackmail."

"Obviously." Holt put some salsa on the cheese nacho and bit into it. He had mistakenly garnered a jalapeño along with it and quickly grabbed the bottle of Negra for a long swallow.

Nikky Dorati laughed.

"Whatsamatter, Rev? Cain't handle the little peppers?" He put three of them on a hot nacho and eagerly devoured them. "They'll put hair on your chest."

"Yeah. And fire in your belly." He took another drink of the beer. "So what you're telling me is that Walter Hargrive could have been killed by a hundred drug addicts who were angry at having their supply dry up."

"Or by a broke blackmailer."

"Swell," he said. Then he paused. "I vote for the blackmailer."

"Why, Rev?"

"Because of the other murders. I don't think they have the M.O. of a dope fiend."

"Wait till I tell you about our old friend Ashton Willis."

"You already mentioned he was gay. Don't tell me he was into drugs, too?"

"Nope. Worse than that, Rev. But there were plenty of people out to kill him, too, and with much more reason than a little missing fix."

"Do I need a jalapeño to listen to this?"

"Probably."

"I'll try it without," the Rev said. "Shoot."

"Ashton Willis was not just gay. He was a switch-hitter, AC/DC, you know."

"You mean bisexual?"

"That's what I said, Rev. He could go either way, and frequently did."

"So what? That's not enough to get you murdered, unless of course you're having sex with both partners in the same marriage."

"He did that, too, Rev. But that's not the kicker."

"Okay, Nikky. I will be appropriately shocked when you tell me. You've done a great job of delaying the suspense. . . . Now what the hell *is* it?"

"Ashton Willis was dying from AIDS." Nikky Dorati paused dramatically. "And he *knew* it."

Lucas Holt stopped chewing and looked up. Dorati was pleased that the news had done its work. He could see the parameters racing through the Rev's mind.

"You mean, he was aggressively infecting everyone he could before he died?"

"Old Ashton didn't like to go anywhere alone, Rev. Not even to Hell."

"How many people do you suppose we're looking at as suspects, then?"

"If you mean how many people did he screw a week, I heard he'd gone on a rampage the last few months after he found out. He hung around all the gay bars and picked up whoever he could, male or female, sometimes both. He was really hacked off about getting it."

"And he took out his hostility on everyone around him."

"Yep. One of our boys—who ought to know—estimates about fifty or sixty people, both men and women."

"But did they all know what he was doing?"

"The word hit the street a couple of days ago, Rev."

"Roughly coinciding with the time he was killed."

"Yeah, but he had somethin' else goin' on the side, too."

"You mean there's more? Now what?" Lucas Holt seemed exasperated.

"Seems like he dealt in fake art stuff in some way. I have some acquaintances that were not, uh, real pleased with what he did to them."

"What do you mean? They bought something from him they thought was real and it was fake?"

"Something like that. More the other way around."

"So explain."

Nikky Dorati was about to speak when the owner of Mother's appeared in the darkness.

"I'm finished here for the night. Here's the key, Rev. Lock up on your way out. I've got another key for tomorrow. Just drop that one off next time you come in to eat; which should be soon, by the way. I haven't seen enough of you, lately."

"Thanks, Charles. We'll lock up."

"Yeah," Nikky responded. "And your place'll be safe from now on, too."

"What do you mean?" The owner looked puzzled.

"He doesn't mean anything, Charles. Good night. And put all this on my tab."

"I will. See you around."

The two heard the back door close. They replenished their supply of beer and continued.

"You were about to tell me something about Willis's art scam."

"Yes, I was." Nikky Dorati leaned forward on his seat. "You see, certain people would bring certain things to him to make copies of, you know?"

"And then he would sell the copies like originals?"

"Yeah, that's it. I think that's the way it went. Anyway, he got greedy these last few months. Guess he wanted to go out in style. Well, he did. That casket he's gonna be buried in? It musta cost him plenty."

"It cost him his life." Lucas Holt wondered how much his own life was worth. He wondered if greed was so obvious in him and what it was that drove him to the kind of life he lived. He wondered how God would judge between himself and Ashton Willis. Finally he wondered if there really were *any* "Saints of God." "So there are even more people who would want him dead?"

"Yep. You practically gotta stand in line to knock off *any* of these dudes."

"And what about our Colonel Bradenberg? How many hundreds of venge-crazed killers were out to nail *his* hide to the wall?"

"Well, you already told me the entire security division of the Air Force might have been after him."

"That's just a guess, Nikky. I think he used his covert operations position to do some smuggling business on the side. His house was filled with rare antiques and art pieces that he could never have afforded on his usual salary."

"So maybe somebody made one last collection? Maybe he cheated somebody on the last run he made? Hell, we could be lookin' at a foreigner who came over to get his stuff back or somethin'."

"I don't think so, Nikky. Look at the murder."

"Yeah. It almost looks like a professional hit."

"And that could mean CIA, FBI . . ."

". . . or an old KGB enemy for that matter. Remember, this boy was world famous."

"Or it might mean a contract, Nikky."

"Nope," he said decisively. "No contracts were out on any of those dudes—at least not in Austin. I can guarantee you that."

Lucas Holt looked at his friend. "I'll take your word for it.

So that narrows it right down to only a handful of a hundred or so people, including some from unknown parts of Europe."

"I can't figure it, Rev."

"Which thing can't you figure?"

"Usually there's somethin' in common with this kind of thing. You know, they all get off to the same kind of murder; like they all die of strangling or something. Or they always kill the same kind of people, like hookers or kids."

"Or all the victims have the same kind of interests, Nikky. What do these three people all have in common in terms of interests?"

"Well, they have that hymn you mentioned in common."

"Assuming that's what the two forty-three means, yes."

"Maybe you need to check out what churches they went to. If they're Baptist, maybe one or two was late paying their tithe."

The Rev laughed. It felt good to get some relief from the heaviness of the evening. His eyes focused briefly on the Indian paintings on the wall.

"Whatcha lookin' at, Rev?"

"I think I know what it is they all had in common, Nikky. But I'm not too sure about Hargrive."

"What's that?"

"They all had an interest in *art*."

"Well, it just so happens I can tell you about Hargrive, Rev."

"What?"

"You see, some people in this town read the obits to find out when certain other people won't be home."

"Not one of ours?"

"No, not one of the God Squad. They know you'd hang 'em yourself if they did. But I do know a dude that got busted after breakin' into Hargrive's house the day of his funeral."

"Let me guess. His house is full of artwork."

"Sorry to blow your theory, Rev, but the answer is no. The dude said he had the usual stuff on the wall to take up space and hide the wall safe. But remember this doc was on

he ropes from lawsuits and makin' ends meet with his
blackmail money."

"So maybe he sold it all?"

"Maybe. But I don't think so. I know a fence who—"

"Never mind."

Holt noticed that a car was slowly passing in front of the
restaurant.

"Hit the light, Nikky," he said. "I think a blue and white
spotted it."

"Got it, Rev."

The two men sat in darkened silence while the light from
the police car flashed over the front of the café, barely
missing them in its sweep. The car drove on, but they both
knew it would return.

"What say we call it a night, Rev?"

"Yeah," Holt replied, stretching his cramped body.

They felt their way to the kitchen door and locked it securely from the outside.

"Want a lift home, Rev? One of the boys is on a side
street with the car."

"Don't mind if I do, Nikky. You'll have to drop me a
few blocks away though. My place will be watched carefully by now. I may have to stay with a friend overnight."

"I'm sure she'll . . . I mean, it'll be a more pleasant
evening, Rev. But I'd sure like to see you just walk up to
your house, big as life in front of those cops."

"Save the dramatics, Nikky, and concentrate on finding
that killer. I have a feeling he's going to strike again soon."

"Because the odds are going against him?"

"Yes. And because he's getting sloppier with each one."

The men walked in silence to the waiting automobile.

"There's another reason I need to catch him, too, Rev,"
Nikky Dorati said as if they had not stopped talking.

"What's that?"

Nikky Dorati put his arm around Lucas Holt's taller
shoulder.

"You never know who's *next*."

• Fourteen •

The couple lay quietly in each other's arms, looking at each other as they had many times before, thinking their separate thoughts about what life could be like for them, knowing it never would be that way. They gently stroked each other's bodies, caressing, holding, feeling secure, the touching and wanting, these were the attractions they had known and shared over the years. But without commitment: always their loving had stopped short of that. It had to, for both of them.

The woman had watched him closely tonight, for there seemed a certain sadness in his eyes. He had arrived at her place later than usual with some tale of his house being watched. He was tired, needing comfort, time away from the demands of his hectic life. And he also needed to give to her, to talk to her and listen to her tell of her life, to hold and to love her again.

"What is it, darling?" she asked, caressing his face with her soft, wrinkled hand.

"Nothing," he demurred.

"It doesn't look like 'nothing' to me. What are you thinking about that upsets you so?"

Reluctantly he spoke in a tone that underscored his sadness.

"I was thinking that we . . . we can't go on like this. Risking your career to meet here, having to sneak our time together, never able to be seen out socially."

The woman's small laugh shook the bed a little.

"After all this time, you're not . . . *proposing* to me, are you, my darling?"

"I guess, maybe I am. I . . . I don't know. I just feel so . . . tired tonight."

"You've been through so much."

"*We've* been through so much, or rather *I've* put *you* through so much."

"Now, don't say that, my dearest. You know I'd go through it all again as long as we're together." She put her hands on his cheeks. "We don't have such a bad life, you know. We go our separate ways for a time; then we come together like this. We care for each other. We listen to each other. We make love and we play with each other. Then we part again; but we always know the other is right here, waiting."

"I guess I was thinking . . ." he said as his eyes watered and the lump in his throat thickened, ". . . or wondering . . . what would I do without you in my life?"

She pulled him close to her breast and rested her chin on his head, as she would a hurting child. Softly she whispered, "There, there, my dearest. You and I will be here for a long time to come. We love each other far too much to—"

Gasping for breath, she suddenly began to cough in spasms. The man pulled away from her and, holding her under her arms, raised her to a sitting position in the bed.

"My . . . medicine," she gasped. "It's . . . in the . . . usual place."

"I know," he said. "In fact, I already have a glass of water out here for you." He reached over to the bedside table for the glass and the small capsule lying beside it. "And I have one of your pills out, also."

He handed her the capsule, made certain she had it securely in her mouth, then carefully held the water glass up to her shaking lips. She smiled gratefully and snuggled close to him as they laid back down next to each other.

"Mmmmmm . . . you are so good. And I do love you,"

she said, holding him tight. "Thank you for taking care of me. I feel so relaxed now."

She yawned and breathed a deep, comforted sigh. Then, just before dropping off, she managed to reach up and softly, lightly kiss his cheek.

She did not hear his muffled crying. Nor did she feel his sweaty hand gently touch her neck and slide his fingers down over her jugular.

She did not feel the bed shake with his sobs as the throbbing in that vein slowed more and more, until, in a short time, there was no pulse at all.

The man reached down and kissed her several times on her now still face. He quickly dressed and wiped clean the few objects he had touched in the course of the evening. Just before leaving, he went back to the bed to cover her lifeless body and straighten her tousled hair for when she would be found.

She was so lovely. They had had a good life, such as it was. But this was necessary. It was part of the plan. She was in good hands now. He had seen to that. It was too sad to see her suffer. He had hurt her long ago and spent the rest of his life trying to rectify that sin. Tonight, he had at last done that. With tears streaming down his cheeks, he leaned over and kissed her one last time.

Finally he opened a drawer and located her favorite dusting powder. He dumped a quantity onto the dressing area beside the washbasin and, with the end of a pencil, outlined the numbers "243."

On his way out to the street he read through blurry eyes the too familiar sign: "El Convento del Prado Verde." The Convent of the Green Meadow.

• Fifteen •

Two large men crouched unseen in the black trees behind the small house off West Sixth.

"Able A to base." The blond-haired man spoke quietly
into the small square snapped to his dark green shirt.

"Any sign of life?" the box spoke back.

"None, sir. Able B thought he saw a light, but it turned
out to be passing vehicles."

"Continue," the box commanded.

"Approaching target now."

He motioned to his dark-complexioned companion, and
the two men stealthily ran in the cover of night to the back
door of Lucas Holt's house.

"Kick the damned thing in," the dark one said.

"Too much noise." The crew-cut blond pulled a tool
from his utility belt. "This will do."

"Able B entering."

"Radio silence," the box said.

"A and B out."

"A" switched off his microtransmitter as both men entered the open door.

"Here," the dark one said, pointing to the next room.

His companion motioned up with his hand and took the
wooden staircase by threes.

Upstairs, in Holt's bedroom and study, the blond man
pulled books from their cases, plunged his serrated knife
deep into the mattress and pillow slips, and overturned desk
drawers, beaming his small, high-powered light over the
contents.

In the living room the man stopped suddenly at the sound of a creaking board. Trained to remain absolutely motionless, the dark man waited, heard the sound again, and silently moved toward the kitchen with his knife clasped tightly in his teeth.

Like a shadow, he slid around the doorway, saw the back of a tall, thin figure, and reached for the knife handle. From the corner of his eye he glimpsed a raised object to his right. He spun to counter, but the blackjack slammed him into unconsciousness. As he fell, he knocked a chair into the glass cabinet.

"One down," Nikky Dorati whispered across the kitchen to the nervous Eddie Shelton. "Now go upstairs and get the other one."

"Hell, no!" Shelton replied. "*I* got this one. *You* go get the one up—"

Both men disappeared into separate rooms as they heard hard boots hit the stair landing.

Shelton found himself plastered against the wall below where the huge blond man stood, and watched as the figure pulled on night binocs.

Shit, he thought to himself. He's got those damned green vision things. And me with frigging prison glasses.

He heard the steps creak under the weight of his adversary.

Sucker must weigh 260, Shelton thought as he jumped out from his safe enclosure, holding his .38 aimed at the hulking figure before him.

"Who—no, *what* the hell are you?" the blond-haired man sneered.

"Just don't move."

The man whirled and kicked. Shelton's gun flew across the room. Eddie swung, but his fist was stopped in midair. Nikky Dorati peeked around the corner in time to see Shelton follow the route of the gun.

"I hate it when that happens," he murmured as the huge blond man yelled, then hurtled toward him. Dorati hit the floor, buying the needed edge to pump two silenced shots into the flying man's thighs.

The big man twisted in the air and landed squarely on his broad back, knocking out his wind. Dorati swiftly bound him with tape, gagged him, then went to check on Eddie Shelton.

"How the hell are you?" he said to the groaning figure under the front window.

"Where's my piece?"

"Right here propped against the wall next to you. I think he tried to get two 'leaners.'"

"Funny, Dorati," Shelton said, rubbing his aching arms.

"How'd you stop the blond gorilla?"

"Did his legs."

"You can still *do* that?"

"Some things . . ." Dorati smirked. "Like ridin' a bicycle."

Minutes later the two green-clad men were securely bound, the one with bandages around both legs.

"Hit 9-1-1, Eddie," Nikky ordered. "And say *'Help me! Help me!'* like that guy in *The Fly*."

"You're sick, you know that?" Shelton dialed the emergency number and complied.

"Now, let's get the hell outta—" Dorati began. He was interrupted by a squawk from the dark-haired man's shoulder.

"Base to Able B. Base to Able B. What's going on there? Do you copy?"

"Yeah," Dorati said, yanking the small boxes from each man's uniform. "We copy, you mothers." He smashed each box against the floor with his blackjack. "That ought to cover the damage you done to the Rev's place, you shits."

Distant sirens hurried them out the back door.

Susan Granger grabbed the phone after one short ring. She recognized the voice and signaled the officer just outside her door. Then she spoke.

"Where the hell *are* you, Lucas Holt? My people have been looking for you all night. The least you could do is to check in."

"Susan, stop it. I'm not going to hang on long enough for you to trace this call so if you want to hear what I have to say, be quiet."

"No, dammit! You listen to *me*! You may think it's cute to create a diversion and slip out from the watch I had on you. But you better get your ass back under that watch and soon."

"Why? What happened?"

"He struck again."

"Where? Which one was it?"

"The 'Shepherdess on the green.' "

Lucas Holt's voice dropped.

"Who was it?"

"The Directress at the Convent of the Green Meadow. It's out 2222 by the lake."

"He killed a *nun*?"

"Yes. A 'Sister Marguerite,' I think her name was. Did you know her?"

"I didn't know her well. I'd met her recently at a clergy conference. She was way ahead of her time; very progressive and ecumenically minded."

"She must have been something to get that far up in the hierarchy of the Catholic church. They just didn't promote women like that back then. Most convents were really run by men."

"That's right," Holt replied quickly. "As a matter of fact, I heard that when she got the appointment there was scuttlebutt that the Archbishop had been under pressure from someone to give it to her. She deserved it anyway, but whoever it was managed to threaten the powers that be into doing the right thing."

He looked at his watch—eighty seconds before the three-minute trace period was up.

"How did she die?"

"According to her doctor's report, she had cancer. Bad. Our boy merely substituted a cyanide capsule for her pain medicine. She died instantly. Never knew what hit her."

"How'd he get that close?"

"He got a hell of a lot closer than that, Lucas," Granger replied, looking at the tracer. He shook his head. "Listen to this," she stalled. "The lab says they'd had intercourse just prior to her death."

"Yet another mistake on his part."

"What do you mean mistake?"

"I knew a guy got thirty-to-life from one drop of fluid. I assume the semen specimen can be traced like blood type."

"Right. If there's any sperm to find. This guy must have used a condom and taken it with him. But we're checking stains on the sheets that may turn up something."

"Nailed by the wet spot, huh, Lieutenant?" Holt snickered. He knew Susan Granger would recall the same scene as he did, and that she was praying he would not allude to it now. He didn't. "How do we know it was the same killer? The numbers?"

"The numbers. He left them drawn in a pile of dusting powder on her vanity. It was a gruesome contrast to her rather painless, easy death."

"Sounds like he killed someone he loved, Susan. That's weird, but won't it narrow down the list of suspects?"

"Oh, right, Sherlock. All I have to do is go in and ask the good sisters for a list of potential and actual lovers their boss had. I'm sure they'll be quite helpful." She glanced again at the officer outside, who shook his head. "But let me ask you something else."

"Time's up, Lieutenant. I'll call you right back."

"Wait a min—"

The line went dead in her ear.

"Did you get anything?"

"Got the first three digits, Lieutenant. He's somewhere in downtown Austin."

"Get a unit over to St. Margaret's Episcopal Church.

He's probably not there; it's too obvious. But you never know."

Her phone rang. She let it ring two more times to be sure the trace was ready.

"Hello?"

"I'm not *at* the church, Susan. I'm not quite that stupid. So you can call off the squad car there."

"Listen, smart ass, I'm tired of playing with you. Maybe, just maybe, if we hadn't been out looking to save your skin last night, we would have prevented that nun's death. Did you ever think of that?"

"I have." He paused. "Have you thought about the fact that I don't think I need saving? Not by *you*, anyway. Call off the troops, Susan. When I've gotten the information I need, I'll get back with you. I'm already on to some reasons the others might have been killed. I have to check out one more thing and I'll meet you and we'll talk."

"You're damned right we'll talk. And before you innocently assume you're not in need of saving, let me tell you what else happened last night."

"Fine, Lieutenant. Scare me some more."

"I will. If you think in your arrogant, sexist mind that the reason the Austin Police Department is spending its time hunting for you is because *I'm* worried about your sorry Episcopal hide, you're badly mistaken."

"Hurry up about it, Susan. I have to hang up again soon and I don't want to miss this."

"Okay, wise guy," she said. "Get *this*. When you first slipped the tail, I was just plain mad. But then I got a call from the officers watching your house that someone was coming back in. I naturally thought it was you and so had them wait a while and then go in after you."

"But I didn't go back there last night."

"I know. Someone *else* did. *Two* 'someone elses' as a matter of fact."

"Who were they?"

"Oh, yeah, sure. Now he's interested. Maybe *I* ought to

hang up on *you* now, huh?" The officer on the other phone held up one finger. They had the first digit.

"Lighten up, Susan. What the hell happened?"

"Here's what happened, Lucas." She paused for a drink of coffee. "We suddenly got a 911 call to *your* address. My men ran in the back door and found the place ransacked. Drawers dumped out. Books pulled off the shelves. Cushions shredded. Even your fireplace ashes had been messed with."

Lucas Holt felt a chill up his spine. He hadn't counted on any of this. Maybe he *was* in over his head.

"So who . . . was it?"

Ignoring his attempt to hurry the conversation, Susan Granger continued.

"Unfortunately, we can only guess at that, Lucas."

"They weren't there? I thought you said—"

"Oh, they were *there*. The two men were tied up like Christmas packages on the floor of your dining room. One of them had been shot in both thighs—clean shots, right through the skin without hitting the bones." She smiled as the nearby cop held up two fingers. "That sound familiar, Lucas? Remind you of anybody we mutually know and love?"

"Save it for later, Lieutenant." He held up his watch. "You've almost got four digits by now. I need to know who they *were*."

"I can't tell you that, Father Holt," Granger said. "Seems as soon as the officers cut the wrist tape, these two gorillas chop sueyed them into la-la land and split."

"With two bullets in—"

"Seems they *also* had a little help from their friends."

"Did your guys get a description? Who do they think it was?"

"They got a good look at the two men. They were tall, muscular, well trained in martial arts fighting. They weren't street fighters, either. And there's one more thing."

"What's that?"

"They had military haircuts—and wore greens."

Lucas Holt automatically reached back and touched the address book in his rear pocket.

"So," he answered, "they were either Air Force or Aggies."

Susan Granger was aware of the people listening to their conversation. "Cute, Lucas," she said. She had to be careful here. "So, do you think they . . . found what they wanted?"

"I doubt it. I still have my . . . uh . . . wallet with me."

"Then you're still fair game—for both the killer and the other people who want to get hold of you." The cop held up four fingers. "Do you think you need saving now?"

"Not quite yet, Susan. Time's running out again. I need to hang up. I promise you I'll meet you at my house this afternoon. It's ten o'clock now. Meet me there at five. I have some things to say that will help. Besides, you can help me clean up."

"Dammit, Lucas. Let me do this *with* you."

"I can't. Or rather *you* can't. Just meet me there, okay?"

"Do I have a choice? I'll meet you there, I just hope you live till then."

"I will. And Lieutenant?"

"Yes?"

"When you get there, you can help me with my drawers."

Lucas Holt hung up the phone in his church office. Saturday morning there was busy with choir members, altar guild, and church school teachers preparing for the next day's activities. He had gone to Kristen's, then slept the remainder of the night in his office. This morning, unshaven, he had hardly been noticed in his regular street clothes. Only Maxine, working her half day getting the bulletin ready, commented on his attire as he opened his office door, carafe in hand.

"You've always looked good in total black, Rev. Grease up your face and you could rob a bank."

"I may have to do that if we can't think of a way to pay off our debts."

"Lord's Prayer won't work, huh?"

"What?"

"'Forgive us our debts as we forgive our debtors?'"

"It's 'trespasses' in this church, Max, and you know what they say at the bank."

"Yeah, same as at the pen. 'In God we trust—all others pay cash.'" Max grinned. "Other offer's still open."

Holt smiled back. "It's looking more and more tempting." He poured himself a cup of Earl Grey. "I need not to be disturbed a while, Max," he said.

"You got it, Rev. And if somebody comes callin'?"

"I'm not here." He closed his office door and locked it.

The phone call to Susan Granger had shaken him. Dodging APD was one thing. Staying away from the Air Force military police, or whatever branch of government security was looking for him, was quite another. He would have to be extra careful until he again hooked up with Susan. And he would have to get rid of that book.

He took the black leather object out and looked at each page quickly. Now that he understood the system, he thought he might recognize a name more easily than before. He had just gotten to the *T* listing when a small buzzer sounded under his desk. Maxine had hit a foot button to alert him to voices in the outer office.

"Excuse me, but is Father Holt in?"

Maxine stalled, speaking loud enough for the Rev to hear.

"No, *Officer*. I haven't seen him all morning."

The voices continued as he hurriedly glanced through the pages of the address book.

Stall them five minutes, Max, he thought. Stall them five . . .

Suddenly his eyes screeched to a halt. His heart pumped quickly when he recognized the name. How had he missed it before? What in the world was this person's connection with Bradenberg? Was it one that would end in murder?

He wrote down the name and slipped the paper into his pocket. Then he put the book in an envelope, quickly addressed it and attached a note directing Maxine to mail it immediately. Tossing it in his "Out" box he looked up at the sound of someone trying to open his office door.

"You can't go in there, *Officers*!"

"If he's not in there, what's the problem with opening it?"

"Do you have a search warrant?"

"Do you want us to break this door down?"

Maxine stood nose to nose with the six-foot cop. "Listen, sonny," she said, her red hair matching her blotchy face, "I asked you where the hell your frigging *warrant* was."

"You got some mouth on you for a church secretary."

"That time I asked you *nice*."

"Break it down," the cop said to his partner, still staring at the redhead in his path.

"All right! All right!" she said, hoping she had given her boss time to do whatever he needed. "I'll *open* it for you. Wait a minute until I can find the *key*."

She stalled as she looked through the different drawers in her desk.

"I just can't imagine what I *did* with that little critter," she said, knowing they were getting increasingly annoyed.

"You got thirty seconds, lady," the tall cop said. "And I use the word loosely."

Maxine kept her response to herself. She finally opened the center drawer and "found" what she knew was there all along.

"Well, *here* it is after all," she said, going over and slowly inserting the key in the door handle. "Now you two boys can look inside."

The officers hurried into the room and found the sunlit office empty. Maxine noticed that the door to the Rev's private bathroom was closed shut. It was almost always open just a crack. Unfortunately the police noticed it, too.

One officer took out his gun and pressed flat against the wall behind the door. The other slowly advanced directly in front of the door and was about to pull it open.

"I don't know *what* you two expect to find in that *bathroom* there."

He yanked the door open, and his partner aimed the gun at arm's length through the crack by the hinge.

Maxine crossed her arms over her chest.

"Now that you've got the drop on the toilet, sonny, would you like to handcuff the sink?"

The St. Margaret's Treasury was located in the ancient basement of the church. The original 1846 pilings, sunk deep in Texas granite, provided perfect divisions for the displays. Enclosed by thick glass and protected by a series of alarms and backup systems that could only be deactivated by one key, the vast wealth of the Treasury was considered safer than most of the bank vaults in Austin. It was that one key that now turned behind a door known only to one person.

Lucas Holt had found the long-forgotten passageway leading from his office to the basement during his first week as he had reviewed old plans of the church. This passage evidently was one of many that were used to hide slaves, soldiers, illegal aliens, or whoever needed sanctuary for whatever reason over the last 150 years. The still intact passages in the sanctuary walls and ceiling above the church were well known to most parishioners, but this one had been boarded up, nailed shut behind sheetrock, probably declared unsafe and unnecessary decades ago.

Doing office repairs after hours on his own time, Lucas Holt quietly opened the passage, outfitted it with a lock to deactivate the Treasury alarm, a cordless phone, and a lighted stairway. With the door closed and tightly barred from the back, the seam inside was virtually undetectable. With the alarm off, he could safely use the Treasury area as a place of refuge until it opened to the public at noon.

It was just like the secret exit his dad had had in his law office in Smithville. When asked, Ben Holt had told his son that there were simply times when it was better not to be in the office, even if you *were* in.

The Rev wandered through the exhibitions, as he gave the police time to leave the building. It was really the first time he had looked carefully at the many sacred objects there. The jewel-encrusted chalices, the golden pyxes, the silver candlesticks all reminded him of a church of the past. He wondered why the native people had tolerated such extreme poverty for themselves while their religious hierarchy lived in luxury. Nothing but the best for God, they must have believed. And that had left nothing at all for them.

He stopped, mesmerized by the beauty of a particularly ornate cross. The large emeralds and rubies seemed too heavy for its delicate stature. Was it really worth it? he wondered. Should they entirely liquidate this incredible collection to pay for the greed of one man? Would it not be better to find another solution? But what?

Lucas Holt was suddenly aware that he had two problems on his mind at the same time: the murders and the Treasury. For one brief moment he mixed the two together, wondering how they might be intertwined.

The Saints of God.

The Treasury of St. Margaret's.

But how could they be related? The only thing they had in common was . . . maybe that *was* the connection. Maybe they were right last night after all.

Lucas Holt quickly returned to the hidden doorway. He picked up the phone and punched in the digits he had memorized.

"Hello. Nikky?"

"Rev? Is that you? What're you doin' up so soon?"

"It's nearly eleven o'clock, Nikky."

"In the *morning*?"

"In the morning."

"Cut me some slack, Rev. If you remember, last night wasn't over till about four."

"Listen. I need you to come by the church and pick me up."

"Ain't you heard, Rev? They got a brand-new thing in Austin now. They're called 'taxis.'"

"The only taxi I could get right now is a blue-and-white one."

Nikky Dorati sat up in bed. "How soon can I get you?"

"Wait twenty minutes. Then come by the Seventh Street side of the church. There's a small wooden door there in the stone wall."

"Okay, Rev." Dorati swung his feet out of the single bed. "Believe it or not, I know where that is. But don't expect me to drive too good. I ain't got my eyes open yet."

"Just *get* here," Holt said thankfully. "And Nikky?"

"What else?"

"You any good at 'b and e'?"

"Not good at all, Rev. I got three-to-five the first time I tried it. Turned out to be the mayor's house they said I was breaking and entering. Didn't know shit about alarms back then. So I had to go into another business. Why?"

"'Cause we need to do a little b and e this afternoon."

Silence came through the line. Then, "Okay, you got my eyes open now." Dorati stood by the bed and squinted out the window. "So what's the joke?"

"No joke, Nikky. B and e. You and me."

"Great, Rev. I'm outta the joint three weeks and my *priest*, for God's sake, is askin' me to do a heist with him."

"Not a heist, just a little look-see."

"And are you *sure* nobody will be home?" Dorati paused for what sounded like a drink. "If I get popped, I stand to take a *big* fall this time."

"I'm *positive* the owner won't be there."

"Why?"

Lucas Holt smiled as he spoke. "I buried him yesterday."

• Sixteen •

"So we might be right about the connection with the murders, Nikky. It all depends on what we find in there."

Lucas Holt sat in the passenger seat of the brand-new black Beemer, admiring the leather interior.

"Where'd you get this car, anyway? I thought the State of Texas gave you fifty dollars and a suit when you got out." He smiled at his cigar-chewing friend.

"Collected a long overdue debt, Rev." Dorati stuffed the unlit cigar into the ashtray. "Local guy agreed to wait till I got out to pay me. Worked out great, huh?"

"Why'd you get black?"

"Cops don't go after black cars. They look for little bright-colored sports cars. They figure anybody driving a black Beemer like this one, he's gotta be a judge or a doc or something they don't want to mess with." He punched the Rev's shoulder. "Hell, Rev, they might be a priest."

"A bishop maybe, not a priest." Lucas Holt pointed to the next corner. "Turn here."

"Shit," Dorati mumbled as they turned onto Cat Mountain Trail. "You'd better be right about this."

"Drive by and turn at the next block."

They passed the police cruiser sitting in front of the house of the late Ashton Willis.

"Just one in the box," Dorati said. "Probably thought they wouldn't need more than one cop on the day shift."

They drove around the block and checked for other police vehicles, marked or unmarked.

"No sign of any others," Dorati said.

"Park there, behind the house." They casually got out of the car as if they had every right to be strolling up to the rear of the Cat Mountain mansion.

Nikky Dorati got suddenly nervous. "Are you *sure* this is the right time of day to do this, Rev? In broad *daylight*?"

"What time of day did you get busted breaking into the mayor's house?"

"I don't do b and e and I never understood taking that kind of chance. That night I was actually looking for the gardener to ask directions."

"What time was it?"

"Three in the morning."

"Does that answer your question?"

Nikky Dorati was not sure whether it did or not. There seemed to be a slip in the logic somewhere, but he did not have time to think about it. They stood at the back door, ready to enter.

"Okay, Nikky," Lucas Holt said, pointing to the lock. "Do your thing."

"It's not my thing, Rev." The short, greasy-haired man took a small packet out of his coat.

"Then where did you get that?"

"I borrowed it from Frankie Colovas."

"'*Doors*' is in town?"

"Yeah." Dorati selected what looked like the right pick for this type of lock. "When he got out he heard you were here—and that some of the Squad was here—so he landed about two days ago. I been puttin' him up at the Alamo till he gets on his feet."

"Another surprise for Lieutenant Granger," Holt mumbled as Dorati was about to slip the two picks into the lock.

Lucas Holt put his hand over Nikky's and held a finger up to his lips.

"Hold it," the Rev whispered.

"What? You chickenin' out—I hope?"

"No. But I don't think that pick will be necessary."

"Huh?"

"Just turn the knob," Holt whispered. "Quietly."

Nikky Dorati turned the doorknob, and the door easily opened.

"How'd you know that?" He frowned and put away the picks.

"Frankie mentioned it one time." Holt crouched down behind his short companion. "Shhhh. I thought I saw movement through the window." Lucas Holt hunched down to Dorati's height. "There's somebody *in* there."

"Shit. I thought you said he was dead."

"Shhhh."

"Well, it can't be the owner."

"That's the *bad* news."

"I think my car alarm just went off."

"Go on in."

"You first, Rev. So far, your record's cleaner."

The two men cautiously entered the house, trying to make certain their movements would be unnoticed. They slunk through the kitchen and moved down the hallway toward what appeared to be a spacious living room.

Dorati motioned for the Rev to lean closer to him. "I just thought of somethin'," Dorati began.

"What?" Holt whispered nervously.

"You remember that deal the Lyman brothers used to run when they'd break in a place?"

Holt nodded.

"Well, there's no sense *both* of us gettin' killed in here. I mean, what if this dude ain't a cop? What if he's a playmate of the gorillas who broke your house up?"

Holt nodded again. "Okay. I remember the Lymans. Who goes first?"

"*You* do." Dorati winked at him. "Good luck."

The Rev took a deep breath and wiped his sweaty brow on his shirtsleeve. He continued down the hallway alone and turned once to see Dorati urging him on. As he turned back, he did not see the short man slip around a corner out of sight. He also did not see Dorati reach behind his back to find the small pistol hidden under his jacket.

The Rev walked carefully into the living room. It was still marked with crime scene indicators outlining where the body was found and where major pieces of evidence were located. The painting over the fireplace blared out the fateful numbers, demanding attention to its defiant message.

Lucas Holt stood still and surveyed the area. He was not sure what it was he was trying to find, but he knew he would know when he found it. The number of art objects was overwhelming. Either Ashton Willis was an extremely aggressive and rich collector, or he used the house as a kind of a storage place for his "business."

Walking around the room, the Rev looked closely at the various pieces of religious art: crosses, icons, ancient-looking wooden statues, hand-painted and cracking from years of decay. Willis was evidently very good at his ability to transform modern pieces of clay, wood, and precious metals into identical images of ancient and valuable fakes. He mixed his love for religious artifacts with his considerable artistic talents to produce both pleasure and wealth for himself and others. Maybe one of those "others" was the murderer.

Holt had heard the footstep when he first walked into the room. He was pretty sure the other person was waiting behind the partly closed door leading off the living room, just beside the fireplace. He slowly moved in that direction, making sure he was visible as he casually looked at the pieces, pretending to be searching for some specific item. When he reached the proper spot, he turned his back on the door and bent over to observe a small statue on a table. It was then that the expected voice spoke behind him.

"Move and you're one dead white boy."

Lucas Holt did not move.

"Now, just stay bent over like that so you can't do anything funny and tell me what the hell you're doin' here."

The Rev moved his hands to his waist to maintain his balance.

"Don't make no fast moves. Me and this 9mm don't like anything that don't move in slow motion."

"I might ask you the same thing," Lucas Holt said slowly and softly.

"You might, but you ain't got the gun, do ya?"

"I was a friend of Ashton Willis," the Rev lied. "I heard he had some of my art in here that I had him do for me. It was a business deal. I wanted to get it back before the police—"

Lucas Holt felt a deep jab to his kidney. He doubled over with the pain, not daring to shout or turn around. He wondered where the hell Dorati was.

"Don't lie to me, sucka. That creep Willis never done business with you."

The tall black man lifted the butt of his gun over the Rev's back. "If you don't tell me what you're doin' here, I'll—"

"Drop the gun, mo-fo, before I air-condition your chest." Nikky Dorati held his pistol to the man's back.

Holt held his throbbing side and slowly straightened to a standing position. "What took you so long? And didn't I tell you not to bring a gun?"

"You're in a lousy position to complain about the gun, Rev. And I couldn't walk in before—"

"'*Rev*'?!" the black man said out loud.

"Keep the hands where we can see 'em, mister," Dorati demanded. "And keep your damned voice down. There's a cop outside who'd make captain if he got *this* bust."

The black man grinned. "Dorati, is that *you*, you sawed-off piece of sh—"

"Wait a minute," Nikky replied. "Turn around and let me see your ugly face; but do it slowly, bro, I'd hate to spill more blood on this antique carpet."

The man turned around and Nikky Dorati lowered the gun. "I don't believe this shit."

"Yo, homey!"

The two men smiled and embraced like lost brothers.

"Where you been at, Dorati? I heard you was cleanin' up your act, and I couldn't believe it. Not the 'Mafia Midget.' Not one of the best hit men in the business."

"*One* of the best?"

"Well, okay, man, but you been out of circulation a long time."

"Yeah, and it's a damned good thing, Omar. Fifteen years ago I'd have shot first and said 'too bad' later." He put the gun back in his waist holster. "How'd you get onto this place, anyway? I heard you just got cut loose from the joint in Oklahoma last week."

"That's right. But I read about this rich guy gettin' wasted, and I figured it might be a worthwhile sting, ya know?"

"Yeah, but—"

Lucas Holt cleared his throat.

"Excuse me," he said, "but I don't believe we've met. I'd like to know where to send the bill for my renal dialysis."

"Oh! Sorry, Rev," Dorati began. "This is Omar Dewan. We did two-to-four together before you got to Huntsville."

The black man extended his hand to Lucas Holt.

"Omar, this is Father Lucas Holt. The boys call him 'the Rev.'"

"Pleased to meet you, Reverend. I heard a lot about you from some home-boys who did time with Nikky here after I split the State. Took the 'geographical cure,' ya know, and went to Oklahoma. Didn't do me much good, I guess. Here I am again."

"Yes, I see." Holt rubbed his side.

"Hey, man, I'm sorry about that kidney jab."

"Think nothing of it. I'll be okay in a year or so." Lucas

Holt looked at Nikky Dorati. "Listen, I hate to break up this family reunion, but we did come here for a reason and that officer's not going to drink coffee all afternoon."

"What're you guys lookin' for? Maybe I can help. I cased the joint yesterday, and I been all over inside here already."

"That's just it, Omar," the Rev said. "I'm not exactly sure. I came here expecting to see something I'd recognize, maybe something from the church or somebody's name written on a receipt. So far I don't see anything familiar."

"Well," Omar replied, waving his arm in front of him, "you're lookin' at most of the good loot right here. I checked out the upstairs before I was interrupted in my work by you two. Ain't nothin' happenin' up there that *I* can see. Just a few more statues and pieces of metal and like that."

Nikky Dorati took the tall, black man by the arm.

"Now, Omar, this is more your gig than mine," he said. "If you were going to hide something in here that you didn't want nobody to find, where would you hide it?"

Omar Dewan stood back so he could see the whole room. Holt and Dorati got out of his way so as not to distract him. He walked around the room, picked up a few objects and looked at them carefully, then returned to his place with the other two men.

"I got this strange feelin' that the really good stuff ain't in sight," he said. "Now, this is some good loot here, all right, but I think the dude hid what he didn't want nobody to find."

"Right," Dorati said, "but *where*? We don't have much time." He swept over the room with his hand. "Where would *you* hide something in here?"

"Well," Dewan began, "first I'd find me a secret compartment or somethin' like that." He walked over to the wall and looked behind the paintings, one by one. "No, that ain't it. And I already checked out the floor for hollow boards." He turned and looked at the fireplace. " 'Course I ain't gone over that thing yet," he said, walking over and placing his hands carefully on the tiles surrounding the mantel.

Nikky Dorati and Lucas Holt went to help.

"No." Omar waved them away. "This is still *my* gig, remember? You might miss somethin' or distract me."

He stopped and held his ear up to a tile near the top of the mantelpiece. He took out his gun and lightly tapped the butt on the tile. The hollow sound brought the three men quickly to the side of the fireplace.

"That's it!" Lucas Holt exclaimed. "You found it."

"Not so fast, Rev," Omar said cautiously. "Sometimes these babies are rigged to go off if they're opened wrong. They showed me that little trick in 'Nam when they were teachin' me to blow up villages and people and shit. Comes in very handy now and then."

Omar Dewan put his ear up to the tile, moved the ceramic piece very lightly and heard no telltale click that would arm a charge.

"I think this one's clean, Rev. Let's give it a try." He took a wooden statue of an ancient saint from the table in front of the fireplace and held it at arm's length in front of him. "Stand back, you two, just in case."

He pushed the tile gently with the statue, and angled it so that the nose of the saint hooked around the edge of the tile. Then he gently pulled the tile open.

A dart whizzed across the room.

"Good," Omar said. "*Very* good!" He crouched down around under the opening. "Let's hope that's the only one in there." He pulled a handkerchief from his back pocket and wrapped it around his huge hand, then put a thick leather glove on over it.

"Just in case," he said, sticking his hand up to the opening. "Let's just see what's so important that it has to be hid so good."

Omar slowly reached into the small niche and lifted up the

object. He felt a small push on his hand as he retrieved a gold-and silver-plated icon, obviously of Mexican derivation.

"There it is," he said.

"It's beautiful," the Rev said.

"It's deadly," Dewan replied, pointing to the small dart imbedded in his leather glove. He carefully removed it and laid it back in the niche.

"No wonder he hid that, whatever it is."

"It's an icon," Holt said quietly.

"Right, that icon in the fireplace wall," Dorati said. "It makes these other things look cheap by comparison."

"They are cheap," Holt said as he looked around the room. "Because all these are fakes."

The quiet in the room was abruptly broken by the sound of a car door slamming shut.

"Shit," Dorati said. "Let's book."

Without a word they took care of their separate tasks to cover their tracks.

Lucas Holt wiped clean any objects he had touched. Omar Dewan replaced the icon, closed the hidden tile, and checked the rest of the mantel area quickly for other compartments. Nikky Dorati watched out the front window as the officer came closer to the house. He tossed Omar Dewan the gun he'd taken from him earlier and motioned the two toward the back of the house.

"Come on, Nikky," the Rev said. "We still have time to get out the back door. He's just making his rounds."

"Okay, Rev. But we'd better make it fast. I think he's plannin' on comin' inside the place."

The three men hurried to the kitchen where they had entered and pulled the door closed, locking it as they did. They walked quickly to Dorati's car and were about to get inside.

"This is where I split," Omar Dewan said. "I'll see you all some other time."

"Sure you don't want a lift, Omar?" Nikky Dorati offered. "You might get spotted in this neighborhood."

"I do better on foot, Dorati. You ought to remember

that." He turned and offered his hand to Lucas Holt. "Nice meetin' you, Rev. Maybe we'll see each other again some time around town. You'd be good to rob houses with, ya know?"

Lucas Holt smiled. "Thanks for the compliment. But I'd suggest you stay out of that particular house, Omar. It's going to be hotter than usual in a day or so."

"Not bad advice, even if it is from a preacher."

"And stop by the church sometime. I'd like to talk with you."

"Sure thing, Rev."

"Don't bullshit him, Omar," Dorati said. "Come see me at the Alamo Hotel. 'The Door' needs a roomie. Maybe we'll all hold hands and go to church together—if we don't get our asses arrested in the next five minutes." He started the engine. "Come on, Rev. We're in the wind. Bye, Omar."

Dorati maneuvered the car out of the alley and back down Cat Mountain. He and the Rev were nearly back to West Sixth Street before Nikky finally spoke.

"You know, Rev, I been thinkin'."

"I noticed. You haven't said a word since we left Ashton Willis's house."

"Yeah. Well, somethin's been botherin' me about that statue Omar pulled out of that compartment."

"What's that?"

"Well, I only seen that collection of yours once. You know, the one in the basement of the church?"

"The Treasury?"

"Yeah, that's it. Like I was sayin', I only seen it once." Nikky Dorati looked over at Lucas Holt. "And, no, I wasn't thinkin' about liftin' any of it."

"Go on."

"That icon thing he found? Doesn't it look a lot like one in that Treasury of yours? Third case from the right I think."

Lucas Holt paused a second, then looked over at his friend.

"No, Nikky. It doesn't look a lot like it," he said. "It's identical."

• Seventeen •

Susan Granger watched in her rearview mirror as the white Miata convertible pulled up in front of Holt's house. She looked away as Kristen Wade held his face in her hands and kissed him.

What the hell did he see in her?

She looked back in the mirror at the shiny auburn hair and the white car.

That was a dumb question.

Why do I put myself through this? she thought. She knew it could never work with Lucas Holt. It never had in the past. Why would she think now was possibly any different?

That was twenty years ago. They were different people now. Or were they? He was still attracted to lost causes— like Kristen Wade and the God Squad and a failing church—and she was still the grim voice of reality he ignored in his quests.

But still, he seemed somehow changed in these last few days together. Maybe it was the fight with the bishop, or the dead bodies they kept stumbling over. Or maybe she was mellowing toward him.

God forbid she should do that!

Interesting phrase, *God forbid,* she thought as she saw Holt extract himself from the tiny car like a sardine from a can. Why didn't God forbid these horrid murders? Why didn't God forbid Holt from getting into relationships that were doomed to fail?

Maybe that was the attraction? Lucas Holt was the only

man, or woman for that matter, whom she could talk to about God—or about anything of substance—and be taken with utmost seriousness. Was that her hunger, to be taken seriously? Was it to have a partner equal to her? Was it something else?

She watched him slowly walk to her car and felt a stirring deep within her.

Obviously there was another component to the attraction she was trying to ignore. As Kristen Wade drove by her and waved, Susan Granger remembered what it was.

That would have to wait, she thought as the Rev leaned into her open car window, his face inches from hers and the scent of Lagerfeld's wafting like a scarf around her.

She took a deep breath. It didn't help.

"Hi, Susan," he said.

"At least for now," she replied.

"What?"

Granger turned red, rolled up the window, and opened the door.

"Nothing, I was thinking about another case."

"I'll buy you a beer if you promise not to be too angry."

Susan Granger stepped out of the car. She looked tired and upset.

"Well," she said, looking at her watch, "at least you're on time for a change. And I'm not angry, Lucas. Right now I'm absolutely beat from too little sleep in exchange for too damned little evidence."

"Come on inside." He took her arm and escorted her up the steps to the door. "I'll see if I can fix at least one of those problems."

"Kristen wouldn't like it if I slept here."

Holt opened the door and pointed toward the shambles in the living room. "I was talking about the *evidence*, Susan. Go sit down and I'll get you a cold Celis from your favorite local brewery."

She plopped down on the tattered couch and kicked off

her shoes. Lucas Holt appeared with two frosted mugs of the dark Texas beer and sat on the opposite end.

"At least they had the good sense not to break the beer mugs," he said, handing her one.

"God, that tastes good," she said. She turned around and stretched out her legs so her feet landed in his lap. "Start rubbing," she ordered. "For all the trouble you've caused me, you owe me one."

"Keep talking and maybe I'll do *both* of them."

"You'd better." She laid her head back on what was left of the large white pillow. "You're a hell of a lot cheaper than a therapist, and *they* won't rub feet." She took another drink of the beer. "At least the legit ones won't."

"Depends on where you go. Now, I know of a nice little place over on the Interstate . . ."

"Madame La Rouche's Ten-Minute Body Belt and Bang Job?"

"Now, Susan. Those young ladies all used to be employees of Maxine's, and—"

"I know, Lucas. I always wondered just how personally you got involved with . . . OUCH!"

"Don't insult the alligator until you have crossed the river, Lieutenant." Lucas Holt released his hold on her instep. "I still have charge of your feet. So tell me what else is bothering you."

"I've been chasing down dead-end clues all day. The chief is about to have my badge for not coming up with anything more than we've got. He wants to call in the damned FBI. The press is having a field day with the blood and gore and the mass-murderer mystique. They've practically been advertising for every borderline kook in town to give them the exclusive story."

"Any takers?"

"The usual." She arched her back like a cat and rolled her head against the pillow. "Twelve people so far have confessed to being the killer. One of them was paraplegic. God, the next thing I know some enterprising college kid on the Drag will be selling 'two forty-three' T-shirts to the university students." She sipped her beer slowly. "Actually, that may not be a bad idea. I'll need some income soon if I—or rather we—don't catch this space cadet soon."

Lucas Holt massaged her feet, wondering how much he would tell her about what he had learned. He decided it was time she knew it all. He hoped she would not ask how he had gotten his information, as that would just upset her more. Besides that, she already knew.

"So that's been one day in the life of Lieutenant Susan Granger, Austin Police Department—so far, anyway. Wouldn't my daddy be proud?" She looked down at the Rev, who was intently squeezing her toes. "So does this mean you really 'knead' me?"

Holt squinched up his face. "Bad, Susan. Very bad. It means I was thinking, concentrating on what I have to tell you."

"So spill, Lucas. But before you do, get up and get me another beer. And bring some cheese or something, too."

Lucas Holt tossed her legs off his lap.

"Yes, Master." He bowed and scraped.

Susan Granger laughed as he left the room in a hunched over position. She wondered if he ever played like that with Kristen Wade. Before she could give it much thought, Holt returned with a tray holding two more beers, a plate of cheese, crackers, and a piece of paper.

"What's that?" she asked.

"It's what you asked for."

"I meant the piece of paper."

"So did I. Read it."

Susan Granger nibbled the cheese and picked up the slip of paper. She read the name.

"So?"

"So does that name mean anything to you?"

"Only by rumor. I've heard of his reputation—or rather his *legend*. Surprisingly enough, even with all the time I've spent in and out of courtrooms here, I've never met him. Where did you find this?"

Holt pulled her feet back in his lap and took a drink of beer. "I found it in Bradenberg's little black book—right before I mailed the thing back to the Bergstrom Air Force Base Security Division."

"You *mailed* it back to them?"

"You're damned right I did. We got what we wanted out of it. Maybe it'll keep them off my tail now."

"Maybe. Maybe not. If they think you have some knowledge of the killer, they'll still tail you until he's found. I'm sure they want no connections with their entrepreneurial spy left to chance."

"At least they won't try taking me or my house apart anymore—I hope."

"So I assume *you* know this guy?"

"Which guy?"

"The name in the book—*Travis Layton.*"

"I know him as well as anyone can in two months on the Vestry."

Holt related the history of the alcoholic attorney to her as she continued to work her way through the food. He poured her another beer and told her of the list of persons who could have wanted Hargrive, Willis, and Bradenberg dead.

"Would it do me any good to ask how you found all this out?"

"No."

"Then I won't," she said, popping the last hunk of Jarlsberg into her mouth. "Besides, I already know. But there's one thing that doesn't fit the theory, Lucas."

"The nun?"

"Yep. She not only doesn't fit the M.O.—all the rest were violent murders—but how could she have been into anything other than nunning?"

"'Nunning'?"

"Isn't that what you call it?"

"No. But maybe we just don't have enough information about her yet. Anyway, she does fit another possibility."

"What's that?"

"I think another connection might be that all the victims were involved some way with art, particularly religious art."

"Including Dr. Hargrive? I was at his house, and he hardly had anything on his walls that would qualify as art, unless you consider Elvis Presley spray-painted on black velvet 'art.'"

"I know. The theory falls down there, also." Lucas Holt got up and paced in front of the couch. "Dammit, Susan, there's something here that we're missing. What is it?"

"Dessert?"

"Haven't you eaten today?"

"No. I've been out chasing you and all the other criminals in town."

"What do you mean by that?"

"I mean you were seen by a sharp-eyed officer in the neighborhood of Ashton Willis's house. We picked up a black man walking in the area and questioned him, but he claimed he was just looking for work. My guess is he'd already found it. Of course he never heard of *you*. None of them has."

"Would you believe me if I told you I didn't know what you were talking about?"

"No."

Lucas Holt sat back down. He picked up her feet and began messing with them again.

"Hmmmm."

"Kindness will get you nowhere, Lucas Holt. Tell me what you were doing there. I assume you got into the house. Right?" She felt him grasp her heel. "Ouch! Stop that, Lucas!"

"Okay. Okay. So I wanted a look inside. I didn't even know what I was looking for in there."

"And did you find it, whatever it was you weren't looking for?"

"Yes."

"Well?"

"I'm not sure I can tell you as a police officer. Isn't there a law against b and e and tampering with evidence?"

"That never stopped you before. And quit tempting me. What the hell *was* it?"

Holt stopped rubbing and rested his beer mug on her foot.

"Okay, listen to this. I found a secret compartment Willis used to hide important pieces of his art."

"How'd you find that? Who was in there with you?"

"You want to hear this or not?"

"Sorry. I'll shut up."

"Right." He took another drink and put the mug on the table. "Willis apparently parlayed his extensive knowledge of art into a little business of his own. Seems he made fake replicas for people who then turned around and sold the replicas as the real thing. It was a great scam. You could sell your art and have it, too. But he was so good that the people who brought him the originals sometimes couldn't tell the difference between what he made and their actual pieces. Often he made two replicas, gave them both back to the owner and kept the original for himself, either to collect or to sell. He got greedy, somebody found out about it— and he got hit."

Holt wondered if that would satisfy her until he confirmed his other conclusions.

"There's something else you're not telling me. I've known you too long for that, Lucas." She put her mug on the floor and sat up to look at him. "Spill."

"All right. The piece I found in Willis's house is an exact replica—if it *is* the replica—of a piece in St. Margaret's Treasury."

"What?" Susan Granger retrieved her feet and pulled them up under herself to sit upright opposite the Rev. "You mean someone was ripping off the *Treasury*, making dupes and selling them?"

"Or worse."

"What could be worse?" She looked down and thought, then looked back up at him. "Oh, no. You mean they could have made duplicates and then replaced the *duplicates* in the Treasury and—"

"Yes. And sold the original to the highest bidder."

"But who would do a thing like that?"

"Well, we have two suspects for openers, and maybe three."

"Harris Lambert? I thought he wanted to sell it. He's on *your* side, Lucas."

"Yeah, looks like he's off the hook. Plus he stands to lose a lot financially from that kind of a theft. He has the collection insured against theft, fire, and nuclear disaster."

"It will be more than a nuclear disaster if what you say is true. Your last ace in the hole to bail out Maggie Mae's is gone."

"That's right. I can hear the phone call from my friendly bishop now."

Granger changed the subject back to business. *Her* business.

"And the second suspect?"

"The other man in the black book of Bradenberg's. Travis Layton."

"What would *he* have to gain?"

"Money, I guess. And maybe power. He's wanted to be powerful all his life and never has been able to achieve it; first for his stubbornness and then for his drinking. Being on the Vestry he'd have access to the collection with no questions asked."

Granger looked puzzled. "So who's the third person?"

"My predecessor. The guy who bankrupted the church in the first place. If he was crazy enough to juggle the books and spend all the legitimate money, maybe he was nuts enough to rifle the collection and deplete all its worth, also."

"It still doesn't make sense, Lucas. That man's dead. He couldn't be doing all these murders."

"Somebody he *worked* with could be."

"That's true. And whether or not it was him, it would make sense that a church person would know the hymn and its number."

"There's another remote possibility that I shudder to mention."

"No, Lucas, it couldn't be your bishop. Even *I* know he's either buried behind the mounds of paperwork at that grandiose mansion you call Diocesan House over on West Fifteenth, or out in the boonies trying to raise money from cattle and oil people. Unless, of course, he's into murder by long distance."

"'Reach Out and Kill Someone'? Sounds just like his style to me."

"*Now* who's sick?" She wrote a note on a napkin. "But we can check out his travel schedule just to be sure. My guess is that he's been anywhere but near the crime scenes."

"Be interesting to see."

"No, I still think our best bet is a craftily crazy person who wants to be caught. Why else would our man be leaving those numbers like he does?"

"I don't know, Susan. I don't think you leave clues unless you know you're going to get caught—and *want* to be—and you have each murder preplanned and timed so that you get caught when you get to the end."

"Or you think you're too smart to get caught and you want to tweak the noses of those chasing you."

"Or both," Lucas Holt wondered aloud. "Or maybe neither."

"What do you mean?"

"I mean what if . . . ?"

His speculation was interrupted by the sudden ringing of the phone.

"It's probably for me, Lucas," Susan Granger said. "I

told the office I'd be here if anything came in related to the case."

"And I'm sure they believed you."

"They'd better have," she said as she picked up the phone. "Hello? Yes. Lieutenant Granger here."

Lucas Holt took the tray of empty glasses and plates back to the kitchen. He rinsed them off and put them in the already full dishwasher. When he turned around, Susan Granger stood in the kitchen doorway. Her face was pale.

"What's the matter, Susan?" Holt asked, walking over to her.

"Our killer just made another slip," she said.

"What happened?"

"That was Sergeant Edwards. He's over at San Jacinto Hospital Emergency Room."

Lucas Holt's mind went spinning. He wondered who it could be this time? He did not have to wait to be told.

"It's Harris Lambert," she said. "He was attacked by a pack of coyotes."

"The 'Fierce Wild Beast.'"

"Yes."

"What's the mistake?"

Susan Granger turned and headed for the door.

"The mistake is—Lambert's still alive."

• Eighteen •

The light flashed on and off above the door of Room 403 at San Jacinto Hospital on Thirty-second Street. The nurse had just left the patient's room and returned to the unit station. Her cohort for the night looked up from reading a chart.

"What's 403 want *now*? You've been down there every ten minutes since the shift started."

"Probably more pain meds. I keep telling him the doctor only ordered it every three hours, but he says it doesn't help. I think he's more scared than hurt." She picked up a medication tray and started back down toward the room. "I wish his doctor would call back."

"Excuse me, miss." The man with the collar touched the nurse on the shoulder. "I'm Mr. Lambert's priest, and I'm wondering if it's okay to go in and visit him?"

"You bet it is. He needs you more than he needs what's in this syringe here. Maybe you can calm him down."

"What seems to be his problem?" Susan Granger asked.

"Is this your wife?"

The Rev grinned. "Surely you jest."

Susan Granger spoke for herself, glaring at Lucas Holt.

"I'm Lieutenant Granger, APD. We're both friends of Mr. Lambert."

"Well, he's been really upset all night. Since he came in, actually. He says the pain meds aren't helping, and I have a call in to his doctor to try to get them changed. Maybe if you two talked to him, it would take his mind off being here." She walked with them to the end of the hall. "At least it would keep him off the light a few minutes."

They were about to enter the room when Holt stopped the nurse.

"Can you tell us how bad he was hurt?"

"He's a lucky man," the nurse said. She waved the two over to a quiet area across the hall from Harris Lambert's door. "I can tell you, since you're his priest and all. I mean, Father, the Good Lord must have been watching out for him."

"How so?"

"The dogs, or coyotes, or whatever they were?"

"Yes."

"They barely missed the main vein in his throat—the jugular. He'd have died by exsanguination."

"By what?" Holt said.

"Bleeding out," Granger announced with satisfaction in her tone.

"Correct," the nurse continued. "He'd have bled to death if they'd have gouged one inch more to the right."

Holt and Granger glanced at each other briefly.

"Close call, huh?" the priest said.

"Can't get any closer and live," the nurse replied.

"Any other wounds?" the Lieutenant asked.

"Mostly abrasions and hematomas."

"'Bruises' to you." The lieutenant grinned.

"He's also got some really bad punctures from their bites. We wouldn't see signs of rabies for at least three weeks, but we're keeping a close watch on him tonight for infection, just in case."

"Thanks very much, nurse," Holt said. "You've been quite helpful."

"I just hope you can help calm him down. He'll feel much better if he can get some sleep." She opened the door. "As it is now, he'll be up all night and be a wreck tomorrow."

The three walked into the room. The nurse again took his

vital signs and explained she'd get back to him as soon as the doctor returned her call. She then excused herself with a wink to the lieutenant.

Lucas Holt sat in the windowsill next to the bed. He introduced Susan Granger, who pulled up a chair on the opposite side of the bed. Harris Lambert looked and sounded uncomfortable.

"Dammit, Lucas. I've got to get out of here."

"Why? You got a party to go to or something? Just sit tight and rest tonight, Harris. Your business will still be there in the morning."

"I know, Lucas. I know. It's just that I'm not used to being in the hospital. Everything is strange. And everything hurts. The needles hurt. This damned IV in my arm hurts. It hurts when I go to the bathroom through this damned tube." He looked at the lieutenant. "Sorry, ma'am."

"No problem."

"I hurt when I move *anything*."

"Then don't *move* anything, Harris."

"You're a *big* help." He turned to Susan Granger. "How do you put up with being around this man?"

"It's not easy, Mr. Lambert, I can assure you."

"Call me Harris, please."

"Okay, Harris. He's not easy for me to put up with, either." She grinned at the Rev.

"What *are* you doing here with him? I don't suppose there's a law against defending yourself from being attacked by wild coyotes, is there? I *do* have a permit for the gun back in my office if you need to see it."

"No, no problem. I'm sort of along for the ride tonight. Lucas and I have been working on some business together."

"Church business, Harris," Holt interrupted. "I'll tell you about it later." He moved over and sat where he could touch Lambert's hand. "First tell us what happened to you out there."

Harris Lambert tried to sit up in the bed. He was obviously in pain, but the conversation and company seemed to help distract him. He reached for the teapot sitting on his tray table.

"Ouch! Dammit! Lieutenant, would you mind pouring me some of that in this cup? I can't seem to do it without tearing at these damned bandages."

"Of course. Take anything in it?"

"Yes, some milk please."

Holt offered him a straw.

"Get that thing out of my sight, Lucas. If I can't drink my tea out of a cup like a civilized man, then I might as well be dead."

"I just thought you might stretch something, Harris."

"Doesn't matter, really. Just the thought of tea through a plastic straw makes me gag. But you *could* help me hold the cup up here."

"Gotcha." Holt held the bottom of the cup as Harris Lambert sipped slowly. The hot liquid seemed to help; or maybe it was just the ability to do something his own way.

"Amazing what a little thing like that can mean to a man." Lambert rearranged himself with some difficulty into a sitting position. He kept his hand on the cup and began explaining. "I know it was a dumb thing to do. But I didn't think much about it when I went out there."

"Out where?" Susan Granger asked.

"Out to the deer lease that Luis and I own."

"Luis Arredondo?" Lucas Holt glanced at the lieutenant.

"Yes. He and I bought that little deer lease up in Pfluger-ville a couple of years ago. We thought it would be close by and we could use it for business acquaintances." Lambert took another slow sip of the tea. "Anyway, Luis must have gotten delayed, or I got there early, I don't know. With all this medication and pain I'm not sure of much of anything right now."

"You're doing fine, Harris," the Rev said, holding up the cup of hot tea for him again. "You don't have to talk if you don't want to."

"No," Lambert said, motioning him to put the cup back

on the tray table. "It seems to help to go over it. It all happened so fast I . . . can hardly remember . . . it seems like a blur."

"Take your time, Harris."

"Well, like I said, I got there before Luis did. I had just unloaded the supplies from the pickup when I heard the howling."

"Harris," the Rev interrupted. "Haven't you been reading the stories in *The American-Statesman* the last few weeks about the problems in Pflugerville?"

"Oh, I guess I've glanced at the headlines. Something about the animals being forced out of their land by all the development, wasn't it?"

"That's right. There have been reports of coyotes actually going right up to houses and attacking children. With all of the new housing developments up there, the critters have been chased into suburban areas."

Susan Granger put her hand on Lambert's arm. "Ranchers north and west of there are having lots of problems with them. The coyotes are roving in bands and attacking their cattle, especially the new calves."

"Looks like that's just what I ran into. I had just put the supplies out."

"Maybe they got the scent of the food?"

"That's probably right, Lucas. Trouble is they thought the food was *me*. I no sooner reached in the back of the truck to bring out my rifle than there they were."

"What happened?" Susan Granger asked.

"I turned around and saw the pack coming toward me. I did get two of them before they had me on the ground." Harris Lambert closed his eyes and shuddered. "God, it was awful."

"It's okay if you don't want to continue."

"No. No. Let me finish." Lambert took a long drink of the hot tea. "I remember . . . being on the ground and thinking I was going to die. I don't even remember feeling the bites so much as I do thinking about dying. I thought sure this was it."

He stopped for a minute and allowed the Rev to hold his cup. He swallowed hard and continued.

"I remember hearing the sound of another truck driving up. I didn't even think who it might be. I was just grateful that somebody was coming. I wondered if they'd get to me in time. I heard the rifle shots and saw a couple more of the coyotes drop before the rest began to scatter."

"Listen, Harris." Susan Granger began to stand. "You need some rest."

"No. Please. I just get a little winded. So it turned out to be Luis in the other truck. He kept firing at the coyotes to make sure they weren't coming back. He damned near hit *me* a couple times, actually. Then he came over to me to see how bad things were looking." The Rev glanced at Susan. "I think he really was scared—because he moved so fast, and he was cursing a lot. I've never heard Luis curse like that. He put some bandages over the deeper wounds, carried me into his pickup and brought me in here as fast as he could. Far as I know my truck is still up there."

Lucas Holt tried to be reassuring. "If I know Luis, your truck is probably in the parking garage here at the hospital by now. He wouldn't leave it up there on the lease any more than you would."

"I hope you're right, Lucas. I'll need it to get out of here soon."

"When do you think you'll be able to leave, Harris?" Susan Granger asked.

"Last I heard from the doctor, I should be here only a couple of days. It depends on how the wounds heal, whether there's any infection. *I'd* like to be out tomorrow." He moved to reach for the tray table. "Ouch! Damn! That hurts!"

"Make it the day after, will you, Harris?"

Lambert slowly let his arm fall to the bed.

"Maybe you're right, Lucas. Maybe I do need a rest."

"Now, that's good thinking." Lucas Holt wondered if he dare tell Lambert about the statue at Willis's. On the one hand it would be cruel to burden him with more worry while in this condition. On the other, in a weakened state such as this, Lambert might show his real emotions. "And you'll need all the rest you can get, too."

"Why? What do you mean?"

Susan Granger looked at the Rev with a puzzled expression on her face. She wondered what the hell he thought he was doing to this sick, hurting man.

"Harris, I don't want to upset you, but I do want you to hear this from me before somebody else on the Vestry tells you. You *are* senior warden, you know."

"What's going on?" He frowned and turned to the lieutenant. "Will you tell me what's happened *now*?"

"I'm not sure which thing he's talking about, Harris." She squinted her eyes at him. "Go ahead, Lucas."

Lucas Holt looked directly at Harris Lambert.

"Harris, did you know a man named 'Ashton Willis'?"

"Let me think . . . damned drugs dull your memory so you can't . . . let me . . . No, I don't believe I do. Of course I'd have to check my insurance records. He might be an old client. But, no, I remember most of my clients by name if not by face anymore." Lambert looked directly back at him. "Why? Should I?"

"If he was a client of yours, you'd know by now. He was murdered two days ago."

Lambert's eyes widened. "Murdered? How terrible!" His hand shook and Holt steadied the cup of tea for him. Lambert thanked him. "Sorry . . . I am usually not so shaken by the news of death. It is a relatively common thing for me to get phone calls from families regarding the death of a loved one. But tonight . . . having faced my *own* death . . ." He looked down and took another drink of the tea. "I don't think I will ever hear those calls quite the same way from now on." He looked at the Rev. "No, you're right. I'd have been notified already by someone if he was one of mine. Why do you ask?"

"Well—and this is the bad news—it seems that Ashton Willis had an exact duplicate of one of the statues from the Treasury in his house."

Lambert seemed to have composed himself, though he looked puzzled. "Why is that bad news? Isn't it possible that he had one made for himself by someone in town? I understand some of the pieces are quite popular. Do you know we've even had some offers to make plastic replicas and sell them in our church bookstore?"

"This wasn't a plastic replica, Harris. It was an *exact* duplicate." Lucas Holt paused a moment and watched Harris's reaction. "It was *so* exact it could have been the real thing."

Lucas Holt's words took a while to register with Harris Lambert. Perhaps they had trouble making their way through the dulled sensory receptors into his consciousness. Or perhaps, thought Lucas Holt, he was good at bluffing. In any case, when the words did get beyond the veil of Lambert's clouded mind, his eyes widened and his face looked shocked.

"My God, Lucas! What are you saying?"

"I'm saying there could be several possibilities."

Lambert's mind became suddenly clear. "Are you telling me you think that the Treasury . . . has been *stolen*?"

"I'm not sure, Harris, but it looks like it."

By now, Susan Granger was overtly scowling at Lucas Holt.

"Lucas, I think Harris has had enough for one day."

"No, Lieutenant. I *do* want to hear about it. I need to be thinking about this, Lucas. Do you realize how much that collection is insured for? Do you know what that could do to my independent company?" Harris Lambert looked genuinely shaken. "I could sustain the loss, I think, but the damage would mean—"

"Harris, there's no evidence that the Treasury's not all

there, intact and ready to bail the church out of bankruptcy. All we have to do is to have it appraised again."

"I just *had* it appraised, Lucas."

"When was that?"

"Right before you came to St. Margaret's. About three months ago, I believe." He seemed to slump down in the bed. A large man engulfed by a larger white marshmallow of a mattress.

"And who was the appraiser?"

"Let me see. I'm sorry, my brain isn't functioning as it normally does. Normally I'm very good with names . . . I think it was . . . Jacob Benton. Yes, that's correct. You could check by calling my secretary at the office in the morning. She has all the files and the appraiser's notes and report. Just ask her for them."

"If you don't mind, Harris, I'd still like to get the Treasury appraised again." He watched Lambert's face for signs of worry. Finding none he continued. "Is there anyone else you can recommend? I thought of having the Koger firm do it this time."

"Koger . . . Koger . . . Yes, they're good, also. I'd recommend them highly." Harris Lambert was obviously tiring quickly now. "Why don't you call them tomorrow. And please, call me here as soon as you get any results. Will you?"

"You bet, Harris." Lucas Holt patted him on the leg and stood up to leave. "I think it's time to take Susan's advice now and leave you for the time being."

"Well, Mr. Lambert," the nurse said, walking into the room with a full syringe on a tray. "Your doctor called and ordered a change in your medication. He said to give you this sedative to get you through the night." She looked at his two visitors. "Thank you for spending time with him. I'll have to ask you to leave now so my patient can get some rest."

"We were just going anyway, nurse." Susan Granger motioned to Harris Lambert. "Good night, Harris. And don't worry about anything. I'm sure everything will be all right."

"Thank you, Lieutenant. And thank you, too, Lucas, for telling me what's going on. I'd have been very upset if you hadn't."

"I just hope it wasn't too upsetting for you and you're able to sleep tonight, Harris. Good night. Take care of yourself."

"Thank you, Lieutenant. I will." Lambert raised his arm for the nurse to insert the needle. "Oh, and Lucas?"

"Yes?"

"Would you bring me Communion tomorrow if you're not too busy?"

"Certainly. I'll drop by after noon tomorrow."

"Thank you." Lambert turned to the nurse. "I'm ready to go night-night, madame. Just make it quick."

"We'll take good care of him for you in the meantime, Father," the nurse said, shutting the door behind them.

Susan Granger waited until they had safely cleared the hospital and were seated in her car. Then she exploded.

"Damn you, Lucas Holt! Why did you do that to that poor sick man? Couldn't you see he was upset enough without having to worry about his business, too?"

"Now look who's playing the bleeding heart here! Hell, I had to see how he reacted. If he *was* the killer—"

"And do you think he was, Lucas? Really, now."

"I don't know."

"You *don't know*! Did you see him react in any way that would lead you to believe that?"

"No, I didn't. But—"

"But *what*?"

"But our killer is also crazy as hell. He wouldn't react to us if we dropped a bomb beside him."

"Which you did very well, Lucas. And Lambert didn't react the way you expected him to." She paused a moment. "I just think it was unnecessary, that's all."

"Yeah." Lucas Holt settled back into the passenger's seat. "You're probably right." He looked out the window as she drove. "I don't know, though."

Susan Granger reduced her speed and took back roads. She wanted to avoid the glaring lights and hurry of the expressway. Finally she spoke. "It sort of reminded me of my father."

Holt turned his head toward her. "After the shooting?"

"Yes."

Holt knew her father's story backward and forward from their years together at U.T. He had debriefed the details with her, cathexed and catharted until he almost had taken it on as a part of his own psyche. It was clearly one of the most painful parts of her life.

"He was accused . . . and questioned . . . as though—"

"I know. The way I assumed Lambert was guilty and would react if I questioned him the right way."

Granger stopped at a light. She wiped her nose with her hand and snuffed back the drips. "Damn," she said angrily. "Do you suppose this shit *ever* goes away?"

Holt put his hand on her neck. "No. I don't think it does. I think it's part of who we are. Just like my own shit with my dad. I think I learned something about that at the pen."

The light turned green and she proceeded down West Twelfth Street.

"Like what?"

"The shrinks there kept trying to have the prisoners 'work through'—whatever the hell *that* meant—the traumas of their early lives, as though if only they would do that, they would be fine and live great lives and never come back to jail and be upright and successful citizens."

"Yeah." She turned onto West Lynn.

"I don't know. It seemed to me like they were saying the inmates should negate those experiences, or make them okay, or accept them for what they were—all of which was meant to expunge the experiences from their memory banks."

"And?"

"And you can't *do* that." Holt watched a jogger on the other side of the road. "Wherever you go—*there* you are."

"Meaning?"

"Meaning you'll take that experience with your dad to your grave—and maybe beyond. And I'll do the same thing. Hell, I don't know. It seems to me our lives are like that old Carole King album, *Tapestry.*" He took his hand away and turned toward her. "Remember that?"

Granger smiled and nodded.

"Well, all those experiences are indelibly interwoven into the tapestry of your life. They're a part of what makes us us. They can't be torn out or ignored or painted over and made to be something they're not."

The lieutenant glanced over at him. "So I'm doomed to get upset every time I'm in a situation that reminds me of the injustice done to him, and his pain and the suffering and the demise of a good man?"

"I think so, Susan. Probably." He looked to his right at a stray dog digging in a garbage can. "*I* do it. I've just learned to keep the feelings inside and deal with them later, talk with somebody who'll listen to them and try not to let them interfere with the present. I think that's the best anyone can do. It doesn't make them hurt any less, but it does let me be more present right now, so I can see things like Harris Lambert for what he is instead of yet another rerun of my own past."

"I wasn't just rerunning the past, Lucas."

"Sorry," Holt apologized. "I didn't mean that the way it sounded. And I was talking more about myself than you, anyway."

"Okay."

The darkened streets shrouded the two of them in their own private thoughts. Passing street lights briefly illuminated their pensive faces, then the shadows covered them again. It was not until they reached his house that either of them spoke. It was Susan Granger.

"Lucas," she said, turning to look at him. "I want you to promise me something."

"What's that?"

"I want you to let my officers keep you in sight. I want you to let them tail you from here on out, until we catch this murderer."

"Susan . . . come on. You know the God Squad is watching out for me. I'll be fine."

He started to get out of the car, but she grabbed his sleeve.

"It's important that you do this, Lucas."

"Why? What's so different about now?"

Susan Granger let go of his sleeve. She spoke as seriously as she could.

"The hymn—two forty-three. 'The Saints of God.'"

"What?" He closed the police car door.

"The 'Priest' is the only one left."

• Nineteen •

Carolynne Philips waited for her electric garage door to shut before getting out of her dark gray Mercedes 500SL. A "blue norther" had blown in, turning Austin's usually mild November weather, in a matter of thirty minutes, to biting cold. Sitting huddled in the warm driver's seat, she was unaware of the shadowed figure moving quickly under the closing door.

She exited her car, turned off the house alarm, and entered the kitchen of her Travis Ranch townhome. She immediately turned up the thermostat and looked quickly in the refrigerator to be certain she had the milk for hot latte.

She took off her shoes and climbed the thick, carpeted stairs to her bedroom, where she undressed slowly to give the furnace time to take the chill off the house. She turned on the whirlpool and let the tub fill with steaming, soapy water. The splashing, swirling sound obscured the click of the downstairs kitchen door as it opened and closed.

It had been a hard day, and an even harder night. That damned, recalcitrant, prissy bank officer had finally come through with the loan for her new subdivision. It had taken tough bargaining and more than a few harsh words of potential threat to pull it off, but she had done it. She would retaliate later, after the monies started coming back from the investment. She would wait until the amount was just where she wanted it, then she would pull her entire investment portfolio out from under the effete bastards and transfer it to their competitor across the street. They would learn, as others had, not to play games with Carolynne

Philips. She smiled, preoccupied with the day's events, and could not hear the heavy footsteps move slowly up the padded stairs.

Tossing her underwear into the hamper, she moved quickly back to the heated marble bathroom and looked at her naked body in the mirrors that lined the walls. "Mama would be proud," she thought as she turned to view herself from each angle. She worked hard to take care of her forty-one-year-old body, as she worked hard to take care of the fortune her mother had left her years ago.

Carolynne Philips placed one painted toe into the hot soapy water in the sunken marble tub. Her whole body relaxed as she stepped down and lounged back to let the swirling bubbles surround and comfort her. It was the only comfort she would allow herself most of the time. And it was a hell of a lot better than a man—at least the ones she had known lately, the ones interested in her money and her body.

The development business had gotten tougher in Austin as more and more outsiders flocked to the area to score a piece of the action. Of necessity, she had grown tougher with the times, sometimes surpassing her mama's reputation as a hard-nosed businesswoman with an eye for a deal and a drive that never quit.

Even in this warm, embracing sanctuary, her body tensed as she recalled the earlier meeting with the neighborhood association that morning. Stupid, simple-minded people that they were, they could not see the progress that the shopping center would bring to the city. All they could think about was their precious little neighborhood and the park land adjacent to it.

Park land? she wondered as she slowly rotated her head to loosen the stiff muscles in her neck. What the hell could you do with park land? What good was it? It didn't produce anything. It only got trashy and overused. Eventually, she hoped, all the parks would be purchased by developers to be put to some *good* purpose—like office buildings or more parking areas. God knew the city needed more of those than it did another vacant area of dirt, swings, and picnic tables filled with snotty-nosed kids.

She would eventually get that land from the neighborhood, she thought as she closed her eyes and moved her sore buttocks closer to the thrusting jets. It was a matter of time, wearing them down, compromising—or seeming to—and eventually buying them off. Everyone had a price. Everyone except her.

She always—or almost always—got what she wanted. Even if it took leading on the mayor and one or two council members, she could stand an evening or so of expensive dinners and ridiculous flirtations. Such men were easily bought, she remembered, and just as easily dropped when their usefulness ended. Power was always their Achilles' heel, especially their desire for power over her. Just like her momma said, she thought, no man would ever have that again.

Twenty minutes later she emerged from the water, her skin steaming, relaxed, glowing red in the light from the heat lamp above.

She slipped the pink silk nightgown over her powdered body and pulled the quilted satin robe tight around her. She laid back the feather comforter on the bed and plumped the down pillows, readying her nesting place for the night. As she padded down the stairs to the kitchen, she did not see the figure move silently into, and then out of, her room.

As she flipped the button on the espresso machine to heat the water, she flipped through the mail on the counter, opening assorted bills and throwing out all the ads without reading them. When the red light came on, she ran the scalding hot water through the small net of ground coffee in the espresso machine. Turning the steam knob, she thought she heard something upstairs, but the loud noise of steam in the container of milk distracted her attention. She mixed the foamy white milk into the small cup of coffee,

walked into the living room, and curled up in a peach-col-
ored chair. She punched a remote button and the CD
player softly played the haunting chant of *The Lamenta-
tions of Jeremiah.*

The warmth of the cup felt good on her hands as she held
it up to her lips. She slowly sipped the hot, rich liquid and
felt safe and secure.

This is nice, she thought. This is what I work for—what
momma and I worked for. If only she were here to share it,
that would make it perfect.

She had drunk only about half of the coffee when the ex-
haustion of the day caught up with and overtook her. The
thought of being wrapped up beneath the heavy covers of
her bed was deliciously appealing and seemed to hasten the
sleepiness pervading her body.

Carolynne Philips rinsed out the cup, reset the coded
house alarm for the night, and sleepily walked back up the
stairs to her room. She hung her robe over the chair next
to the bed and punched the button that turned out the
lights downstairs. Sitting on the side of the bed for one
last moment, she looked at the faded Mexican icon sitting
on the table beside her. It was one of the many such
pieces in her house that gave her pleasure, partly because
of the beauty and partly because of the cost and great
risk—especially the risk—at which she had acquired
them.

She looked at this one every night before getting into
bed. It was the closest she came to any kind of religious be-
lief. Ironically, it was situated right next to a picture of her
mother, and she was never sure which one was more like
God to her.

A part of her tired mind realized the icon was not quite
where it usually stood. The maid had probably moved it
when cleaning that day, she thought, and made a mental
note to fire her if she couldn't get things exactly back in
their place.

On the other hand, maybe she had bumped it herself

when pulling back the covers. She returned the icon to its place, glanced quickly at her momma's picture, and swiveled around in the bed. She turned off the light, pulled up the comforter, and thrust her legs down beneath it, sinking deep into the fresh-smelling sheets and pillows.

At first she thought her foot had gone to sleep, and that the tingling she felt down there was the blood moving back into the nerves of her ankle and toes. She rolled over, hoping a different position would alleviate the pain.

As she did, she suddenly felt the points of a dozen needles drill into her feet and legs.

Her racing mind told her what was happening, what she had feared and dreaded all her life, but could not tell her why . . . or who! It had happened twice before, with only one bite or sting, and she had recovered. But this . . . there were too many . . . too many needles . . . and they were moving up her legs, under her nightgown! No! This couldn't be happening! Why? Why to *her*?

She tried to move, to reach the pills in the drawer next to the bed or to grab for the phone. But the phone had been placed just out of reach and the more she struggled the quicker the poison spread through her body, numbing her limbs and clouding her puzzled, speeding thoughts.

Her panicked heart pounded in her ears and seemed about to burst through her chest. Her breathing became labored as her lungs quickly stiffened and gasped for air. Through blurred, fading vision she watched, unable to move, as the man walked into her room.

She saw him head directly for her purse and thought, somewhere in the deep recesses of her mind, that he wanted her wallet. Instead he pulled out a smaller object, went over to the large mirror above her dressing table, and scrawled three large numbers in bright red lipstick. Without looking at her, the man tossed the lipstick back into her purse and walked out of the room.

Knowing death was near, tears formed in the staring eyes that could no longer blink or focus. Calling up a final burst of strength from deep within her, Carolynne Philips forced her leaden arm up to the table beside the bed. With her last, excruciating movement, she grasped her momma's picture and knocked the icon to the floor.

• Twenty •

The morning had been particularly busy and distressing
for the Reverend Lucas Holt. The usual parish business had
consumed most of the time; weddings and baptisms to
schedule, not to mention working in funerals and hospital
visits. In between phone calls and counseling sessions, he
worried about the Treasury and tried to think through different options for whether and how Maggie Mae's could
stay afloat.

Finally he took a break, thanks to Max and Earl Grey,
and sat in his office, feet on the windowsill, reviewing the
progress, if you could call it that, he had made. Unlike God
at the end of the seven days, none of it could be declared
"good."

The call to the new appraiser had brought a quick response; the man was able to make a preliminary visit that
day. But devising a secondary game plan to salvage the
church was more difficult than making a phone call. If the
worst were true, if the Treasury *had* systematically been
stripped and replaced with phony copies of the originals,
then the church had no hope of survival.

There were no Diocesan funds for such an occurrence.
Bishop Salas would graciously see to that. There were certainly no grant monies available for bankrupt churches.
And the amount necessary to keep the parish and its programs running until it could again be self-sustaining would
amount to nearly a million dollars.

Lucas Holt had spent the entire morning trying to imagine the different scenarios for the future of his parish—the

parish he had not wanted, but to which he was now viscerally attached. Funny how embezzlement, murder, and intrigue could grab your guts and get you interested in a place, not to mention Kristen Wade and—here he surprised himself—Susan Granger. Wouldn't the ultimate irony be that, having found a niche in Austin, a place to settle in and call home, with people he liked, including the God Squad, that having overcome his initial recalcitrance at the bishop's command, he now would have to leave because the church folded?

He couldn't let that happen. But he wasn't sure yet how to stop it. It was nearly noon and each scenario for survival still looked worse than the last. The bottom line kept coming out the same no matter which route he took—the church would have to close its doors, sell the property and give up its location and ministry in downtown Austin. The worst for him personally would be the call to the smiling bishop.

He threw his pencil down on the desk and stood to stretch his tired body. From the window he saw Travis Layton make his way to the downstairs door of the church. Layton walked briskly against the gusty north wind, his sport coat buttoned and a wool scarf around his neck. He seemed to be walking stiffly, the Rev noticed, as if pained.

Holt opened his office door and waited for Layton to enter. The old attorney had called earlier in the morning to invite him to lunch. Layton had said he had something to discuss that needed immediate attention. The Rev, in his concentration on the Treasury and its possible demise, had nearly forgotten the call until he saw the man walking into the church.

Maxine looked up from her desk. While she did not know the extent of the problem, she surmised that things were not going well, given the look on Lucas Holt's face this morning.

"Rough day so far, Rev?"

"Yeah." He yawned. "And I don't think it's going to get

any better, Max. I just saw Travis Layton coming up the steps to take me to lunch."

"Want me to run him off for you?" Maxine stood and pushed out her considerable chest with her hands on her hips. Her red hair shone in the fluorescent lighting and clashed with the rouge on her face. "I got lots of experience in taking care of angry men who think they know what they want."

The Rev smiled. "Thanks, Max, but I think I'd better find out what's on his mind first." He turned and went back into his office. "But stick around. I may need you later."

Lucas Holt had just dropped onto the sofa when he heard the cigarette voice of Travis Layton in the outer office greeting Maxine. He slowly got up as the man walked through the door.

"God, it's cold out there. That norther blew in last night like a freight train."

"Hello, Travis." The two men shook hands and sat down. "Can I get you some coffee or something before we go?"

"No. Let's go ahead and get down to Sixth Street before the noon rush hits."

Lucas Holt looked at the man getting awkwardly out of the chair in front of him. Something, some connection or scene began to form in his head, something about the death of Alvan Bradenberg. He went back to his closet to get his jacket and spoke, while his back was turned, to Travis Layton.

"Good grief, Travis, where's that old overcoat you wear all the time? You sure need it today."

The man seemed hesitant to answer.

"I . . . I guess I left it at home this morning. You know how that goes. You go out early in the morning thinking the weather is the same as last night. Well, that's what I did. Got in the car and drove to work before I knew it was cold out."

Holt guessed that the real reason was something other than the cold. There was one other thing to check out—the stiffness in the man's upper body. He returned to the attorney's side and put his arm around Layton's shoulder to lead him out the door. The response was just what was expected.

"Careful, Lucas! That's my bum shoulder."

"What's happened to it, Travis? It wasn't that way the other night at Vestry."

Again, Layton hesitated in his reply.

"Well, it's just arthritis, Lucas. You know how us old men get when the weather changes."

Lucas Holt looked at him directly.

"Arthritis?"

"Well . . . okay, Lucas. I had a little too much to drink last night and, well, I had a little accident."

"What happened?"

"Nothing much, actually. I just lost my balance and fell against some cabinets, that's all."

"Have you had a doctor look at it?"

"Good God, no! Do you know what those bastards charge for a visit nowadays?"

"I just think it would be well to have it looked at, that's all." Holt thought he'd like to have a look at it himself, to see if it was a bruise—or a graze wound. "Maybe you'd like Max to have a look?"

"I'll be just fine, Lucas. Don't worry about me." The lawyer turned and headed out the door. "Come on. Let's go to lunch."

The Rev spoke to Maxine on the way out. She was holding the phone to her ear.

"Max, we'll be about an hour. Just hold calls for me, okay?"

Maxine put her hand over the receiver and spoke softly.

"This one's for you now, Rev. It's Lieutenant Granger at APD. Says it's important she talk with you."

"Tell her I just stepped out to lunch with Travis. I'll call her as soon as I get back."

"You got it, Rev."

Travis Layton's voice trailed out the door as the two men left the red-haired secretary talking on the phone.

"That Granger woman, Lucas? What's she calling you about that's so all-fired important?"

The weather occupied most of the walking time between St. Margaret's Episcopal Church and El Mercado on Sixth Street. Lucas Holt unobtrusively watched Travis Layton favor his left shoulder as the man stiffly walked against the cold. The Rev remembered the picture Susan Granger had painted of the Saints of God murderer getting careless in the killing of Bradenberg. The shoulder wound would not have had time to heal by now. It would even be worse if left untreated.

But what was the connection with Layton and Bradenberg? And why was he in the man's black book? Holt's questions came to a screeching halt in his mind when the two sat down at the restaurant. Without looking at the menu, Layton ordered for them both.

"Queremos dos Comidas Mexicanas, con dos cervezas, por favor."

"Cual cerveza?" the waiter asked.

"Kind of beer make any difference to you, Lucas?"

"No. Unless they've got Negra Modela."

"Dos Negras Modelas, por favor."

"Sí. Gracias." The waiter departed.

"I don't have a lot of time to waste on this, Lucas. That's why I went ahead and ordered."

"That's fine. I usually get the Mexican dinner anyway." The Rev watched Travis Layton's face slowly metamorphose into a frown. "What's on your mind?"

"I think you know very well what's on my mind, Lucas. I want to talk to you about that Treasury."

"What about it? I thought the other day you hadn't made up your mind yet. You seemed to be open to whichever plan we needed to accomplish to keep the church open."

"I was. But the more I got to thinking about it, the more I hated to see that stuff tampered with. It's been in our church for a long time. It's the pride of the community. It brings in business."

"But if we don't raise the money, Travis, there won't be anything around to bring business *into* anymore." Lucas Holt watched the lawyer's face and wondered if there was another reason Layton didn't want the Treasury touched. "I think we ought to have it appraised soon."

"No! Dammit, Lucas. I've given this a lot of thought. A lot of those items, the chalices, the vestments, the crosses, came from my daddy's place, as I'm sure you know."

"Yes. You told me. And a lot of other people donated things, too. In fact, people are still occasionally bringing things in to us. Why, just the other day—"

"I don't give a good damn about the other day! I'm telling you you can't sell it, Lucas. There's a lot of us on the Vestry that feel the same way. There's a lot of hot feelings about this issue from several of us in the parish."

"Who's feeling the hottest, Travis. Besides you, I mean?"

The waiter brought their beer and dinners.

"Los platos estan muy calientes," he said. He held the hot plates with a white towel and placed the plates in front of each man.

"Gracias," Travis Layton said. He poured a glass of the Negra and gulped it down. *"Pelo del perro."*

"Hair of the dog," Holt translated in his head.

"So, to answer your question. First of all there's Luis Arredondo."

"You already told me he'd be against it."

"I know I did. But I don't think you know how vehemently he feels about keeping the Treasury. His hot temper could lead him to do some unfriendly things, Lucas." Layton took a large bite of the enchilada and continued talking. "He's a big contributor and he carries a lot of weight in the Hispanic community, as you know."

Who else?" the Rev asked, rolling a flour tortilla and scooping up the refried beans.

"Well, I think Harris Lambert isn't all that happy about it, either."

"You've got your stories mixed up on that one, Travis. I talked to Harris just last night and he's in favor of selling the Treasury." He watched Layton carefully for signs of recognition. "He recognizes it's the only thing to do."

"Then he's crazy, too, Lucas. I tell you I won't let you *do* it. I've talked to too many people in the congregation who want it left alone. You don't understand what that Treasury means to these folks." Layton's voice suddenly became an echo of his emotion as he raised it loudly. "There are people in this town who'd *kill* to keep that collection intact."

Customers at other tables turned to see what the argument was about.

"Keep your voice down, Travis," the Rev cautioned. "People think you said something about 'killing me.' "

Travis Layton's bloodshot eyes looked across the table at Lucas Holt.

"Don't make light of that option, boy. This is still Texas, you know, and some people—if they get pushed far enough—sometimes take care of difficulties with a Colt." He paused between bites. "It *has* been mentioned."

The Rev felt a familiar shiver move up his spine. He knew from his time at Huntsville that the threat was real. More than one prisoner was doing life for commanding the business end of a gun.

"Where exactly did you hear that, Travis?" Lucas Holt tried to sound casual as his insides reacted violently.

"The usual unnamed source, Lucas."

Holt put his fork down. "So do you *really* expect me to change my mind about what to do with the Treasury because of a threat like that?" He took a drink of Negra and decided it was time to turn the tables on the old attorney. "I like you, Travis. You're one hell of a good old boy, but let me assure you, and any others you may—or may not—represent, that I will do *whatever* is necessary to keep St. Margaret's open. If it means selling that bunch of religious gaudiness downstairs, I'll *do* it."

It was the Rev's turn to raise his voice. "And I don't give a good damn *whose* daddy's ranch it came from. That was a long time ago, Travis, and I don't mind telling you I'm getting damned sick and tired of having that albatross around my neck. The church has got to do its job *now* in this city. It can't be tied to the past anymore. If that means losing a group of alleged supporters like yourself, then don't let the door slam your ass on the way out."

People were now looking around at Lucas Holt. It was time to play his last trump card and see the reaction in Travis Layton's face.

"Now calm down, Lucas, and wait a min—"

Holt leaned across the table and lowered his voice. "I haven't told anybody this, Travis, but I called a private appraisal company this morning. They're coming out today to do a preliminary inventory for me to bring to the Vestry meeting next week."

Layton's face conveyed his shock at the news.

"You can't *do* that, Lucas! I'm telling you, you need the sanction and approval of the Vestry to bring in anybody."

"And if there are no—irregularities—in the pieces—"

Layton's countenance changed from shock to what looked like surprise.

"What makes you think there are 'irregularities'?"

"Well, I don't know. It's been a long time since anybody's actually gone through there and looked at each item to check out its real worth."

Travis Layton stood and threw his napkin down on his plate.

"Dammit, Lucas! Stop this nonsense before it gets out of hand." He pushed in his chair and moved away from the table. "I'm warning you. Leave that Treasury alone." His voice changed to a whisper. "Or you'll regret it."

Lucas Holt watched the old man walk out of the restaurant and into the cold gusty wind. The stiffness was still in the shoulder as he made his awkward way through the lunchtime crowds on Sixth Street.

Maxine had taken a longer lunch break than usual and asked Cora Mae Hartwig to sit at the desk for her until she returned. Lucas Holt's cheeks were bright red when he walked in and saw the small, white-haired woman in a blue Adidas running suit sitting there reading. Her jogging shoes were propped up on the desk.

"Hello, Cora," the Rev said. He took off his overcoat and walked up to the desk.

"Hello, Lucas dear," Cora Mae Hartwig said, without looking up from her book. "Just a minute," she said as she finished the paragraph she was reading.

Holt looked at the title of the book.

"Cora, where did you get *Lady Chatterly's Lover?*"

The old woman put her feet slowly down onto the floor, placed a bookmark in the book, and carefully laid it on the desk.

"My, your cheeks are nice and rosy. I got the book at the library, of course." She smiled her squinty smile at him, the one that made her face look like a potato doll. "They allow it there now, you know. They didn't when it first came out, as I remember."

"And you're just *now* getting around to reading it?"

"Oh, heavens, no, Lucas," she said. "I've read it several times before."

Lucas Holt smiled and was about to make a comment.

"But now I'm reading it as a part of my master's thesis at U.T."

"You're working on a master's degree?"

"Of course, Lucas, dear. A body has to do something to keep the mind in shape, don't you know?"

Holt was constantly amazed at this woman's ability and tenacity.

"And I know what you're thinking, dear, so go on ahead and say it."

"What's that?"

"The same thing everyone thinks when I tell them what I'm doing."

"And that is?"

"That they hope I'll be around long enough to finish it!"

The Rev laughed and the laugh felt good after the angry exchange at lunch. He was about to comment on her tenacious qualities when he noticed the number of pink slips in front of her.

"Those messages for me, Cora?"

"Well, they're not for *me*, Lucas," she said, handing him the papers. "I hope you can read my scrawly writing, dear."

Lucas Holt looked at the perfect script on the pieces of paper and smiled.

"The arthur-itis, you know." She put the book in her backpack. "And I used to have such good penmanship." She held up a small rectangular box for him to see. "Of course, I seldom need that skill now that I've got this lovely notebook computer."

The Rev waved the slips. "Anything important in here?" he asked.

"There's one from a young lady with a very pleasant-sounding voice, Lucas. I believe it was a Miss Wade or something like that."

Holt flipped through and noted the time. Kristen had called half an hour ago. Maybe she was free tonight.

"Then there was that very . . . strange one."

"Which one?"

"The message from Lieutenant Granger."

"She *is* strange, Cora," the Rev said, leafing through the pink messages.

"Now, be nice, Lucas. Remember she has a very difficult job to do."

"Yes, ma'am." Holt stood corrected by his elder. "What did she want?"

"You'll find it on the bottom, dear."

"Thanks," he said, glancing through the slips as he walked into his office.

He pulled the one from Susan Granger off the bottom and stopped still as he looked at the message: "Call immediately. The 'fierce wild beast' was a *scorpion*."

• Twenty-one •

The drive out to Travis Ranch Estates took longer than he anticipated, but Lucas Holt was glad for the time to think. His mind felt overwhelmed with the pace of events, events that at first seemed separate, then parallel, and now intersected. His concentration was reflected by the deep frown on his face and nearly caused him to run a Stop sign. As he hit the brakes hard, a sustained beep further distracted him.

The phone had been installed yesterday.

"Shit, where is that thing?" he said aloud. He looked down between the seats and pulled the receiver to his ear.

"Hello?"

"YO! REV!"

"Nikky?"

"Yeah! This is *great*, Rev. You just joined the twentieth century!"

The driver behind him honked.

"Beep it out your ass!"

"What?"

"Wait a minute, Nikky," Holt said. He dropped the phone on the passenger seat as he pulled through the intersection and parked on the side of the road. "There, now we can talk."

"Rev, you didn't park the car, did you?"

"Sure I did. Dangerous to drive and talk on the phone. I grew up where all you did on the phone was use the *phone*, not dry your hair and trim your toenails and balance your checkbook and make love and *most certainly not drive the damned car*, for God's sake."

"S'cuse me, Rev. But are you hacked off about something?"

"I can't figure this damned thing out, Nikky. I'm relatively sure there's a connection between the killings and the Treasury. In fact, I know there is."

"Yeah, Rev. We figured that out a long time ago. Too many coincidences. And there ain't no such thing as a coincidence."

"Then why the hell didn't you tell me?"

"Didn't want to give up too much too soon. Besides, you'd get into trouble with Lieutenant Granger—and to tell you the truth, we weren't exactly one hundred percent sure."

"And now you are?"

"Yeah, pretty much."

"So?"

"So the first thing we gotta do is get you back on the road."

"What?"

"Start up the car and get back on the road—we'll talk, real slow like, and you'll get the hang of this and you'll feel better and you'll get to your appointment with Granger in a better mood and don't worry, me and the boys are workin' on it."

"I think you're nuts."

"Start the car and we'll see."

"If I have a fatal accident—"

"We'll find a good place to dump the ashes."

"Thanks," he said, starting the car. He pulled back onto Ranch Road 2222 and headed toward the lake. "How do you hold this stupid thing up to your ear? I can't drive at a forty-five degree angle."

"Punch the Speaker button."

"Oh, that." He still held the phone.

"Now put the phone down and just talk like I was sittin' in the passenger seat beside you."

"Right." He put the phone down. "This is weird."

"You'll get so used to it you'll want a portable one on you at all times."

"That'll be the day."

"I'll remind you of that when you get one."

The Rev shook his head. "Okay, I'm driving. So talk."

"You talk. I just called to say there was some funny business with your buddy Lambert."

"What kind of funny business?"

"That stuff about the coyotes was plausible, but those babies aren't stupid. They don't usually come around for no reason. And Lambert ain't got that much meat on him anymore that they'd be real attracted to him."

"What are you saying?"

"I'm saying that I asked Omar to check out the scene of the attack."

"Because of his 'Nam experience."

"Right. If Omar can't track 'em, can't nobody track 'em."

"This is getting easier. So far I only ran over one old lady and a couple of squirrels."

"Great, Rev. You're gettin' the hang of it."

"It works better if I forget you're on the phone."

"Also if you forget about the bill."

"Talk fast, we're already bankrupt."

"Right." Dorati paused for what must have been a swallow of something Holt wished he had with him right now. "So anyway, Omar went out there and—to make a long, expensive story short—found traces of meat."

"Meat?"

"Yeah, like bait."

"Shit." Holt swerved to the right.

"Don't get so excited."

"I just ran a red light. Hope there are no cops around."

"Now you know how *I* feel all the time."

"I hate this phone. So about the bait?"

"Yeah. Looks like someone put some very attractive-smelling bait out to attract the coyotes—and bring them to Lambert."

"It doesn't make sense."

"Which part?"

"The part about the 'Fierce Wild Beast.' Lieutenant Granger told me this Carolynne Philips was killed by some animal."

"So he missed Lambert and got her instead."

"Still—the connection with the Treasury? I see how Bradenberg and Willis were connected, but what about Hargrive, the nun, and now this developer?"

"I'll tell you the thing puzzles me."

Holt turned off 2222 onto Loop 360. "You're fading on me, make it fast."

"Cheap phone, Rev. You deserve a better one."

"I may need you guys to rob a bank to pay for it."

"Anything for the Lord, Rev." Dorati's voice smiled.

"What puzzles you?"

"That hymn thing. I don't get it. I've known some of these mass crazies. Most of 'em are pretty smart, but their thinking is more convoluted than a roller coaster. So I been wonderin'—did this guy pick out the victims randomly—or did they conveniently fit the pattern of the people in the hymn?"

"I don't think there's anything random about it." He passed the sign marked TRAVIS RANCH ESTATES and slowed the car.

"Then we gotta ask what Lambert and this dead developer chick have in common—that one is replaceable by the other."

"I'll keep that in mind when I see her."

"I think the answer's in that hymn, Rev. Just none of us has figured it out—yet."

"You're fading on me, Nikky. I'll call you when I get back to the church."

Holt punched the button and put the phone back in its place. He turned onto a street with numerous police vehicles and silently hummed each verse of "The Saints of God." He got out of the car, walked around the other vehicles, nodded politely to the officers he was now coming to recognize, and went up to the front of the house. As he walked through the open door and saw Susan Granger giving orders in the next room, he simultaneously finished the last verse of the hymn.

"Hello, Father Holt," the lieutenant called across the room.

Lucas Holt stood in the middle of the living room, staring at the floor. He knew something had fallen into place but was still out of consciousness, just beyond reach. It was something, he thought, about the last verse. The last verse.

"Lucas Holt! Are you on drugs or what?" Susan Granger walked over to him and looked down at the floor in front of him. "That . . . is a floor. It is used to cover the ground so that houses can be built on it. This particular one is known as a 'living room floor.' "

"Be quiet, Susan. I'm thinking."

"Then could you do your deep thinking somewhere else? We happen to be in the middle of a crime scene here."

"It's in the last verse, I know it."

"What's in the last verse?"

"The clue to the identity of the killer."

"What are you talking about?"

"I don't know what I'm talking about, Susan. If I did I'd tell you."

"Well," she said, leading him over to the staircase, "while you're thinking about it, come upstairs and check out the latest travesty on the word *murder*."

The two walked side by side up the stairs.

"And, Lucas, I have some information that will clear up that little problem of the relationship between Alvan Bradenberg and Travis Layton."

The mention of Layton's name jostled Lucas Holt from his thoughts. He stopped the lieutenant on the upstairs landing.

"What's the connection with Layton? I just had lunch with him and he practically threatened my life if I even touched that Treasury, much less thought of selling it. And there was one other thing."

"What's that?"

"He had a shoulder wound of some kind."

Susan Granger pulled a small notebook out of her back pocket and flipped through the pages until she came to the information she wanted.

"I don't know if it would be enough to *kill* over, but Layton served as Bradenberg's attorney in setting up his estate. If anyone knew the accounts and the amounts of money Bradenberg had—and possibly how he acquired them—it would be Layton."

"Layton was his lawyer?"

"Yes. We checked the courthouse records for any and all transactions by Bradenberg, and every one was done by Travis Layton. Apparently, he was paid well for his services, too."

"How do you know that?"

"We checked his bank accounts to see whom he had listed as beneficiaries."

"Good work! Why didn't I think of that?"

"Because, for the one millionth time, you are not in the detective business."

"Oh, that."

Granger continued. "Bradenberg's estate goes mainly to family in Texas, but there is a small percentage left to Layton. And Layton's own personal account is nothing to sneeze at, either."

"Travis Layton has money?"

"Sure he does, Lucas. Just because he dresses like a bum doesn't mean he's broke. How do you think he manages to be so choosy in the cases he takes? He doesn't have to rely entirely on them for income."

"Then what would be his motive in killing Bradenberg— or any of the others for that matter?" Holt said mainly to himself.

"Unless the two of them had some agreement related to that Treasury of yours, I don't know. Certainly the amount of the inheritance wasn't enough for a man as wealthy as Layton to take that kind of risk."

Lucas Holt looked out over the living room from the vantage point of the balcony. Suddenly several objects downstairs stood out in his mind.

"Susan, look at the number of Mexican religious relics this woman had collected."

"Yes. She was known for having that interest. What about it?"

"I hate to tell you this, or maybe I hate to tell myself this, but I've seen most of them before."

Susan Granger looked at the many objects below them, then over at the Rev.

"The Treasury?"

"Yes. Nearly all of these things are from that collection. I wonder if these are the copies or the originals?"

"We'll keep a special eye on them as evidence, Lucas. You'll need to have that appraiser you hired come out here and check them out." Susan Granger turned to go into the bedroom of the slain woman. "Have you heard anything from him yet?"

"No. I'll call from here in a few minutes." He followed her toward the room.

Holt walked into the bedroom and his eyes fastened on the bright red numbers emblazoned upon the mirror. The hymn, he thought. The last verse of the hymn. It was in there somewhere.

"As you can see, Lucas, the scene is the same as the others with respect to the numbers. What's different is this," she said, pointing to the rumpled bed covers.

"What happened?"

"You read my note?"

"Yes, of course I read it. But what exactly happened?"

"Well," Susan Granger began. She delighted in being the one to lecture Lucas Holt for a change. "We think the killer came in through the garage. Either he was waiting there when she came in or he snuck in while she sat in her car waiting for the electric door to close."

"Doesn't this place have an alarm system?"

"Sure it does. But she shut it off when she came in the house to take a bath. While she was in there"—Susan Granger pointed to the bathroom—"he probably came in from the garage and walked right up the steps. The carpet is so thick you could bring an elephant up here and no one would hear it."

"Yeah, but you sure could *smell* it. Speaking of which, what is that smell in here?" he grimaced.

"Vomit." Granger pulled a handkerchief from her pocket and put it over her face and pointed to the mess on the bed. "And feces." She handed an extra to Holt.

"My God! What did he *do* to her?" Holt clamped the white cotton cloth over his nose and mouth.

"Nothing. He didn't touch her."

"Then what *did*?"

"These." With one hand, Susan Granger opened the top of a shoe box on the table by the bed. It was filled with stinging scorpions. "Careful where you step in here. We think we got most of them, but you know how that goes." She put the lid back on the box. "He must have dumped this nest down at the bottom of her bed while she was having a drink somewhere else, maybe in the bath. She came out, got into bed, and thrust her legs right down into the middle of the nest."

Holt tried to remove the handkerchief, but could not stand the stench.

Granger added, "Needless to say, the little darlings did the rest."

"Wait a minute, Susan," he protested. "You don't *die* from scorpion stings, not even from a whole nest of them. At least adults don't. If you did, you couldn't walk barefoot in your house in Texas."

"You do if you're allergic to the venom."

"Anaphylactic shock?"

"You do know some big words. Congratulations!" She pulled out the drawer in the bedside table. "The venom shut down her central nervous system. She was paralyzed in a matter of seconds, before she could reach the epinephrine pills she kept right there beside her. And the phone had been placed where she couldn't get to it."

"So the smell?"

"Anaphylaxis results in loss of bladder and bowel control along with severe emetic convulsions."

"God, that's horrible. This guy really is crazy."

"Some part of him is pretty rational, Lucas. He had to know her well enough to know she was allergic to the venom."

Holt bent over to pick up the icon on the floor by the bed.

"Here's another—"

"Let that one sit, Lucas."

"Why?"

"Seems our killer didn't know her all that well." Susan Granger showed him the picture of Carolynne Philips's mother. The glass was now shattered and the frame bent. "The lady picked up this picture and knocked that thing over with it just before she died. It must have taken nearly superhuman determination."

"She wanted to leave us a clue?"

"I think so. Now if we can just figure out what the hell she meant."

"I . . . uh . . . need to make a phone call, Susan. That appraiser should know something by now." He started toward the door. "Can I use the phone out in the hallway?"

"Sure, Lucas." Susan Granger followed him out, watching him closely. "Are you sure you're all right? You look a little pale."

Lucas Holt leaned on the balcony railing as he made his way to the phone.

"I'm . . . okay." His head swam. "Really. Thanks."

"I'd be glad to call downstairs and have them fix you some tea or something."

Lucas Holt turned to her and stared in disbelief.

She looked at him, perplexed. "Are you going to puke?"

"Wait a minute," he replied.

Granger called to an officer for assistance.

"No, wait." Like tumblers falling silently into place deep inside a bank vault, unheard at the surface but allowing the mammoth door to be wheeled slowly open, the series of events, conversations, and, most important, the last line of the hymn suddenly clicked deep within the mind of Lucas Holt.

"Susan, that's it! You've *said* it!"

"What's 'it'?" She waved the officer away. "Said what? What the hell are you babbling about?"

Holt turned around to the telephone.

"Let me make that call and I'll tell you." He quickly dialed the number of St. Margaret's Episcopal Church. "Maxine?" he said when the phone was answered. "This is Lucas. I'm fine. Listen, Max, is that appraiser still around there? Good. Can you put him on the phone for me? Thanks."

"Lucas, will you tell me what the hell is going on here? If you've figured something out, tell me, for God's sake."

"I will. I will. Just let me check this out. I'm almost sure this appraiser is going to say that . . ." He turned his attention back to the phone. "Hello. Mr. Koger? What have you found out so far?"

He listened to the news as Susan Granger frowned at him.

"I see. That's exactly what I thought. I'm sorry to hear that, too, Mr. Koger. No. Go ahead and finish your appraisal and leave the preliminary report on my desk when you leave. Yes. Thank you very much for your help. Goodbye."

"Well, what's the bad news?" Susan Granger asked.

"Just as we both thought, Susan," Holt said dejectedly. "The Treasury's pretty well decimated. Turns out, according to the appraiser anyway, that most of the pieces are duplicates of the originals, and of course worthless."

"Sorry, Lucas. I know what this means for you."

"Maybe, Susan. But if what I think is true, we may have been led on a chase to recover most of it."

"What are you talking about?"

"Your kind suggestion to me a few minutes ago pushed my consciousness over the edge, Susan. I've been wondering since I walked in here what that clue was in the last line of the hymn."

"And?"

"And we talked with the murderer together less than twenty-four hours ago."

"Who? Where?"

"At San Jacinto Hospital, Room 403."

"Lambert?" She wrinkled her face in disbelief. "Harris Lambert?"

"Right. We met him, as the hymn says, 'at tea.'"

"I don't get it, Lucas. In fact, I think the stink in that room got to your brain. You said it couldn't be Harris Lambert for about a million reasons, all of them greenbacks." The lieutenant picked up the phone and dialed the hospital switchboard. "Give me Room 403, please," she said hurriedly.

Lucas Holt looked at her as she listened for the reply, then hung up the phone without answering. She stared at him, her eyes narrowed in disbelief.

"Harris Lambert checked out a.m.a.—"

"'Against medical advice'? When?"

"Twenty minutes after we left last night."

• Twenty-two •

November dusk came early on Sixth Street, shading the neon harshness with quiet, hazy tones; it was the dull calm before the sensuous night blared in with loud sounds and thick smells and a crush of people looking for a good time, or something like it. Not yet filled with its ageless jostling seekers, "Old Pecan Street" was nearly naked save for one man with a determined gait. He ignored each club or restaurant he passed, knowing clearly who he sought.

The Buffalo Barn Grille commanded the corner of Sixth and Brazos. It was the last club on the street, and it was here that he entered. The man moved slowly, so as not to attract attention or arouse more suspicion than his black shirt and white collar already did. He sat silently on a stool for a minute, then motioned to the woman tending bar.

"Billie Gayle?"

She smiled, straightened her tight-fitting halter top, and walked over in front of his place.

"Hiya, Rev! What's happenin'?" She leaned over the bar and pecked him on the cheek. "Can I get you somethin' tonight?"

Lucas Holt winked, but spoke seriously.

"I sure hope so, darlin'." He took out his pen and wrote a name on the cocktail napkin. "And I'll start with some information."

"Depends on what and who, Rev."

He turned the napkin around. One of the first things he had learned at the prison was that names were never mentioned aloud anywhere. Walls had ears, even prison walls. So did barstools, mirrors, and beer bottles, it seemed.

"Know where he is?"

The woman turned her bare back to Holt and proceeded to the cash register. She wrote something on another napkin and stuffed it in her halter while she waited on several other customers. Drawing up a draft beer, she returned to Holt's place, removed the napkin and placed it under the glass before him.

"Will this do?" she asked.

"How much?" he replied, without looking down.

"This one's on the house, Rev. I owe you one—at least."

Lucas Holt picked up the glass of beer.

"Thanks," he said, lifting it to her and downing a large swallow. "Next one's on me."

"I'll hold you to that, Rev." She winked and cleaned the bar with a wet rag. "Y'all come back, now."

The woman served other customers at the bar as the Rev held on to his glass and looked around the room. He absently reached for the napkin, wiped his mouth with it, and slipped it into his jacket as he took another drink of the cold, foamy liquid. Leaving a small quantity in the bottom of the glass, he slid off the bar stool, nodded politely at Billie Gayle, and went out the door.

Holt had just passed by the front window with the picture of a large buffalo in an even larger barn when the bartender glanced knowingly at a dark man huddled in a smoky corner booth. She slowly nodded her head. Without hesitation, the man arose and walked through the kitchen to the rear entrance and the alley.

Lucas Holt put his hands in his jacket pockets and turned down San Jacinto to Fifth Street toward his car. As he walked, he withdrew the napkin and read: "So. Congress House." He took his keys from his other pocket and had just leaned over to unlock the car door when he heard the deep voice behind him.

"Get in the other side," the man said with an inflection that could not be disobeyed. "I'll drive."

Holt left the keys in the door and walked around the car without directly looking at the tall figure in the stocking cap. It was another tactic he had learned from the inmates. If you look directly, you may look your last. Look without looking. Observe everything peripherally.

The man unlocked the passenger door and motioned the Rev inside.

"You a present from Billie Gayle?" Lucas Holt said to the hulking figure next to him. He noted the baseball-mitt hands and cement-block feet. "I didn't know she cared."

"I'm your escort service, Rev," the man interrupted. He started the car and lurched down the street toward South Austin. "Billie Gayle knows you cain't go near that house on your own. I'm just makin' sure you get there all right. Once you're in—you're in. From then on it ain't my bidness." The dark man grinned. "Hope to hell you're a good talker."

"I can manage." The Rev breathed a sigh of relief and canceled plans to jump out at the next light. He looked over at the huge man holding the steering wheel like a toy and wondered if his insurance covered "giant damage."

Minutes later the car jerked to a halt in front of a house on South Congress Avenue. "Need to get that clutch checked." The big man handed his captive the keys and smiled.

What's left of it. "Right."

"I'll just make sure you get in the door, Rev."

"Thanks," he said. "I've heard the bouncers don't have much of a sense of humor."

The man looked down at him.

"Sure we do, Rev. Just not about people nosin' around where they ain't wanted."

The two men walked to the side entrance of the old wooden two-story house. Lucas Holt knocked on the door.

The clone of the man behind him opened it, looked at his cohort, and waved the Rev inside.

"You two separated at birth?" Or from the same test tube?

"Night, Rev."

The garish red room assaulted his eyes as smoke from several different kinds of cigarettes overcame his lungs. He had stopped coughing when a woman in a pink jumpsuit approached him.

"Welcome to our house, Rev," she said, putting her arms around him and kissing him squarely on the lips.

Holt hugged her back and returned the kiss.

"God, Annie, I hardly recognized you. I didn't know you were back in town."

The young woman wiped her red lipstick off his face with a small hankie. "Been here a couple of months, Rev, 'bout as long as you have. Made parole last summer and just haven't had time to look you up." She backed away and held him at arm's length. "You look good as ever, though. Still the best holy bod in town."

Holt put his arm around her waist and walked over to the couch.

"Is it okay to talk in here?"

The woman looked square in his eyes. "Rev, it's okay to do anything you want in here."

"What I meant was—"

"I know what you meant. I just like to play with you. To pull your . . . you know." They sat down on the orange velvet couch. "Things don't start hoppin' for an hour or so yet. We got a couple of customers upstairs tryin' to beat the rush." She smiled at him. "No pun intended of course."

Holt grimaced. "Well, I've got a couple questions for you. This'll be a quickie."

"My favorite." She laughed. "Go for it, Rev." She took his hand and held it between hers. Her long nails were painted different colors and her skin smelled of the strangely attractive mixture of smoke and strong perfume. "Oh, can I get you something to drink?"

"No, thanks, Annie. This is a short visit."

"Too bad."

"Yes, well, anyway, what's with the escort service to get in here?"

"Election year, Rev. Some South Austin yo-yo is tryin' to clean up all the houses in this district. We've had some bad times in here lately with undercover cops and narcs and some just plain mean cowboys playin' that self-righteous crap. Even had a couple of the girls beat up. Nothin' serious. It'll all be over in a month or two," she said philosophically. "Comes and goes with the election. Ten minutes after they're voted in, they're back down here celebrating with the ones they swore to run off."

Three young women in tiny shorts and half T-shirts meandered past the couple on the couch. They seemed unruffled by the presence of Lucas Holt's collar, as if they'd seen such things many times before. Annie whispered in the Rev's ear.

"Nothing much bothers them, Lucas. They probably think you're Catholic." She nipped his earlobe. "You sure I couldn't interest you in a little—something?"

"Thanks, Annie. This is purely business."

She smiled seductively at him. "Me, too, Rev. And don't kid yourself—ain't nothin' pure about business."

"That's not the kind of 'business' I meant."

"Me, either."

The Rev pulled away from her. "Here's the deal. I'm looking for an acquaintance of mine; a member of my parish, actually." He told her the name. "Have you seen him?"

"Course I have, Rev. He usually—you'll excuse the expression—comes early." She snickered and stood in front of the priest, bending over slowly as her ample bosoms strained at the front of her low-cut dress. She lifted him gently up from the couch with her hands under his reddening face. "Up the stairs, Rev. It's the second room on the right." She moved her hands down his shirt and around his waist and put her head on his chest. "Of course, if you'd like to make a little stop on the way?"

Holt took a deep breath to compose himself. "Bye, Annie," he said, extracting her hands and kissing her quickly on the nose. "I owe you dinner. Stop by the church and we'll make a date for it."

"Bye, Lucas." She smiled as she watched him go up the stairs. "It's a business doing pleasure with you."

The Rev shook his head as he walked down the dimly lighted hallway. The thin, faded carpet had a musty smell that mixed easily with the strong odors of smoke and liquor and sweat. He wondered what it was like to have sex in this place. He pictured himself in bed with Annie and imagined her soothingly sensual—and incredibly intimidating. His fantasy vanished at the sound of a familiar voice behind the door in front of him.

He knocked, then quickly opened the door and walked in. Two naked women flanked the man who sat bolt upright in the bed—with a gun aimed directly at Holt's face.

"Geez, Rev! You got one hell of a sense of timing!"

Lucas Holt smiled and tossed the man's pants from the chair.

"Get dressed, Nikky. I need your help."

• Twenty-three •

Lieutenant Susan Granger slowly cruised the streets around Harris Lambert's northeast Austin home. She doubted that the man would be likely to appear at his residence, but she also knew from experience to expect the unexpected, especially with maniacs like Lambert.

But was he really a maniac? He had seemed pretty gentle, even fragile when she had met him at the hospital the other night. He was said to be independent and outspoken with Lucas Holt, but that was bravado typical of men of his age and upbringing. Be tough. Don't admit to pain. Be independent. Be successful. Was it just Texan genes that imprinted these characteristics, or was it typical of Depression Era families? All these traits that were indigenous to Lambert were also found in her own parents—especially her dad—for that matter.

The street lights cast shadows on the live oaks still grasping their leaves, shadows that slipped over her car like a lace tablecloth. She thought of her dad, of her home and her own upbringing. She had received those same injunctions, the same commands and expectations. But she had avoided them, sought her own way, on her own terms—or had she?

She stopped at a corner and glanced in both directions. Was she in fact living up to the same demands in her life? Was she success- and money-oriented; and just how far would she go to obtain the things that her parents wanted for her, and that she wanted for herself? Would she lie, or cheat? Would she kill? The .45 police Magnum in its holster felt suddenly heavy. Maybe she was closer to the mind of Harris Lambert than she wished to admit.

She took the lid off her 7-Eleven coffee and turned the corner slowly, pretending she were the outlaw. Where would she go if she were running from someone like herself? Would she go to the least obvious place—home? Or would she get lost in a crowd of people? Would she head for the airports, which she knew would be covered? Or would she risk taking her car on the back roads and avoid the interstate surveillance by state and county police?

She dimmed the headlights and cut back through an alley. What if Lambert was not trying to run? Suppose his crazy mission had been accomplished and he was now waiting to be caught? Didn't he want to get caught? Didn't the numbers left at each murder point to that?

She wondered, as she rounded the corner in front of Lambert's house, how he would arrange his own capture. He seemed to have engineered everything else quite well, kept the police *and* Lucas Holt and his God Squad at bay while systematically completing the list of persons to be killed.

Granger inhaled the pleasant, familiar aroma of the coffee, then drank as she flashed the car beam into the dark crevasses between the houses. She remembered that the list was not yet complete. There was still the matter of the "Priest." That was why she had had Holt closely watched, for his own protection, whether he wanted it or not.

She pulled her unmarked car to the curb in front of Lambert's house and turned off the engine. She looked intently at the darkened house, and a more frightening thought occurred to her. What if that was to be Lambert's final accomplishment? What if he were to lure Holt into "capturing" him, only to turn the tables and effectively *finish* the list?

Susan Granger grabbed the radio from the seat.

"HQ, this is APD Twelve. Over."

"HQ by. Over."

"Any word from APD Ten on the whereabouts of clergy? Over."

"Subject last seen entering a house on South Congress Avenue. Over."

"What kind of house? Over."

The voice hesitated, then announced to all the police radio channels in Austin: "A house of prostitution, Lieutenant. Over."

Susan Granger squinted her eyes in the direction of Lambert's house. Had she seen movement in there or was it the play of the shadows on the window? And what the hell was Lucas doing down there unless it was to contact that damned God Squad? Her thoughts were interrupted by the squawking radio.

"Did you read, Lieutenant? Over."

"Ten-Four. I'm on my way back downtown. Tell me when he leaves that house. Over."

"Subject not seen leaving at this time. Will do, Lieutenant. Over."

Susan Granger had just started the engine when something peripherally caught her attention.

A lamp came on in the house.

The Green Light Café was the last holdout of old ownership on Sixth Street. Other proprietors had sold their properties at outrageous prices to yuppie businesspeople who gutted the historical stone buildings, then spent millions to make them look "old." The Green Light maintained its tradition of live mariachi bands, no air conditioning, the greasiest barbecue in town, and C&W music by old-timers with stubbled faces and red eyes. The place still catered to skinny, hunched-over, squinty-eyed men who smoked and drank and played Shoot the Moon on Texas domino tables, with small slate boards at each place and a little shelf on each leg for longnecks.

An embarrassment to its classy neighbors, the Green Light accommodated blacks, Chicanos, and Anglos in a way that none of the newer clubs could. It was the oldest and least segregated bar on the Street. The only identification cards needed were age and tradition, being down and out but not beaten, and having a loneliness to talk with other people like yourself. The place smelled of Bugler and Lone Star and rumpled flannel shirts sporting stains of both. It was a safe place—for many kinds of people.

The plodding sounds of C&W punched through the thick smoke in the back room of the Green Light Café. Sitting at a small, round table, Nikky Dorati huddled over a telephone, waiting. He and Lucas Holt had left the house on South Congress over an hour ago through a covered rear exit. The short man grinned as he visualized the unmarked police car still waiting in front of the house for them to come out. If they were to find Harris Lambert, it would not be with a police tail on them. Besides, Dorati thought to himself, the kinds of people he needed to contact got real nervous at the sight of cops in any form.

He had sent the Rev off to search out the areas of Sixth Street Lambert might be likely to frequent. Sometimes a man on the run tried to lose himself in a crowd, go to a familiar place, or, he thought as he listened to the old men slapping their ivories down on the tables, seek out the company of old friends.

He doubted if Harris Lambert was doing any of those things, and knew Lucas Holt had his own contacts to follow, but he wanted the Rev highly visible tonight. If Lambert was going to complete the sixth murder from the hymn, Nikky Dorati wanted him to have an easy target. Too easy.

The God Squad had been rounded up with a few calls before he and Holt left the house on South Congress. Annie, Nikky, Omar, Max, and Eddie had contacts in the underground network of the city that saw and knew things hidden from the "square" population of Austin, including the police. They relied now on the expertise of prostitutes, ex-

cons, dealers, and skids to find Harris Lambert before he
found Lucas Holt. They bet the Rev's life that they could.

Dorati got up and drew himself off another mug of hot
coffee from the urn behind the bar. He returned to the back
room table and opened another pack of unfiltered cigarettes. His mouth desperately craved a cold Shiner from the
tap, but he knew this was one night he had to maintain
every bit of control and clear thought he could muster. The
man had eluded them through the course of five murders; it
was entirely possible that he might complete the sixth.

The plan was an easy one. Each God Squad member had
his or her own territory to cover, contacts to make and
places to alert. Each was armed with a description of Lambert and the necessary means to stop him—temporarily or
forever. When located, they were to call the number at the
Green Light Café before taking any action. Like a nervous
father in the waiting room, Nikky Dorati paced and
smoked, trying not to watch the silent phone.

To purposely distract himself, he wandered over near the
bar door and listened to the band thump its way through
"Redneck Mother." He was about to take another sip of the
now lukewarm coffee when he realized he had been distracted too well.

The phone was on its third ring.

Diving for the table, Nikky grabbed the receiver and
shouted:

"Where is he?"

He listened carefully to the reply, crushed out his cigarette, then answered.

"Make sure he stays there."

Unlike his trek down Sixth Street earlier that evening,
the late-night darkness was filled with neon promises and
hopeful people. Taking care to avoid the blue-and-whites
cruising the area on their normal rounds, Lucas Holt had
moved with the crowds coursing down the sidewalk. His
maroon cloth jacket was zipped to the neck; his white collar

was stuck in his shirt pocket. He kept to the inside of the sidewalk so he could see into the clubs or peel off and wander up to bars and survey the customers for a large man sitting alone.

In the short two hours he had spent looking for Harris Lambert he had several interesting propositions, one from a person of unknown sexual identification, and a couple of opportunities to purchase the latest shipment of Colombia's best export.

Having closely observed the clubs of the main area of Sixth, Holt decided to try the side-street establishments that were less crowded. It was then that he noticed the figure behind him.

Why the hell hadn't he seen him before? Although the man was keeping distance and stopping into doorways so as not to be obvious, Lucas Holt knew he himself was the object of the man's surveillance. But who was it?

It could be one of Susan's officers, but she still thought he was back on South Congress. Or did she? Did they raid the house to see if he was still there? Or was this Nikky's idea of keeping tabs on him? The man did not look like anyone he knew from the God Squad and in fact seemed too old to be doing this kind of thing.

Holt's heart suddenly got a shot of adrenaline. He walked faster as the man—who looked amazingly like Harris Lambert—started to catch up with him. Rather than risking anything in the crowded area of the street, the Rev decided to lure him around the corner to St. Margaret's. As they moved quickly up to Seventh Street, the crowd thinned to only one or two other persons. Lucas Holt readied his master key for the plunge into the safe darkness of the church.

Just before entering, Holt glanced behind at his pursuer. The man was clearly winded now but was also closing the distance between them. Leaving the front door open, Lucas Holt left a trail of lights behind him and headed for the basement of the church—and the Treasury.

The large man opened the door and moved slowly down the carpeted stairs, using the time to catch his shallow breath. He followed the direction of the lights constantly downward and listened for signs of the priest he sought tonight. Hearing none, he reached into his pocket and pulled out a silver object that glinted in the darkness. He had come to a long corridor that he knew lead to the Treasury. Holding the object in front of him, he headed into the darkness, feeling his way very slowly along the glassed-in walls.

The man took one step at a time, listening for movement, cautiously holding on to the wall behind him. He had moved most of the way down the corridor when a door burst open behind him. The man wheeled around, turned on the bright silver flashlight, and beamed the bright light into the Rev's eyes.

Lucas Holt, temporarily blinded, fell to the ground to avoid the beam, but it followed him there, too. The man came closer, reached down and grabbed him by the shoulder.

"Reverend Holt?" The large man's thick voice was much different from that of Harris Lambert.

The Rev, about to spring for the man's throat, relaxed from his crouching position.

"What do you want?"

"Nikky Dorati had me tailing you, or actually watching after you tonight in case somebody tried to take you off the count. You know what I'm sayin'?"

"Yes, I do. But—"

"Well, right before you started runnin' from me I got the word to get a message to you."

"Come here first."

Lucas Holt stood up and flashed the beam of light in front of them, leading the man back down the corridor. When they reached the lighted area, the Rev turned to look at his pursuer. The man before him was indeed of the same build as Harris Lambert, but his unshaven face and blood-shot eyes told of a very different background.

"Sorry for the chase. I thought you were someone else."

"I know. That's what Nikky told me to tell you."

"What's that?"

"One of the boys found him."

"Where?"

"At the Driskill Hotel. Nikky says for you to meet him there right now."

• Twenty-four •

The Driskill Hotel was one of the few remaining buildings from the mid-1800s that was still standing. Named for Civil War hero Colonel James T. Driskill, it had been slated for destruction many times and had barely escaped the demolition ball through the intervention of the Heritage Society and various moneyed citizens. It now boasted a clean, sandblasted pink granite exterior, newly renovated rooms with twelve-foot ceilings and rotary fans, and a wealthy clientele that went there to enjoy its famed, historic luxury.

Except for one.

Harris Lambert had chosen Room 327 of the Driskill both for its view of Sixth Street and for its balcony. The view allowed him to observe the major thoroughfare approaching the hotel; he would easily see any police cars, marked or unmarked, such as Lieutenant Susan Granger's which was now screeching to a halt in front—indicating that she had gotten the note at his home. The balcony, on the other side of this corner room, overlooked the alley and would prevent any surprise intrusions from that direction.

He removed the antique Tiffany lamp from the polished round table and set it on the floor. Dragging the table to the center of the room, he placed the tacklebox on it as his shoulder pulsed with pain. The table would divide the room in half. When Lucas Holt found him and entered the room the table would be between them.

Just as he planned.

Expecting at least one person to accompany the priest Harris Lambert placed two comfortable chairs with embroi dered cushions near the door and set one for himself by the wall between the balcony and the Sixth Street window. As he envisioned it, they would come to the door, enter slowly, and sit in the chairs while he talked to them. He would sit across the room against the wall, viewing both the street and the alley, and the table with the green metal tacklebox would sit in the middle of the room between them.

He opened the box one last time, adjusted its delicate contents, and carefully closed and latched the lid. Walking over to the large, overstuffed chair against the wall, he sat down and poured himself a large bourbon and branch. He took a long drink, sighed deeply, and settled into the soft cushions for a final moment of rest.

All was in place, people taking their positions, converging on the Driskill and upon this room. It felt good to sit and do nothing but wait, he thought. There had been so much activity up until now to carry out the plan, to bring it to its logical, its poetic conclusion tonight. The pain from his wounds both wearied and stimulated him. Like St. Sebastian, he thought, the pain would purge him of his sins.

But had he really sinned? he wondered. The lives he took were all "deserving" of death; except the one. And she? No, he could not think about her. He could not allow emotion to cloud his intention for this night. He had, with near success, he thought, touching his throbbing shoulder, executed the entire plan. In a few minutes the final scene would begin, and all would be brought to completion.

He slowly sipped the sweet-smelling bourbon and glanced at the green box on the table. Then he took the remote control device out of his coat pocket and clicked the switch to "On."

Susan Granger entered the white marble lobby of the Driskill Hotel and walked up to the dark oak reception desk. A mustached man with red garters on his puffy sleeve turned around to greet her. She felt as if she had walked into a Louis L'Amour novel.

"Evenin', ma'am. Can I help you?"

"Yes. I hope so. Do you have a Mr. Harris Lambert registered here?"

The man pointed to a marble pillar by the house elevator.

"Room 327, ma'am. Those gentlemen over there by the elevator just asked the same question. Maybe they can help you."

She turned to see Lucas Holt and Nikky Dorati vehemently gesturing to each other.

"Thank you," she said.

"Y'welcome, ma'am, I'm sure. But could you tell me what exactly is going on?"

Granger pointed to the uniformed cop behind her. "He'll explain it to you. We're cordoning off the hotel lobby and the entire surrounding block. There's a murder suspect upstairs."

The sweating clerk picked up the phone to call his manager.

The lieutenant turned to the officer. "Seal the hotel."

The two saw her coming and stopped their conversation.

"What the hell do you think you're doing here, Lucas?"

"Now, Susan. Don't be mad just because we found—"

"You were supposed to keep me informed every damned step of the way."

"I did! As soon as Nikky notified me, I had you called."

"The last I heard you were holed up in a whorehouse, pardon the pun. It's a good thing Lambert anticipated my watching his house—at least *he* left me a note saying where I could find him. Maybe he also anticipated that you wouldn't tell me."

Nikky Dorati cleared his throat.

"Excuse me, but could you two have this fight later? We did find the man and he *is* in Room 327 upstairs. Besides, you rudely interrupted a little disagreement we were having about how to approach this loony dude."

Susan Granger turned to Nikky Dorati.

"Look, Dorati." She stared down at him with menacing

eyes. "Where do you get off taking the law into your hands? Who the hell do you think you are?"

"Right now, *Ms*. Lieutenant," Dorati replied acidly, "I'm the guy who found the perp you cops couldn't track down and who also has the room guarded from all directions so he can't escape. So lighten up and don't strain your vocal cords thankin' me."

"Okay," Holt said. "Nikky's right. We can have this fight later. Right now we have to decide how we're going to get into that room."

"Has anybody called up there?" Susan Granger asked.

"Not yet. We waited until you got here to make sure the place was secure."

"Well"—Granger's eyes widened—"thank you so much! I can't believe you actually included me in a major decision." She took the pocket radio from her belt.

Dorati mumbled, "I can't, either."

"Granger to Ortiz. Over."

"Ortiz by. Over."

"Is the area cleared and cordoned off yet? Over."

"Ten-Four, Lieutenant. But crowds are gathering around the police barricades. And the media have started to arrive. Over."

"Call for backup. Get the P.R. queen out there to leash the cameras and keep them out of the hotel. What about the other buildings? Over."

"SWAT team effectively deployed. Over."

"Ten-Four, I'm going up."

Nikky Dorati spoke to the lieutenant. "Does that mean what I think it does?"

"That depends." She punched the Up button. "If you think it means we have SWAT personnel in the buildings across the street aiming weapons at the windows of Room 327, then you're right."

Dorati looked at Lucas Holt.

"So what's our strategy?" he asked.

Granger ignored him. "First of all, it's not *our* strategy. It's police business and both of you are out of here."

"No bet, Susan."

"Listen to me, Lucas, and try for once to be reasonable about this." Susan Granger worked hard to tone down her voice. "I think it's you he wants in there. That would complete his insane 'mission' or whatever the hell it is he's got going with that hymn. So that's our hole card. We don't let him have you."

"That's what I been tellin' him, Lieutenant. But he ain't buyin' it."

"Both of you listen to me a minute," Holt said as a bell sounded and the brass doors of the elevator opened. "He's *my* parishioner. I can't let you just go in and blow him away. At least give me a chance to talk to him."

"Hold that elevator, Dorati," Granger ordered. "And stop the drama, Lucas. Nobody said anything about blowing him away."

"So what does the SWAT team do for a living, kill flies?"

"They're just for backup, in case things get out of control. In case he starts shooting."

"Do you really think that's likely?"

Granger hesitated a second, then said, "No, I don't. But I can't take the chance with the public out there."

"And I can't take the chance that the cops will make a mistake with a member of St. Margaret's."

"I could order you not to interfere, Lucas."

"Yes, you could." He nodded at Dorati. "And I could also have Nikky tell the God Squad to go in after him right now."

Granger glanced at her watch. "We've got the floor secured and that can't happen."

The voice from the elevator replied: "Wanna bet, lady?"

"Granger to Campbell. Over."

"Campbell by. Over."

She stared at Dorati. "Is third secure?"

"Not exactly, Lieutenant. Over."

"What the hell does that mean, exactly? Over."

"Means we can't exactly get in the fire doors from the stairwells. And the elevators won't stop on that floor for some reason. Over."

"Damn you, Dorati. That's obstructing police business."

"But say the word, and the floor shall be ours, dear lady."

Susan Granger pursed her lips and thought a moment. "We go up there together on one condition."

"What's that?"

"You only talk to him outside the door."

Holt stepped with Granger into the elevator.

"We'll see," he said.

As the doors closed, Dorati yelled: "Fix the switch, Omar! We're comin' up to three!"

Nikky Dorati was the first to step off.

"Let the cops in, Eddie." He nodded to the woman. "You, too, Annie. Omar, watch our back."

The lieutenant fumed over the radio. "Granger to Campbell. By."

"Campbell. By."

"Cooperate with persons opening doors. We'll negotiate charges later. By."

"Ten-Four."

"Where's the room?" Granger asked.

Omar Dewan pointed to the right.

Room 327 was located at the end of the richly carpeted hallway. The crystal globe above the door illumined the entire area and shone now on the strange combination of heavily equipped riot police and the casually dressed God Squad.

Susan Granger waved them out of sight as she, Dorati, and Holt approached the door.

The Rev knocked, and the familiar voice from inside responded.

"Is that you, Lucas?"

"Yes, Harris, it is."

"And who is out there with you?"

He looked at the other two.

"Nikky Dorati, an old friend of mine." He hesitated a moment, then continued. "And Lieutenant Susan Granger, of APD."

The voice inside seemed pleased. "Excellent, Lucas. Excellent."

Holt proceeded. "What do you want us to do, Harris?"

"I want you to slowly, very slowly, open the door and enter with your hands over your head."

Susan Granger shook her head "No" and grabbed the Rev by the shoulder.

"I won't let you do this, Lucas."

Omar Dewan stepped forward behind the lieutenant. "The Rev will do what he thinks is best, lady."

"Back off, sonny," one of the riot cops said. "She's running the show here, not you."

Dewan stepped back, ready to strike.

"Stop it!" Granger ordered.

The voice inside interrupted. "And Father Holt?"

"Yes, Harris?"

The man inside took either a deep breath or a long drink.

"Please leave your weapons outside in the hallway. I think your SWAT team has quite enough munitions aimed in this direction already."

Holt looked at Granger and whispered, "I have to go in there, Susan. Neither one of us has a choice. Besides, don't you want to know why this all happened?"

"Yes," she replied, "but I'd like to live to tell about it."

"I think I'll meet you two down in the coffee shop in about an hour." Nikky Dorati turned to go. "You both forget, this guy's nuts. I've done nuts before. They're unpredictable. They live on another planet and they think *you're* the friggin' alien that needs killin'."

"Your call, Nikky. Either way is okay with me," the Rev

said. He pulled away from the lieutenant and put his hand
on the polished brass doorknob, turning it very slowly.

"That's it, Lucas. Come right on in. Sit in that chair
there, on that side of the door." He smiled at Susan
Granger. "And you, Lieutenant, thank you for joining us, as
I thought you would. You can sit over there on that other
chair."

A reluctant Nikky Dorati straggled in behind them both,
his hands also held high in the air.

"Mr. Dorati," Lambert said calmly. "I had not anticipated your presence here."

"Neither had I, spaceball," Nikky mumbled.

"I'm afraid you will have to bring that chair over from
the bed there. That's right. And put it right in front of the
door."

"Excuse me, Lieutenant, ma'am," Dorati said sarcasti-
cally. "But none of your good ol' boys are gonna spray a
few shots through this door any time soon, are they? 'Cause
it would cause me a great deal of concern sitting here if I
thought they were."

"They have been told to hold their fire."

"I hope they can hold it until we get out of here."

"I believe you will come to no harm, Mr. Dorati," Harris
Lambert said. "Thank you all for coming here today. You
may put your hands down now, but please keep them on
your knees where I can see them."

The scene was exactly the way Lambert had envisioned
it. The three captives were against the far wall next to the
closed door. He sat across the room from them in a chair
overlooking both the balcony door and the other window,
but out of sight from either and therefore inaccessible to the
gunsights of the SWAT teams. The small round table with
the green metal tacklebox sat like an altar in the middle of
the room.

"First, let me explain something to you," he said. "The
box there between us contains five sticks of dynamite
wrapped in a plastic explosive with an electronic firing

mechanism. My finger is over a button on this remote-control device. The rest, I believe, is obvious."

"So you're going to blow us all to hell after you tell us why you did it?" Susan Granger snapped.

"Let's just say, Lieutenant, that I want you to stay right where you are for a while; at least until I"—he looked directly at Lucas Holt—"*finish* my task. And I don't want you to make any fast moves or have your people interrupt us. Is that clear?"

"Perfectly," she replied. "Do you mind if I repeat the explicit order to hold their fire? It will also make Mr. Dorati a bit more relaxed."

"Not at all, Lieutenant."

Susan Granger slowly removed the radio from her belt.

"Attention all units. We are in Mr. Lambert's room, and he has an explosive device with an electronic remote control in his hand. You are under direct orders from me not to shoot." She paused, then spoke again. "Repeat. Do not shoot or attempt to take him captive. Over."

"Well put, Lieutenant," Harris Lambert said. With one hand he poured another bourbon over the ice and added water from the antique pitcher on the table by his chair.

"I would offer you some of this fine old bourbon, but I would guess you wouldn't accept anything from my hands now."

"You'd be right about that," Nikky Dorati answered.

"Too bad, actually. It's excellent. This really is a wonderful establishment. So well appointed." Lambert took a drink and settled deeper into the chair.

"Before I begin, are there any specific questions you would like to ask?"

"Yeah," Nikky Dorati said. "When was the first time you knew you were nuts?"

The Rev and Susan Granger glared at him, wide-eyed.

"What he meant was—" Lucas Holt began.

"I know what he meant, Lucas," Harris Lambert said. "And he's right. At times I thought I must be crazy to have done all of this." He took a long drink of the bourbon and branch. "But I think you will see that there was, as they say, 'a method to my madness.' "

"Why don't you just start at the beginning?" Susan Granger asked.

"'In the beginning was the word,' " Lambert said, wistfully. "The 'beginning'? I often wonder when that was. I seem to have forgotten exactly. I do remember the first time I knew I was in trouble."

"When was that?" Holt asked.

"It was after I had taken two or three of the pieces from the Treasury and had Ashton Willis make duplicates of them. My business had been in trouble for some time, Father Holt. With all the big companies coming to Austin, I was losing some of my old clients to younger insurance people with better deals than I could offer. At first I took the pieces and sold the duplicates to make up for the losses. I thought eventually I could pay the church back."

"But then you came to like the money?" the Rev offered.

"Yes. I liked the money and the prestige, being seen around town again at the clubs with all my old friends, dressing well, knowing important people. I've worked at this business all my life, you know. I couldn't let my career end in ruin. It would have been too great a loss of face for me."

"So how did Bradenberg fit in to all this?" Susan Granger asked.

"I'd heard about Bradenberg through another insurance agent who happened to mention to me how much the colonel was worth. I knew he must have used his under-cover work to develop quite a black-market business of his own. He agreed, for a percentage of course, to take the duplicates with him and sell them in other parts of the world."

"That way you didn't have to worry about a local fence, either," Nikky Dorati added.

"Correct, Mr. Dorati. But it wasn't long before the duplicates were not bringing in enough money to support my newly acquired tastes."

"So you started replacing the Treasury with the duplicates and sold the originals?" Lucas Holt asked.

"Yes, Lucas." Harris Lambert rearranged himself in the chair. It was obvious he was still in pain from the animal bites as well as from the graze wound that now spotted his coat.

"You could have covered the thefts indefinitely. You were the one who had them insured to the hilt, and you were the one who had them appraised every year." Lucas Holt hesitated.

"So you must have paid off the appraisers," Dorati said, interested.

"That's correct. As you know, there are people who will do most anything for money."

"I agree with you, Lambert," Dorati said. "Exactly how much would it take for you to let us out of here alive?"

"You are free to leave at any time, Mr. Dorati." He nodded toward the woman. "That goes for you, also, Lieutenant. The only person I really need to remain here is Father Holt. He is my—'priest'—you know."

Susan Granger tightened her hands on her knees. If only she could reach the table, she might toss the box out the window before it exploded.

Harris Lambert caught her glance. "It won't work, Lieutenant," he said, smiling. "I'd press the button before you hit the table, and we'd all be killed."

"Well, I can't leave Father Holt in here alone with you."

"You will have no choice, when I am ready."

The Rev ignored the comment and hoped to distract Lambert from the button he was nervously fingering as he talked.

"The thing that started the killing, Harris. What was that?"

Lambert's face tightened as he recalled the scene in his mind.

"Your damned predecessor, of course, Lucas. If it hadn't been for him, I would have gone to my grave without anyone knowing of the thefts."

"When you heard that the church was bankrupt, you knew we would have to start selling off the Treasury collection," Lucas Holt concluded.

"Not exactly. It was partly coincidental. Actually, the bankruptcy came second. I still might have been able to raise money through friends and foundations to bail out the church for a while. But just before you came to St. Margaret's, someone else found out what I'd been doing and wanted money to keep quiet about it."

"You were being blackmailed?" Lieutenant Granger sounded surprised.

"Yes." Lambert emptied his glass of the brown liquid and, his hand shaking now at the weakness from pain and the loss of blood, poured another one. "By someone who was himself in trouble financially and, I might add, personally."

"Ashton Willis?" the Rev asked.

"No. It was—"

Before Lambert could speak, they jumped at the loud pounding on the door.

• Twenty-five •

Harris Lambert sat upright in his chair, his hand holding the detonation device tightly in front of him.

"Who's there?" he shouted.

A strong, deep voice came back through the door.

"This is Captain Dixon, APD. I want you to let me come in and talk to you."

"Oh, God." Susan Granger sighed. "He's trying that old hostage negotiation crap he learned ten years ago."

"Shall you talk to him or shall I, Lieutenant?" Harris Lambert asked, trying to maintain his composure.

"I will." She slowly leaned around in her seat and spoke toward the door. "Captain, this is Lieutenant Granger. The man knows what you're doing and it won't work. Get away from the door. He has a bomb in here and it's wired to him. If you come through that door, he will set it off and we'll all be killed. Stop playing hero and get the hell out of here."

Silence fell on the other side of the door.

"Did you hear me, Dixon?"

"Yes, I did, but as your superior officer, I—"

Granger yelled: "The only thing the Promotions Board thought was superior about you over me was that pencil between your legs."

"That's insubordination, Lieutenant!"

"Campbell!" she shouted, still facing Harris Lambert.

The voice from the hall: "Yes, Lieutenant?"

"Please allow Mr. Dewan to keep watch on Captain Dixon. There's a commendation in it for you."

"Right!"

There was a loud thump against the wall.

"Secured," the cop said.

"Harris," Granger continued, "if it's all right with you, I will reach over and turn the lock on the door."

Nikky Dorati frowned at her. What the hell did she think she was doing, locking them in with this nut case?

"I believe Mr. Dorati can accomplish that task, can't you? Just do it slowly, please, and do not turn your back on me."

Nikky reached behind his chair and bolted the door.

Lucas Holt, seeing the tired Lambert relax, continued the talk.

"I believe you were about to tell us the name of the person blackmailing you, Harris."

"Yes, I was," he said. "It was Walter Hargrive."

"But how did he know?"

"His father was a jeweler in Tarrytown, Lucas. A very prominent family and wealthy enough to send their son to medical school even when he couldn't get a scholarship. Walter Hargrive was not a brilliant man, you know."

"He was one hell of a drug dealer," Nikky Dorati added.

"That he was, Mr. Dorati. And that is partly the reason for his need for the money. Over the years Hargrive had spent his family fortune on the style of living he could not maintain. His patients eventually dwindled and his own attachment to cocaine increased with his age."

The large man paused to replace a bandage that had fallen off his neck. That wound also felt bloody and infected. His pain increased with the unraveling of the story, but he knew he had to get it all out and do it soon. The police outside would not wait forever, he was sure.

"It seems Dr. Hargrive was viewing the Treasury one afternoon with his Sunday School class when a particular piece caught his eye. It was a golden chalice. Having worked for so many years in his parents' store, he recognized some flaws in the reproduction. He came to me to tell me about it, and I'm afraid he very quickly figured out what my hesitation meant. For a price, he agreed to keep quiet."

"And so you killed him," Susan Granger said.

"One death in return for what number, Lieutenant? How many people do you think his surgical ineptness killed? How many people were misdiagnosed and then led into long involved treatments to pay the bills for his drug habit?" Lambert paused to catch his breath. "Yes, I killed him; and with his own scalpel, too."

"And Ashton Willis?" she continued.

"Of course, Lieutenant. You can clear the books of many things with his death. And there will be one less person with AIDS viciously spreading his disease among the un-suspecting in town." Lambert took another drink, looked at the box on the table, and addressed Susan Granger. "Just like Bradenberg, he cheated me. Bradenberg got greedy and lied about the amount he was getting for the duplicates. Ashton Willis tried to give me back the duplicates and keep the originals for himself. He thought I couldn't tell the dif-ference, but I showed him, too. You will find many of the original pieces of the Treasury hidden in his house, I'm sure. And quite a few other artworks that are currently on your missing list are there, also, Lieutenant."

"Thanks for the tip."

"I hope we live to take it," Nikky Dorati said.

"You will, Mr. Dorati, I assure you. In a minute I am going to ask you to leave."

"You're what?" Susan Granger looked at the man whose eyelids seemed to be growing heavier. She still thought she could make it across the room before the button could be pushed. If not, she could at least knock the box behind the table.

"I said I am going to ask you two to leave. But please don't interrupt me. There is one more person you will want to know about."

Lucas Holt scanned over the list of people. Then he re-membered.

"Carolynne Philips. What was her connection with the Treasury?" he asked.

"Very good, Lucas." Harris Lambert painfully reached over and drained the decanter of bourbon into his glass. Taking a long swallow, he made the effort to continue. "She made the fatal mistake of purchasing a large number of the original items. She bought some directly from me but soon found a cheaper market in Willis." He shifted in the chair. "She was a despicable woman, you know. Her plan was to pave everything from Austin to San Antonio. Her kind only want to use this city for their own greed—just as she wanted to have the Treasury pieces all to herself to look at and own. If you search her house carefully, I believe you will recover the majority of originals there. Some are lost forever, and for that I am truly sorry. I tried to lead you to the ones I knew about."

"I knew the sequence felt like a trail, Harris," Lucas Holt responded. "I just didn't know what we were finding in each place."

"But what was the purpose of the hymn and the numbers at each killing?" Susan Granger tried to distract him from noticing that she was leaning forward on the chair, decreasing the distance between herself and the green tacklebox.

Lambert's mouth drew up to a grin. "Well, Lieutenant, that's what makes me think Mr. Dorati is right in his assessment of my mental state. In one sense it was a game. I wanted to be caught. I realized that the people fit nicely into the categories in 'The Saints of God,' so I used it as a way to play with you—and to let you win, eventually. I presume you know I wanted you to stop me—but I couldn't let you interrupt my plan. You couldn't catch up with me until I was finished. I knew I had to do it. My business would be in ruins anyway, and they had all cheated me in some way." He took a drink of the bourbon. "Besides, I'm sure you know that they deserved to die, each one of them."

Harris Lambert was becoming unnerved, but not distracted.

"And if you don't sit back on your chair, Lieutenant, I promise you will be in Paradise with your friends sooner than you wish."

Susan Granger sat back and put her hands on her knees.

"What about the nun?" she asked fiercely, sensing that she had little time left to make a move if any was to be made. "What had she done in your supreme omniscient judgment to warrant a sentence of death?"

Harris Lambert was visibly shaken by the memory of Sister Marguerite's dying moments. He bolstered himself back up in the chair and spoke to Susan Granger and Nikky Dorati.

"This is where you make your exit." He pointed to them with the hand that held the device. His finger nervously patted the detonator button. "I want you, Lieutenant, and Mr. Dorati to stand up, again with your hands above your heads, and slowly back toward the door."

"And what if we refuse to leave, Lambert?" Susan Granger said. "You know this is a friend of ours and we will not leave him to be killed by you."

"As I said, you have no choice, Lieutenant," Lambert replied, reaching down behind the chair and holding up a .45 Magnum. "You can choose to die while he watches you, here and now, or you can walk out that door and try to think of a way to stop me before I kill him."

Harris Lambert cocked the hammer.

"Which one will it be?"

"I'm stayin'," Nikky Dorati said defiantly.

Lambert aimed at Dorati's chest and began to squeeze the trigger.

"Stop it, Harris!" Holt turned to the others. "You both are going, and now," Lucas Holt replied, looking at neither of them. He waved them off and stared at Harris Lambert. "Let them leave, Harris. I believe there is still a part of this story that only I can hear. Is that right?"

"Absolutely, Father Holt. And thank you for understanding. Now, if you two will just slowly rise and leave me with my priest, I will greatly appreciate it."

"Lucas, you can't stay here—" Susan Granger began.

"Go, Susan." He pushed her out of the chair into a standing position.

"Listen, Rev—"

"You, too, Nikky. Get out of here and leave us alone. I'll be all right—regardless of what happens. Just go."

"But before you do," Harris Lambert interjected, "please take out your handcuffs, Lieutenant."

Susan Granger carefully uncapped the holder on her belt, removed the steel cuffs, and held them in front of her.

"Now what?" she asked.

"Put one on Father Holt's right hand and the other around the arm of the chair."

"I don't like this, Lucas," she said.

"Just do it and go!" the Rev replied.

Susan Granger did as she was directed, then turned and held the door open for Nikky Dorati.

"Yo, Rev," Nikky began. "Remember the Guadalupe brothers?"

"No, Nikky," Holt replied. "Thanks, but no."

"See ya in a little bit, Rev," he said.

"Right."

"Be careful, Lucas," Susan Granger said softly. "I'll do what I can."

The two slowly edged out the door as the people waiting in the hall held their fire.

"One more thing, Lucas," Harris Lambert directed his captive. "Reach over with your free hand and bolt the door again, please."

Awkwardly Holt complied, then turned himself around to sit in the chair again.

"I assume you want to make your confession, Harris, is that right?"

"Something like that, Father Holt. There is a story I have never told anyone that I want you to know. In a way it underlies these bizarre events because it formed my entire life here."

"And it's about the nun?"

"Yes. Sister Marguerite. Her real name was Suzanna."

"Tell me about her."

"Yes. I will." Harris Lambert took another long drink from the emptying glass. "I met her when I was just a boy, back in Tennessee. We dated through high school, then went into our separate professions after that. But we stayed in touch and saw each other from time to time, illegally of course. She could have gotten into serious trouble for meeting me back in those days, you know. The novitiate was quite strict."

"And?"

"And the impossible happened. I got her pregnant." Lambert slowed his speech as the remembered pain coursed through his being. "At first I was happy. I thought she could leave the Order and we would get married. But she said her parents would be mortified, and, of course, her vocation would be ruined. Lucas, you must remember the times. Things like that just weren't done then." He paused for a moment, then said: "And neither were some other things."

Lambert hung his head, stifling back tears.

"You arranged an abortion?"

The large man lifted his head and looked at Lucas Holt.

"Yes. It was awful. She was late in her second trimester, and I saw the fetus as it came out of her. I'll never forget that sight."

"Yes, but in some cases, Harris, abortion is the only viable option, especially for two people in your situation."

"No, Lucas, it was more than that. We should have stayed together, forgotten our career plans, and spent our lives together. We just didn't know any better. It was the times, the society that we bought into and believed and let shape our lives forever. We should have gone off together. We would have made it somehow. People seem to do it now, don't they? As it was it was horrible. She had to be drugged, I don't even know with what. We didn't know if the woman—she was Oriental—was a real doctor or not. Suzanna was sick for a long time. Due to the inexperience, or perhaps the drunkenness, of the doctor, Suzanna suffered irreparable tissue damage. She had to have subsequent surgeries to correct the butchery. The emotional cost was deep and indelible, and the physical cost remained with her until she—died."

"God, Harris. You've held on to that all this time?"

"Of course, Father Holt. Who could I tell? I never married. I felt ashamed all my life for aborting that baby and for affecting her life like that. I vowed never to inflict myself on her again and moved here to Austin to start over where nobody knew me. I had lived here for years before the impossible happened again."

"You found her here?"

"Her Order had made her Superior of the convent over on Exposition Boulevard. At first I phoned. But then I had to see her, and eventually we—fell back in love. I saw her more and more often. I loved her more than ever and wanted to make so much up to her."

"Then why did you kill her?"

"She was suffering, Lucas. She had developed uterine cancer. It had spread to her lungs. The vibrant woman that she was was slowly being sucked dry by the disease. I had caused enough suffering in her life, and I wanted to be her deliverer from further pain. Then, too, I had selfish motives. I wanted to make sure she got to heaven without knowing about me, about what I had done. And I wanted her reunited with our baby. I couldn't stand the thought of—of leaving her behind again."

"Leaving her behind?" Holt gently pulled at the handcuff on the chair. It would not budge. "What are you talking about?"

"Not yet, Lucas. First I must have your absolution."

The large man slowly slid out of the chair down to the

floor on his knees. He was still careful not to come in view of the window or the balcony. His hand still firmly on the detonator, he bowed his head in Lucas Holt's direction.

"Forgive me, Father, for I have sinned gravely."

Holt made the sign of the cross and replied: "The Almighty God, Father, Son, and Holy Spirit, forgives you all your sins."

"Amen," they said as one.

Slowly, with severe pain, Harris Lambert pulled himself to his feet and walked toward the wood and glass doors leading outside.

"Get away from the window!"

"Thank you, Lucas. I'm sorry, but this is the way it must end."

"*No! Harris! Stop!*" Holt yelled and tried to stand from the chair. "You don't have to do this!"

"Yes, I do." He lifted the detonator high over his head and walked outside to the balcony.

Onlookers below gasped, then screamed as the air exploded with rifle shots.

Holt watched helplessly as the bullet-riddled body of Harris Lambert twisted and jerked in a macabre dance of bloody death. Wrenching backward over the short balcony railing, the body fell like some contorted diver from a high board, three stories down to the street.

The room door burst open as a squad of people rushed into the room. Ignoring Holt, they threw a thick metal blanket over the tacklebox. At the same time Nikky Dorati hurriedly lead the Rev, still attached to the chair, out into the hallway.

"Get him the hell out of those things," Dorati said.

Granger worked on the handcuff lock with her small key. After opening it, she rubbed the circulation in his hand and, without regard for anyone around her, hugged him close.

"Shit, Lucas . . ."

"I'm okay, Susan." He hugged her back and kissed her

gently on the neck. "Thanks for the help. Though I'm not entirely sure it was necessary."

"What are you talking about?" she said, pulling him away. "That man was going to blow us to kingdom come."

"Lieutenant?" A voice from inside the room called to her.

"Yes? What is it?"

"Could you come in here please?"

Susan Granger, Lucas Holt, and Nikky Dorati turned and went back into the room. The rest of the God Squad came in from the hall. The sound of sirens screaming in the background told them Harris Lambert's body was on its way to the city morgue.

The green tacklebox lay open on the table. The bomb squad leader held its contents in his hand.

"Any of you know what this is?" he asked.

Lucas Holt stepped up and took the object from him.

"We all do." He took the small gilded statue of Mary in his hands and looked at Granger and Dorati. "It's an icon from the Treasury."

• Twenty-six •

The Reverend Lucas Holt sat at his desk with his black Tony Lama bullhides propped up on the windowsill. The red prayer book sat in his lap as he flipped through the pages of the Service for Burial. The sun shone down on the people passing his purview on Sixth Street and contrasted with the grayness he felt inside.

The last few days had been incredibly draining, filled with violence, fear, and death. As he looked out the window at the warm November day and thought about the task ahead, he longed for time to be alone, to think, to put his life and his job back in perspective. There had been no time for that lately, and there was no time for it now.

The funeral service for Harris Lambert would begin shortly. He was disobeying the direct order of his ecclesiastical authority by doing the service in the church. The bishop seemed to be worried more about the adverse publicity than the man's right to be treated as a member of St. Margaret's. Lucas Holt was sure Emilio Casas would change his mind, especially after the phone call the Rev had gotten earlier that morning.

The service had been worked out last night, after they all had left the Driskill Hotel, after he had gotten home and had a drink and talked to Kristen Wade. Having not been able to sleep until the early morning hours, Holt had come in late to find Max waving a phone message in front of his face.

The call had caught him totally unaware, as Harris Lambert knew it would. Even in death the man managed to control events. Lucas Holt closed the book and swiveled around to his desk to look over the order of service, the readings, and the music. He was about to review one particular Psalm when a light knock came at his door.

"Come in?"

The door slowly opened and Susan Granger entered, followed by Nikky Dorati. They were both dressed for the funeral, and the lieutenant held a cup of steaming tea in her hand.

"Mornin', Rev," Nikky said.

"Hi, Lucas." She put the mug on his desk. "This is compliments of Max. She said you looked like you needed it."

"I swear that woman should have been my mother. She does a better job."

He took the tea and motioned them to the couch.

"Sit down. I was just going over the service."

"Rough night?" Susan Granger asked.

"No night, nearly," the Rev replied, sipping the hot tea and inhaling its minty scent. "It took a while to write the sermon. How do you eulogize a man who's murdered five people?"

"Six if you count himself," Dorati added.

"Yeah, you can definitely count himself," Susan Granger said. "The whole 'bomb' threat along with the statements about killing you to finish his plan—it was all a setup to get us to kill him when he stepped out on that balcony."

"I'm sure you're right, Susan." Lucas Holt reached over on his desk and handed her a pink phone slip. "Check out this message."

Susan Granger read the name and number on the pink slip and handed it back to him.

"Isn't that the name of Lambert's insurance company?"

"Yes. An agent called this morning."

"What about?" Nikky Dorati asked. Then he laughed. "Did he make you the beneficiary?"

Lucas Holt looked at him and nodded. "As a matter of fact, he did."

"What?" A shocked Susan Granger sat back on the couch. "Why would he name you?"

"Well, not me exactly. It seems that St. Margaret's Episcopal Church is the party that is listed first on his life insurance policy." Holt did not reveal all that the agent had told him. "Lambert had changed the beneficiary only thirty days ago, just within the required time to take effect. The former beneficiary had been the Sister Marguerite that he killed."

"That's strange," Granger said. "Why would he kill someone he'd previously made beneficiary?"

"He told you in confession, so you can't tell us, can you, Rev?" Dorati said.

"Under the stole," Holt replied. "Suffice it to say he thought he had good reasons for doing both."

"Well," Susan Granger continued, "might I ask how much money St. Margaret's will get as a result of this—you should excuse the expression—'windfall'?"

"You might, Susan." Lucas Holt took another drink of his tea. "For the past few years while Harris Lambert was paying off a blackmailer and making some rather lucrative sales from the original Treasury items he was stealing, he also managed to buy a whole lot of insurance on his life. He could afford the premiums and he was in excellent health, so his underwriters never batted an eye."

Susan Granger held her hand up in front of him.

"Enough history, Lucas. Give us a figure."

Lucas Holt leaned back in his chair.

"Would you believe a million dollars?"

It was Nikky Dorati's turn to be shocked.

"Holy sweet Jesus, Rev."

"My words exactly," Holt replied, smiling.

Susan Granger still did not speak. She was obviously deep in thought. "And if it's ruled by the coroner to be accidental death," she said, "the policy is doubled."

"So he knew all along he'd be caught, Rev, and he provided the backup for when it happened."

Susan Granger came out of her distant space. "That's

right, Nikky, he used us all in his little plan. Especially the police."

"He knew," Nikky Dorati continued, "that if we caught him before he led us to all the pieces, or before he killed everyone he was out to get, that the church still would be able to go on with the money from his insurance."

"Correct, Nikky," the Rev said. "The worst case was that we would find him sooner and the church would collect the money but not the pieces. The best scenario was that we would get both. And that's the one he managed to accomplish."

The three were momentarily silenced by the bizarre, yet logical workings of the mind of Harris Lambert. Their quiet was broken by the rasping intercom.

"Father Holt?"

"Yes, Max?"

"Cora Mae Hartwig is out here to see you."

"Send her in, Max. Thanks."

The old woman opened the door and walked into Holt's office. She wore a dark blue dress and a matching blue hat with a veil. Her white gloves showed the wear of the many years she had served on the Altar Guild.

"Hello, Nikky, and Lieutenant Granger," she said. "Hello, Lucas dear."

"Good morning, Cora," the Rev replied, then frowned. "How do you know Nikky?"

"Mr. Dorati and I met one day as he was leaving your office, Lucas," Cora Mae explained.

"He don't need to know everything," Dorati grinned. "Does him good to wonder."

"He's teaching me how to win at poker, Lucas." The old woman furrowed her already crinkled brow. "He's a very smart man, and he's been instrumental in my success at the Senior Activities Center."

Lucas Holt shook his head. "Nikky, we'll discuss this later." He turned to Cora Mae. "Is everything set up?"

"I think so, Lucas. I wanted to tell you there are a lot of

people out there waiting to hear what you have to say about Mr. Lambert."

"I'm sure there are, Cora. I hope they will be appropriately appalled and disappointed."

Cora Mae Hartwig's smile lit up her wrinkled face.

"I'm glad you're doing this, Lucas dear. I think it's the right thing, under the circumstances."

"Thank you." Lucas Holt stood up and put his tea back on the desk. "Well, I guess we really should be going up to the Sacristy, right, Cora?"

"Certainly." She turned toward the door. "You don't have much time to vest and get ready. Burt Lister has already started the preliminary music."

Susan Granger and Nikky Dorati also stood to leave.

"You know, Lucas," the lieutenant said, "there's still one little thing out of place in all of this."

"What's that?" the Rev said absently as he picked up his Prayer Book.

"Everything else was so perfectly programmed. The one thing that he didn't pull off was your murder." She held up her hand. "Not that I wanted him to, you understand. It's just that the final piece of the puzzle doesn't quite fit."

"Yeah. I've thought about that, too," the Rev began.

Cora Mae Hartwig closed the door and took her hand off the doorknob. She turned and addressed them all.

"I believe I may just have that final piece to your little puzzle then, Susan dear."

"What do you mean, Cora?" Lucas asked.

"As you all know very well, I am probably the oldest member of this congregation. I may be the oldest person in Austin, Texas, as a matter of fact."

Cora Mae Hartwig cleared her throat and walked over to take a drink of the Rev's tea.

"Thank you, Lucas dear. In any case, you may have eventually guessed that—because I've been here so long—I knew Harris Lambert when he first came to Austin. We even had dinner a few times over the years—strictly as friends, I assure you—and I got to know him better than most people ever did. We remained somewhat close all these years, until very recently, that is."

The octogenarian was obviously moved by Lambert's death, and had to sit down for a moment.

"It's okay, Cora. Here's some Kleenex," Lucas Holt said, handing her the small box to hold.

"He . . . told me never to tell while he was alive. But I guess I can say it now." Her eyes began to tear.

Lucas Holt looked at her. He glanced at Susan Granger and Nikky Dorati.

"What is it, Cora?" he said.

"The Saints of God Murders *are* complete, Lucas."

Susan Granger came over and put her hand on the woman's arm.

"Are you telling us that—"

"Yes, Susan dear," Cora Mae Hartwig said as she broke down and cried. "Harris Lambert was a *priest*."

• Twenty-seven•

Cora Mae Hartwig took some time to compose herself, then sat straight up in the chair.

"I know I must look a fright," she said. "Please excuse my outburst. I've kept that secret hidden for so long. It felt good to finally tell someone. I'm sure Harris would have wanted you to know."

"I'm sure you're right, Cora," Lucas Holt said. "I think he wanted us to know he had completed the task he started out to do."

Nikky Dorati looked at the Rev. "In some ways, it was the 'perfect' crime. It went just the way he planned it."

"Can you tell me more about him, Cora?" Susan Granger asked gently. "What kind of priest was he?"

"He was a Roman Catholic, Susan. He had left the church for some reason before he came to Austin. He never would tell me what that was, though."

The lieutenant looked at Lucas Holt.

The Rev glanced back at her.

"I guess that's one loose end that we'll never clear up Lucas dear."

"I guess so, Cora," the Rev said, patting her on the shoulder.

He looked at his watch, then grabbed his Prayer Book from the desk. "They'll be waiting for us out there, Cora Do you think you're ready to go to work?"

Cora Mae Hartwig dabbed at her eyes with the tissue Throwing her head back and breathing deeply, she stood and took the Rev's Prayer Book from him.

"I'll meet you in the Sacristy, Lucas dear. I'm sure you'll need some help serving all those people. I'd be pleased to help with the chalice, if it's all right with you." She paused for a moment. "I took the liberty of using a very special one."

"Which one is that, Cora?"

"The old one from the Treasury. The one returned from Ashton Willis."

Susan Granger and Nikky Dorati looked at the Rev for his reaction.

"I think that will do just fine, Cora."

He was about to say something else when Maxine opened the door.

"Sorry to interrupt you again, Rev, but I thought you'd want to take this phone call that just came in."

She handed him a piece of paper and winked at him.

"Thanks, Max. You're right, as usual." He looked at the others and said: "If you all will excuse me, I'll take this call and then see you out in the service. Max, please tell the caller I'll be right there."

"You got it, Rev."

Nikky Dorati, Susan Granger, and Cora Mae Hartwig all started to leave. The Rev stopped them just before they walked out his office door.

"I have one request, though."

Nikky Dorati turned around.

"What's that, Rev?"

"Would you meet me back here after this is all over? I think I'm going to need a beer at Mother's."

"I'll buy it for you, Lucas dear. And I may drink it for you, too." Lucas Holt smiled as the door closed behind them. Sitting on the front of his desk, he reached for the phone and punched the blinking button.

"Hello, Bishop," he said.

"Good morning, Lucas."

"You sound in a much better mood than last night when

you were reaming me out for doing this service today. My guess is that someone called you with the news."

"As a matter of fact, that's what I called about, Lucas. I wanted to apologize for my behavior toward you then, and sincerely ask for your forgiveness. I was rushed and I didn't have all the facts at my disposal."

"You certainly didn't, Emil, or you wouldn't have threatened me the way you did. I don't much like that, just like I don't much like being told what a failure I am because I couldn't keep the church afloat and come up with a way to salvage St. Margaret's."

"I understand your feelings, Lucas."

"No, I don't believe you do, Emil. I don't believe you have any feelings where people are concerned. You've been stuck in that damned office for so long, you've forgotten what it's like to hurt with hurting people, to listen to their lifelong fears and guilts, to support them no matter what your personal disagreements may be."

"Now, Lucas—"

"But let me tell you one thing you will understand, Emil. That million or so dollars that Harris Lambert left to us was left entirely to St. Margaret's. The attorney I talked with made it clear that none of that money was to go to the Diocese. I guess Harris knew you even better than I did."

"Father Holt, you are bordering on insolence."

"Compliments will get you nowhere, Emil. You know damned well you wanted to rub my nose in the downfall of this place. Well, this inheritance will let us do the kind of ministry that needs to be done here, not just the kind that looks good on Diocesan reports to your superior."

"This matter isn't settled yet, Father Holt."

"Yes, it is, Emil."

"You have a responsibility to the Diocese."

"I have a responsibility to carry out the terms of the gift, Bishop. And I intend to do that in ways that will unnerve you for years to come. It must be the work of the Holy Spirit. She's got a sense of humor."

"Now, you listen to me, Father Holt—"

"No, I don't think I will, Emil. I have a funeral service to do that I understand is making national news. You can read the eulogy in tomorrow's paper, Bishop."

"Father Holt, you had better not—"

"Good-bye, Emil."

The Rev hung up the phone. He looked for a moment at the sunshine pouring through his windows, warming the couch and carpet. He would stay at Maggie Mae's. He would stick with the God Squad—or let them stick with him. The grayness inside was beginning to lift, but there was one more task to accomplish.

Leading the green palled casket up the main aisle of the packed church, Lucas Holt wondered about the motivation of the people there. Some were clearly present out of curiosity, others to mourn an old friend or business acquaintance, still others angrily awaiting his eulogy.

Processing to the front of the church, Holt turned to face the congregation. As they sang the opening hymn, he felt the usual nervousness about what he was about to say. Should he have done it this way? What would be the repercussions of the words he would speak about Harris Lambert? Instinctively he scanned the congregation as the second verse brought him closer to the time he would step into the pulpit and begin.

At first he did not see them. Then, locating them halfway back on the right, he saw Susan Granger flanked by Nikky Dorati and the rest of the God Squad sharing hymnals. He glanced over his shoulder to see Cora Mae Hartwig blurrily looking at the magnificent chalice on the high altar.

The Kingdom of God indeed, he thought, as the third verse of the hymn began.

The singing continued as Lucas Holt turned and slowly ascended the steps into the pulpit. He set the hymnal down and unfolded the notes he had written the night before, as the congregation came to the last verse of Hymn 243.

The final line of the hymn would be the opening statement of the eulogy:

"And I mean to be one too."